DARK SKY

ALSO BY C. J. BOX

THE JOE PICKETT NOVELS

Long Range
Wolf Pack
The Disappeared
Vicious Circle
Off the Grid
Endangered
Stone Cold
Breaking Point
Force of Nature
Cold Wind

Nowhere to Run
Below Zero
Blood Trail
Free Fire
In Plain Sight
Out of Range
Trophy Hunt
Winterkill
Savage Run
Open Season

THE STAND-ALONE NOVELS

The Bitterroots
Paradise Valley
Badlands
The Highway
Back of Beyond
Three Weeks to Say Goodbye
Blue Heaven

SHORT FICTION

Shots Fired: Stories from Joe Pickett Country

DARK SKY

A JOE PICKETT NOVEL

C. J. BOX

G. P. PUTNAM'S SONS
NEW YORK

PUTNAM
— EST. 1838 —

G. P. PUTNAM'S SONS
Publishers Since 1838
An imprint of Penguin Random House LLC
penguinrandomhouse.com

Library of Congress Cataloging-in-Publication Data
Names: Box, C. J., author.
Title: Dark sky: a Joe Pickett novel / C. J. Box.
Description: New York: G. P. Putnam's Sons, 2021. | Series: Joe Pickett |
Identifiers: LCCN 2020050216 (print) | LCCN 2020050217 (ebook) |
ISBN 9780525538271 (hardcover) | ISBN 9780525538288 (ebook)
Subjects: GSAFD: Suspense fiction.
Classification: LCC PS3552.O87658 D37 2021 (print) | LCC PS3552.O87658 (ebook) |
DDC 813/.54—dc23
LC record available at https://lccn.loc.gov/2020050216
LC ebook record available at https://lccn.loc.gov/2020050217

Printed in the United States of America
10 9 8 7 6 5 4 3 2 1

Book design by Elke Sigal

For Paisley Woods
. . . and Laurie, always

For a moment of night we have a glimpse of ourselves and of our world islanded in its stream of stars—pilgrims of mortality, voyaging between horizons across eternal seas of space and time.

—Henry Beston
The Outermost House

Technology . . . the knack of so arranging the world that we don't have to experience it.

—Max Frisch
Homo Faber

DARK
SKY

Mountain Money

O dark dark dark. They all go into the dark,
The vacant interstellar spaces, the vacant
into the vacant.

—T. S. Eliot
"East Coker," from *Four Quartets*

ONE

Wyoming game warden Joe Pickett stood on the edge of the tarmac with his hands thrust into the pockets of his parka and his gray Stetson clamped on tight against the cold wind. It was a week until his birthday and his leg hurt and the brisk chill made him feel all of his fifty-one years on the planet.

His first glimpse of the $65 million Gulfstream G650ER private jet was of a gleaming white speck high above the rounded, snowcapped peaks of the Bighorn Mountains to the west.

It was a cloudless mid-October morning, but it had snowed an inch during the night and the ten-mile-an-hour breeze cleared the concrete of the runway, rolling thin smoky waves of flakes across the pavement of the Saddlestring Municipal Airport. The timbered mountains had received three to five inches that would likely melt away in the high-altitude sun, but the treeless summits looked like the white crowns of so many bald eagles standing shoulder to shoulder against the clear blue sky.

"Cold this morning," Brock Boedecker said.

"Yup."

Boedecker was a fourth-generation rancher whose land reached up from the breakland plateau into the midpoint of Battle Mountain. He had a classic western look about him: narrow, thin, with deep-set eyes and a bushy black mustache, its tips extending to his jawline. It was the kind of weathered look, Joe thought, that had once convinced the marketing team at Marlboro to hire the local Wyoming cowboy who'd brought them horses for their ad shoot instead of the male models they'd flown out from Hollywood.

"Not quite ready for snow yet," Boedecker said while tucking his chin into the collar of his jacket.

"Nope."

"About a month early for these temps."

"Yup."

"It's supposed to warm up a little later this week."

"Yup."

Boedecker asked, "Are you sure this is something we want to do?"

"Not really."

"Damn. I feel the same way. Is there any way we can get out of it?"

"Nope."

"I could do it without you," the rancher said. "Hell, I do this all the time."

"I know you could. But I wouldn't feel right letting you

down at the last minute. I'm the one that got you into this, remember?"

"How's your leg?" Boedecker asked.

"Getting better all the time."

It was true. The gunshot Joe had sustained was healing on schedule due to months of rehabilitation and physical therapy, but he still walked with a limp. On cold mornings like this, he could feel it where the rifle round had punched through his thigh—a line of deadness rimmed by pangs of sharp pain when he moved.

Boedecker sighed. It seemed like there was something he wanted to say, so Joe waited. Finally: "Well, them horses you ordered are all trailered up and ready. I'll wait for you inside, I think."

Joe nodded. He turned to watch Boedecker make his way toward the glass doors of the old terminal. The rancher wore a weathered black hat, a canvas barn coat stained with oil, and a magenta silk scarf wrapped around his neck. His back was broad. The scarf reminded Joe that cowboys, even the crustiest of them, always displayed a little flash in their dress.

"Thanks for helping me out with this, Brock," Joe called out after him.

"You bet, Joe," he answered with a wave of his hand. He paused at the door and looked over his shoulder. "I wasn't sure I'd get here on time this morning. Did you know the sheriff has a roadblock set up so only authorized people can get to the airport?"

Joe said, "I heard about that."

"I guess they were worried about a mob scene. That's what the deputy told me. This guy is some big shot, huh?"

"That's what they say."

"I can't say I support what we're doing," the rancher said. "I wish we weren't doing it."

"I know," Joe said. Then: "It's supposed to be a big secret, so I'd appreciate you keeping it between us."

"Word's already out," Boedecker said.

"I don't know how," Joe said. The only reason he'd told Boedecker what he was about to do was because he'd needed to rent horses and tack from the rancher.

"I'm just not feeling too good about this guy," Boedecker said.

Joe nodded his understanding. Up until the week before, he'd been in the same boat. His wife, Marybeth, had needed to explain to him who the man was, even though everyone—especially their three daughters—seemed to know all about him.

"Are you still convinced we'll have 'em all back down by the time the cattle trucks show up? The horses, I mean?"

"Absolutely," Joe said. "We'll be back down by Friday."

"Good, 'cause I loaded up my best mounts. Nothing but the best, you said."

"Thank you," Joe said with relief. "Did you remember to stop by our place and load Toby?"

"Yup."

Toby was Marybeth's oldest and most seasoned mount. He was a tall tobiano paint gelding who still displayed boyish enthusiasm, especially when he was taken away from the barn and corral and shown mountain trails.

"Any of these dudes ever been on a horse before?"

"They claim they have."

"Those types always claim they have," Boedecker said. He shook his head as he went inside.

Joe turned back to the west. The Gulfstream was now in profile, streaking left to right across the sky in order to make the turn and line up with the north-south runway.

He rocked back on his boot heels and tried to conjure a sense of anticipation, the feeling of excitement he used to feel as a younger man just prior to setting out into the mountains on an adventure. He'd toss and turn in bed the night before and be up hours before dawn to get ready, filled with a kind of primal joy.

Joe dug deep, but he couldn't find it now.

He was dressed as he always was for a day in the field, in his red uniform shirt with the Wyoming Game and Fish Department pronghorn antelope patch on the sleeve and his J. PICKETT name badge over his breast pocket. Under his uniform shirt and Wranglers were lightweight wool long underwear and socks. He wore a dark green wool Filson vest under his olive-green uniform parka.

He'd been instructed not to wear his holster and .40 Glock semiauto weapon, or his belt containing handcuffs and bear spray. The lack of weight under his parka made him feel airy and incomplete.

He squinted against the reflection of the morning sun on the perfect white skin of the Gulfstream as it taxied toward the terminal building. The twin tail-mounted jet engines emitted a high-pitched whine that hurt his ears.

The pilot of the jet did a graceful turn so the passenger door lined up with the entrance of the terminal before he cut the power to the engines. The turbines wound down into silence and the only sound was the light wind. Joe could see the profiles of several people inside moving about.

A moment later, the door opened and a stairway unfolded to the surface of the tarmac.

And there, not quite filling the opening, was a pale, gangly man with a boyish face and wispy ginger hair. He waved as if there were a crowd to greet him and not just Joe.

This was Joe's first glimpse of thirty-two-year-old Steven "Steve-2" Price, the Silicon Valley billionaire and CEO of Aloft, Inc. and the principal behind ConFab, the social media site.

Joe's job was to take him elk hunting.

Price was dressed in state-of-the-art high-tech outdoor hunting clothing, but despite that, he hugged himself against the cold as he descended the stairs. When he reached the pavement, he stopped and looked up and around him, theatrically taking in the wide-open sky and the mountain ranges on three sides.

Price opened his arms as if to embrace it all and he cried, "*Nature!*"

Joe stifled a smile.

Behind Price, another person emerged: a fidgety overweight man, bald on top with tufts of black hair above his ears. He came down the stairs so quickly Joe thought he might tumble to the concrete. The man quickly shouldered past Price and strode toward Joe until Price called to him.

"Tim!"

The man called Tim stopped dead in his tracks and turned around. Joe had spent the past week exchanging scores of emails with Price's point man, whose name was Timothy Joannides. Joe assumed this was him.

"Did you get that?" Price asked Joannides.

"Did I get what?"

Price fixed a look of disdain on Tim. "My first reaction?"

"No," Joannides said. "I was behind you and—"

"Tim, your job is to document this experience. We talked about that, didn't we? Do I have to explain it again?"

"No."

Tim seemed to Joe to want to say more, but he didn't.

"Are you ready now?" Price asked.

"Yes, sir."

Price waited impatiently until Tim found his phone and raised it to eye level.

Price held up his camo glove for a moment, then climbed the stairs of the plane and reenacted his actions from a minute before.

"*Nature!*" he called out again with his arms spread. Then he froze in mid-pose.

9

"Got it?" Price asked Tim.

"Got it."

"Make sure you get a panorama of the mountains," Price directed. "Then cut that in before we post it."

"I'm on it," Tim said as he stepped out of Price's way and raised up his phone to video the surroundings. He spun around slowly as he did so.

Joe was so preoccupied with the interplay between Price and Joannides that he hadn't seen a third man exit the plane until the newcomer was headed straight toward him. The man was heavy, squared-off, and built low to the ground. His stride was smooth and purposeful, almost a jog, and his shoulders and head were bent forward. His arms were held out away from his body in a way that gave Joe the brief impression that he was about to be tackled.

The man didn't stop until he was inches away from Joe.

"I need to pat you down for weapons." He had a deep bass voice and spoke with a blunt Eastern European accent.

"I left 'em in my truck," Joe said, feeling both angry and violated. The man was just too close. "Isn't that what I was supposed to do?"

"Sorry, it's my job," the man said without a real apology, and Joe found himself being expertly patted down, all the way to the top of his lace-up hunting boots. When the man was done, he stepped back.

"You're clear," the man said.

"I already told you that."

Joe and the bodyguard stared at each other for several beats. The man didn't blink. He had a wide Slavic face, close-cropped black hair, a downturned mouth, and a square jaw not quite as wide as his thick neck. Joe could only guess the man was armed because of the bulges and protrusions beneath his matte black–colored tactical coat.

"Please forgive Zsolt," Price said with an embarrassed grin as he joined the two. He pronounced the name *Zolt*. "He kind of overdoes it sometimes, but he's a good man to have around."

"I'm law enforcement," Joe said through gritted teeth.

Price arched his eyebrows. "I thought you were a game warden."

"Game wardens *are* law enforcement," Joe said to Price.

"If you say so," Price said, obviously unconvinced.

Joe didn't move. Inside, he seethed even while he offered his hand to Price.

"And you must be Joe," Price said with a grin. "'Good old Joe,' I've been saying."

Before Joe could confirm it, Price chinned toward the jet. "Is the wrangler waiting for us somewhere?"

"His name is Brock," Joe said. "Yup, he's waiting inside for us."

"You can call me Steve-2," Price said. He pronounced *Steve-Two* as a two-syllable word. Instead of grasping Joe's hand in return, he offered an elbow bump. It was an obvious holdover from the pandemic. Either that, or Price was a germophobe, Joe thought.

"That's Tim out there with the camera," Price said. "He's my personal assistant. You've met Zsolt Rumy. As you probably guessed, he oversees security."

Rumy nodded at the mention of his name. Joe nodded back.

Price sidled up close, man-to-man. "I know you're probably asking yourself why a dude like me needs security."

"Not really."

"I sometimes wonder myself," Price said.

One of the crew of the jet had opened the cargo hold door and Joe could see what looked like dozens of large duffel bags, gear boxes, and backpacks inside.

Joe narrowed his eyes. "I'm sure Tim told you we're taking horses."

"He did. I'm really looking forward to it."

"We may need to winnow down some of your stuff if it's too much."

"Are you saying we don't have pack animals?" Price asked with a look of genuine concern. "My understanding is we'd have pack animals to transport everything we need."

"We've got horses and panniers," Joe said. "They're waiting for us in the parking lot. But we need to limit the weight on each animal to no more than thirty percent of its body weight. We've got five packhorses in addition to the horses we'll ride."

Price frowned. "How much does a horse weigh?"

"Depends on the horse."

Price closed his eyes and took a deep breath, then slowly reopened them. "I was under the assumption all of this was already sorted out in advance."

Joe said, "I told Tim to limit your baggage to five hundred pounds."

Price glared at him. "You know, *good old Joe*, I can do math in my head. In fact, I'm quite good at it. I'm a coder and a programmer and I've designed world-class proprietary algorithms. Are you telling me that your packhorses can only handle a hundred pounds each? I find that hard to believe, since most human riders weigh well above that."

"They do," Joe said. "But we need to plan for the weight of hauling elk back down the mountain."

"Oh."

"We'll get it figured out," Joe offered in an attempt to be conciliatory. As he said it, Joannides approached the group.

Price turned to his assistant. "If we need to leave things behind, they'll be yours."

"Yes, boss," he said through gritted teeth as he turned and walked away.

Joe felt embarrassed for the man, which Price seemed to pick up on.

"I hope that's not the first of many misunderstandings," Price said. "Sometimes I think Tim tells me what he thinks I want to hear rather than what I need to hear."

Joe was glad Joannides was out of earshot.

"Since you've been communicating with Tim," Price continued, "it's important that you know I'm not some kind of prima donna. I take what we're about to do very seriously and it's extremely valuable to me. I appreciate you and the wrangler taking your time to do this."

Joe nodded.

"As I hope Tim conveyed to you, I only want to participate in an authentic, fair-chase hunt. Pretend I'm just a normal person who hires you to guide him."

Joe started to say that he didn't usually guide hunters at all, but Price was on a roll.

"I've had hundreds of opportunities to just shoot an animal, if that's what I wanted to do. I'm talking absolute trophies. But that was on land owned by friends and colleagues, or worse, game farms. That is the last thing I want to do.

"I want real," Price said. "I want the actual experience. Did Tim communicate this to you clearly?"

Joe was torn how to answer without throwing Joannides under the bus.

"I get it," Joe said.

"Wonderful," Price said. "Now, do you think you can go get the wrangler and help us unload all of that gear? And be very careful. Some of it is really delicate."

Joe turned and pushed through the double doors into the terminal. He found Boedecker sitting on a plastic chair reading the Saddlestring *Roundup*.

The rancher looked up as Joe approached. He said, "Are you sure we can't get out of this?"

"I'm pretty sure."

Boedecker put the paper aside and looked around to make sure no one could overhear what he was about to say. His eyes were unblinking.

"You can go," the man said. "No hard feelings on my part. In fact . . ."

Joe cocked his head as he waited for more.

"I'd really advise you to go home," Boedecker said finally. "I can do this without you."

Joe was puzzled. "I signed on for this."

Before Boedecker could continue, Joannides stuck his head in the door. He was frantic.

"We need to get this show on the road, gentlemen," he said.

Boedecker gave Joe a long look that Joe supposed was designed to tell him something. Then he stood up and the two of them walked through the tiny terminal toward the waiting plane.

Joe looked up from the tarmac. A procession of dark clouds scudded across the sky from the north. Soon, it looked like, they'd envelop Battle Mountain.

TWO

Two and a half weeks before, Joe had sat in a leather-backed armchair across from Colter Allen, the governor of Wyoming, in the newly refurbished capitol building in Cheyenne. Game and Fish Department director Rick Ewig was with him.

They'd both been summoned to appear before the governor. Joe had left a telephone message on Ewig's phone asking if the director knew what the meeting was about. Ewig hadn't called back.

"Why am I here?" Joe asked Allen.

"I'll explain," Allen said.

Governor Colter Allen was in the midst of completing his third year in his first term of office. His term had been wracked with problems including a #MeToo scandal, as well as revelations that he'd falsified his résumé *and* he'd been backed by donors of questionable character, including Joe's own mother-in-law. Additionally, Governor Allen was thought by general consensus within the state to have fouled up the response to the onset of the coronavirus pandemic by lurching from strict shelter-in-place orders to a full-blown reopening within weeks, then issuing no guidance at all for months while the virus raged.

Joe's relationship with the Republican governor was nothing like it had been when Spencer Rulon held the office. Although slippery at times, Rulon had enlisted Joe to be his "range rider" and he'd sent him out to different places in the state on special assignments. And when Joe had gotten into trouble, which was often, Rulon had backed him up.

Allen had assumed office with the misconception that Joe would do *anything* he asked, including gathering dirt on his political opponents and spreading misinformation on his behalf. When Joe had refused, Allen retaliated. If it weren't for Rulon stepping in as a private-practice attorney and representing him, Joe would have long been out of a job and possibly indicted.

Although there had been rumblings about the possible impeachment of Allen—Wyoming's first ever—the bills to start the proceedings had been killed in committee by the legislature. According to the *Casper Star-Tribune*, the house of representatives and senate seemed to have concluded that rather than play hardball with the governor, they'd simply wait him out and elect someone new.

By his very nature, Joe was nonpolitical. He'd done his best over the years to avoid trips to the capital city and especially during the short sessions of the legislature when nothing ever seemed to happen. He had no doubt that he'd taken the right path, especially now when the finances of the state were in a tailspin and all the committee hearings and general sessions seemed filled with anger and acrimony.

Joe thought that Allen had aged in the past three years. The governor's once-broad shoulders had slumped and his salt-and-pepper mane was thinning and turning snow-white. His movie-star good looks—which he'd once parlayed into a few scenes in a soft-porn pseudo-western feature called *Bunk House* that no one had known about until his #MeToo scandal broke—were filling out and softening. Jowls like the beard of a tom turkey hung down from his jawline and jiggled when he talked.

"If you've been paying any attention," Allen said to both Joe and Ewig, "you'll know that we're facing more budget cuts. No one is safe, including your agency."

"I'm aware of the situation, Governor," Ewig said. Unlike Joe, the director was duty-bound to testify during the legislature and defend the department's budget. Joe didn't envy him.

Wyoming was unique because its financial health was determined almost solely by the boom-and-bust mineral industries and the taxes they paid on extraction. Citizens paid very little. There was no income tax, and property taxes were some of the lowest in the nation. When coal was booming—as it had been in previous years—the state was flush with cash. That was no longer the case, and lawmakers were trying to figure out how to deal with the downturn.

It wasn't going well.

The legislature was dominated by Republicans, and there were good ones and bad ones, as well as ideological factions that might as well comprise different parties altogether. Groups of legislators could best be defined, according to some, by how loudly they said no to any new ideas. The mayor of Saddlestring had put it best to Joe—the one thing the Wyoming legislature specialized in was inertia.

"I plan to run again next year and I need a win," Governor Allen declared to Joe more than to Ewig. "You need to help me get it."

Joe shifted uncomfortably in his chair.

"Coal's dying, oil prices are low, no one wants new taxes, and the Cowboy Congress isn't going to help me at all," Allen said. "As we've seen, they'll do absolutely nothing to diversify our economy or bring in new revenue. They'll just sit around blowing hot air while I twist in the wind so they can make the case for a new governor next year. They'll point at me and say, 'The state went to shit with him in office.' That's their brilliant strategy."

Ewig took a deep breath and let it out slowly. Joe guessed he'd endured Allen's rants before. Joe tried to keep his own face blank while he listened. A new governor, he thought, *wouldn't* be the worst thing in the world.

"All of our revenue streams are tied to dying concerns," Allen said. "The legislature prefers to rub its hands and gnash its teeth while watching them die. They're all hoping against hope for something good to happen, like a war in the Middle East that would raise the price of a barrel of our oil."

Joe tried not to react to that.

Allen spun in his chair and pointed to a large map of the United States. "Either that," he said, jabbing his finger at the states of Washington, Oregon, and California, "or we need the West Coast to break off and fall into the ocean and drown all of those lefty politicians who won't let us export our coal to Asia. The Chi-Coms want to buy our coal. We want to sell it to them, but we need a seaport to do it. The environmental wackos on the West Coast won't let us. We're between a rock and a hard place, gentlemen."

He turned back around. "Have either of you ever heard of Steven Price?"

Both Joe and Ewig shook their heads.

"Have you ever heard of Aloft, Inc.? Or a social media site called ConFab?"

"ConFab sounds familiar," Joe said. "I think my youngest daughter uses it."

"Your youngest daughter and tens of millions of other people," Allen said. "It's the fastest-growing social media platform in Silicon Valley."

"It's a mystery to me," Ewig confessed. "I don't even do Facebook."

"Another reason we're in trouble," Allen said with derision. "My state directors are wallowing around in the twentieth century while the rest of the world passes us by."

It was an unnecessary insult, Joe thought. Rick Ewig was a former game warden and had proved himself to be a very competent director of the agency. Allen's reputation for disparaging his own people was being demonstrated right before Joe's eyes.

"Steve Price was a billionaire before he was thirty," Allen said. "That was before he invented ConFab. Now he's a multibillionaire—one of the wealthiest men in America. And it's all happened really fast."

"Okay," Joe said. He couldn't tell where the conversation was leading.

"My people have learned a little about Steve Price," Allen said. "He's absolutely brilliant, but he's a nerd. He's a unique talent and he's very quirky, like a lot of those tech moguls. He eats weird, drives weird cars, has weird friends, and he believes in all kinds of new age voodoo crap. But one thing very interesting about Price is that he's into self-improvement. He's pledged to himself to try to learn everything he can about everything. He wants to be the wisest human being on earth, and he thinks he can get there by devoting himself to learning new things.

"Every year," Allen continued, "Price focuses on something he knows absolutely nothing about and he tries to master it before he can move on. One year he spent learning Mandarin Chinese until he could speak it fluently. Another year he decided to seek out and eat every kind of pepper grown anywhere in the world. He doesn't ever want to die, so he poured millions into research two years ago and learned everything there is to know about extending the aging process. He spent an entire year walking door-to-door in Iowa, talking to farmers so he could get a better understanding of 'how Middle Americans think,' as he put it.

"Do you want to know what his newest thing is?" Allen asked.

He answered his own question before either Ewig or Joe could guess.

"Steve Price is spending the year producing all of his own food. He's got his own garden, his own cows and goats, and even a brewery and distillery. When I say 'producing,' I mean he does everything himself. He dug up the dirt, planted seeds, watered and weeded, and harvested his own personal crop. When he wants protein, he kills one of his herd and butchers the meat himself. He's vowed to consume nothing this year unless he produced it himself."

"That's kind of admirable," Joe said.

"Crazy, is what it is," Allen said. "But he's a billionaire, so who can argue? Anyway, to complete his journey, he wants to hunt and kill a big-game animal with his own hands. He wants to process the meat and eat it. He wants to get his hands dirty and really understand the relationship between wild animals and human beings who kill and eat them. So when Price's people reached out to us about setting up the perfect big-game hunting experience, I came up with a brilliant idea, if I do say so myself. And that, gentlemen, is where you come in."

Governor Allen pointed directly at Joe. "More specifically, Pickett, that's where *you* come in."

To which Joe responded, "Why me?"

Allen deflected Joe's question with a wave of his hand and continued on.

"Aloft, Inc. is in the planning stages to build the largest server farm in North America. It'll cover miles and miles of ground, and the whole thing will be powered by the biggest single renewable energy project—wind, solar, all that crap—in the world. It's a multibillion-dollar venture.

"What Aloft and Price haven't determined is where to locate this monstrosity," Allen said. "Everyone assumes it'll be Texas, Nevada, California, or Washington State, but the determination hasn't been made."

"You're thinking it should be here," Ewig said.

That's what Joe had concluded as well.

"Damn right," Allen said. "We've got the land, we've got cool temperatures to keep those servers running, we've got cheap labor with all our unemployed energy workers, and we've got . . . *me*! I'll do just about anything to land that project, with or without our do-nothing Cowboy Congress."

This would be his big win, Joe thought. *This is what Allen thinks might propel him to reelection, despite his unpopularity.*

"We need to get this state on Steve Price's radar," Allen said. "We need him to love us. Most of all, we need a commitment to get those construction dollars and new jobs before the peasants decide to revolt or the legislature shows me the door."

Allen said to Joe, "I asked Rick for a recommendation on who should take Price elk hunting. I said I needed someone rock-solid. Despite my well-known feelings about you, he said your name. I know you have a ton of elk in those mountains of yours."

Joe said, "There are plenty of actual hunting guides I could recommend. Good ones."

"I thought about that," Allen said. "Then I dismissed it. I don't like the idea of some local rube taking him hunting. What if the local says he doesn't like the Internet? Or what if he says this server project is ridiculous? That could screw up our chances. No, I need someone who works directly for me. Someone who'll say nice things about me and the state and be totally accommodating."

"Someone you can fire if it doesn't work out," Joe said.

"Exactly. And not only fire, but defund his entire state agency in these dire days of budget cuts."

Joe glared at Allen.

"Could you live with the knowledge that your actions resulted in the unemployment of hundreds of colleagues?" Allen asked.

Joe felt his face burn.

"There are plenty of yahoos in the legislature who would support cutting entire state agencies," Allen said. "Especially ones that some people feel have gotten too big for their britches."

Joe closed his eyes and reopened them. He had a real urge to throw himself across the desk and throttle Colter Allen. Unfortunately, what the governor had said about some lawmakers wanting to defund state government had more than a grain of truth.

"We don't really have a choice here, Joe," Ewig said softly. Now Joe knew why the director hadn't clued him in beforehand.

In the hallway after the meeting, Ewig asked Joe for a moment. They ducked behind a standing mount of a huge grizzly bear, stepping out of view of the receptionist's desk that led to the governor's inner office.

"I'm sorry, Joe," Ewig said. "I'm sorry to put this all on you. It isn't fair."

Joe shrugged. His boss was correct.

"Don't do it for him," Ewig said. "Don't do it for me. Do it for all of your colleagues and the state."

"That's a lot to ask," Joe said.

"I know it is. But when the governor asked me for a recommendation for a guide, I couldn't help but think of you. You've got elk experience, and you know how to keep your mouth shut. I needed someone I could trust to do this."

"Thanks for that," Joe said, looking away. "But what if the hunt goes pear-shaped? Weather could be a factor, or maybe we just can't find the elk. Or Price gets a shot and misses. Or worse, he wounds an elk and we spend three days trying to track it? You know how it is in the mountains. Anything can happen."

Ewig put his hand on Joe's shoulder. "I know it sounds ridiculous, but I hope you can minimize the risks. I hope you can get this done and get everybody down safely out of the mountains with an elk and nobody hurt."

"I hope so, too," Joe said. "I don't like being away from my district for a week during hunting season. It makes me nervous."

"I'll assign somebody to cover it," Ewig said. "Maybe I'll even do it myself."

"It's five thousand square miles," Joe said with skepticism.

"I'm aware," Ewig said.

"What about licenses and conservation stamps for Price and his crew? What about him passing a hunter's safety course?"

All hunters in Wyoming had to have a valid hunting license for the correct area as well as an annual conservation stamp. In addition, hunters applying for the elk license drawing were required to have completed a hunter's safety course.

"We got a license from the governor's allotment," Ewig said. "I bought the guy a conservation stamp myself—all he has to do is sign it."

"Hunter's safety?" Joe asked.

"Price took an online course in California. We have reciprocity with them. Everything is legal, Joe. You don't have to worry about that."

Ewig reached back and pulled a folded piece of paper from his back pocket and handed it to Joe. "Price's contact details are all on here. His point man is named Tim Joannides. You'll need to work through him to coordinate the trip."

"Not Price himself?"

"That's not how it works out in Silicon Valley, I guess," Ewig said.

"What happens if Price decides to locate his server project somewhere else?" Joe asked. "Despite what happens on this trip?"

Ewig ran his fingers through his hair. "I don't know. Your guess is as good as mine. *I can* speculate that it wouldn't be good for you or the agency."

"Gotcha," Joe said. His face was burning again.

"Keep me in the loop," Ewig said. "I want to know how it's going. Don't be afraid to ask if you need anything."

Joe shook his director's hand.

"Don't let us down, Joe," he said.

"I think I got that point real clearly," Joe replied.

THREE

After removing the rear seat of a rental Suburban to make enough room for all of the gear they'd brought with them, after waiting for Zsolt Rumy to pat down Brock Boedecker and the SUV driver to make sure they posed no threat to Steve Price, and after Price had insisted that Tim Joannides take a photo of him standing in front of the horse trailer with Joe on one side and Boedecker on the other, Joe ambled toward his green Ford F-150 pickup. He would lead the caravan to the trailhead at the base of Battle Mountain, followed by Boedecker and his eight-horse trailer and the rental SUV with the hunting party.

As he opened the door, Joannides appeared. He was out of breath from running across the parking lot from the Suburban.

"Do you mind if I ride along with you?"

"Nope."

"I want to make sure we're both on the same page in regard to everything we discussed," Joannides said. He dis-

28

played a miniature iPad. "I've got it all on here. I thought if you forgot something, we could stop in town and buy whatever we need to."

Joe looked at him. "Steve-2 just told me he wanted this hunting trip to be as authentic as possible. He said he wanted a real no-frills deal."

"What Steve-2 says he wants and what he expects are often different things," Joannides said. "It's not his fault. He operates on a different level from the rest of us. But that's why I'm here: to make sure we're well-prepared for anything that might come up. You received my grocery list, correct?"

Joe said, "I got everything on your list except quinoa and pili nuts. Those things were nowhere to be found."

"You're kidding. Please tell me you're kidding."

"This is Wyoming," Joe said.

Joannides pursed his lips. "Well, let's just hope it doesn't come up."

"Fine by me."

Joe climbed in and started the engine while Joannides settled himself in the passenger seat with the iPad on his lap. The man started to speak, then stopped short. Joe looked over to find Joannides staring at the .357 Colt Python revolver and other gear on the seat between them.

"What?" Joe asked.

"Do we really need a gun around?"

"We're going hunting."

"Yes, I know. But Steve-2 brought his compound bow. I know I told you that."

"You did," Joe said. "And I'll do my best to help him get his elk with it. But elk aren't the only animals up there, Tim. We've had some serious problems with grizzly bears. Half a dozen hunters have been mauled or killed in the last year. I'm bringing my big pistol, and my shotgun loaded with three-inch magnum slugs."

Joannides stated, "Steve-2 doesn't believe people should have weapons of war."

"Maybe he should tell that to the grizzly bears. And Zsolt."

"That's different."

"What's with the name? Steve-2?"

"It's his nickname from college and it stuck," Joannides said. "You know, after Steve Jobs. Jobs was Steve-1, and our Steve wanted to be Steve-2. Now he nearly is."

"Interesting," Joe said. "Did you bring bear spray for everyone?"

"It's illegal in California."

"Well, it's necessary here. I don't want to see any of you without it at any time."

Joannides looked suddenly distressed.

"Don't worry," Joe said. "I brought canisters for everybody."

"Thank you."

"What about PLBs?" Joe asked.

Personal locator beacons weren't a legal requirement, but they were a good idea, Joe thought, especially since the Aloft team wasn't experienced in the wilderness.

"Those we found," Joannides said. "Skiers and snowboarders use them, I guess."

As they took the exit to the state highway from the airport, Joe's cell phone chimed with three messages, one after the other. He dug the device out of his breast pocket and checked the alerts on the screen. He was alarmed to have received such a sudden onslaught. Was it some kind of emergency?

The texts were from two of his daughters and his wife.

Lucy, his youngest at twenty years old and a sophomore at the University of Wyoming in Laramie, wrote:

You're with Steve-2? OMG. I nearly fainted.

The text was studded with emojis of rolled eyes, emojis laughing hysterically accompanied by tears, and Lucy's own face emoji looking seriously shocked.

April, his twenty-two-year-old who had recently graduated from Northwest Community College in Powell and was purportedly taking a couple of months off to figure out her future, wrote:

How can the most uncool man in the world be hanging out with Steve-2? The world is upside down.

Joe knew April wasn't referring to Boedecker as the most uncool man in the world.

Marybeth, who must have sent her text from her desk at the Twelve Sleep County Library, where she was the director, wrote:

This is a photo I never expected to see! Good luck and I hope you get your elk. Call when you can.

Xoxoxoxoxoxo,
MB

Joe turned to Joannides. "How can my daughters know what we're doing all of a sudden?"

Joannides said, "We posted it. Steve-2 will be thrilled to know your kids use the platform."

"I thought this hunting trip was supposed to be below the radar?"

Joannides grinned. "Nothing Steve-2 does is below the radar. When he posts to ConFab, all of our users get the image. He's a very high-profile individual. I'm surprised you didn't know that."

"I didn't."

"Maybe you should talk to your daughters some more."

Joe sighed. At least Sheridan, his oldest, hadn't texted him. He wasn't surprised. Since taking a job with Yarak, Inc. as an apprentice falconer the year before, she was often traveling or in remote locations with bad cell service.

"Is this whole hunting trip going to be posted to social media for all the world to see?" Joe asked.

"What do you think?" Joannides replied.

"Is that wise?"

Joannides paused to consider the question. Finally, he said, "Steve-2 made the call. He thinks it's important to expose our users to aspects of real life they probably don't know, like the hunting culture. His life is an open book. Sometimes it's hard to restrain him when he gets enthused about a new topic. He knows there'll be some serious pushback from users who hate the idea of hunting, but there has been serious pushback before and our users keep growing. ConFab has grown two hundred and fifty percent this year alone. We're taking on Facebook, Twitter, Instagram, Snapchat, and all of the 'dinosaur platforms,' as Steve-2 likes to put it."

Joe nodded. Joannides had answered the wrong question.

"Aren't there people out there who don't like him?" Joe asked.

"Sure there are. There are always negative people and haters, especially on social media. But we like to think of them as users who just haven't been persuaded yet."

Joe nodded again and drove on. In the past, he'd been accused of appearing naive at times. But it was nothing compared to Steve-2's crew, he thought.

But then again, as Governor Allen had said, Steve-2 was a billionaire tech mogul. Joe was a Wyoming game warden.

The pavement gave way to gravel, then eventually narrowed into a two-track road. The pine trees closed in on it and branches swept by and sometimes scratched the exterior of Joe's pickup. Each time it happened, Joannides flinched as if he expected a branch to break through the windshield and impale him.

Joe drove slowly and cautiously as the trail switchbacked up the mountain. At clearings he slowed to look ahead for oncoming vehicles—there were too many places where trucks meeting on the road would have no place to pull over or back up.

As they made a sharp turn to the right on the side of the slope, the Twelve Sleep Valley opened up to the east. The vista was almost overwhelming, even for Joe, who had experienced the view many times before. Depending on the weather, the time of day, and the cloud cover, the look of the valley changed every time. The tree-clogged river zippered through the bottom and the small town of Saddlestring shimmered in the sun in a distant cluster of sun-glints. Thirty miles away, another mountain range emerged from low-hanging clouds.

The magnificence and vastness of the scene was lost on Joannides.

"I brought the green smoothies for tonight since you said we might be getting to camp late," Joannides said, not even looking up. "You don't need to worry about that."

"Good. I packed a sandwich."

"Monday, tomorrow, is green/red day. Veggies and red meat."

"Got it."

"Tuesday is chicken paprikash and spaetzle," Joannides said with a roll of his eyes. "Zsolt insisted on it and he claims he makes the best dish you can find outside of Budapest."

"I bought all the ingredients," Joe said.

"And Wednesday we fast."

"You can fast all you want," Joe said.

"Thursday I've written down 'fresh elk.' Will we have fresh elk meat by then?"

Joe shrugged. "It depends on our good fortune and Steve-2's aim."

"If not, you bought free-range chicken?"

"Either that or roasted pine grouse," Joe said. "There's a bunch of them up there where we're going."

Joannides made a pained expression at the deviation in his menu.

Joe said, "Look up and you'll see a little bear."

In fact, a small black bear, likely a yearling, was running up the middle of the road ahead of them. Its coat shone in the morning sun and the pads of its feet looked like pink slipper soles.

"A what?" Joannides said.

"A little bear."

The assistant glanced up from his iPad just as the bear ducked into the timber to the left. "It didn't look very scary," he said.

"It isn't a grizzly."

Joannides shrugged and continued. "Friday is oily fish night."

"There are a dozen cans of sardines in the panniers," Joe said.

"Sardines? I asked for wild-caught oily fish."

"I didn't have a lot of options at the grocery store. We're a long way from the ocean."

Joe didn't want to bring up the fact that all of the food he'd purchased for the ConFab group had been paid for out of his own pocket. Eventually, perhaps, the state would reimburse him. Marybeth had been concerned about it since it was the middle of the month and their budget was already stretched—they had a car repair bill due on her van and Lucy's tuition payment. It was an issue that probably hadn't even occurred to Joannides or Steve-2.

"Maybe we can have more fresh elk meat on Friday," Joannides clucked while he updated the dinner schedule on his iPad. "Then we get to Saturday. We should be done and back on the jet by then, right?"

"If it all goes well," Joe said. "No guarantees."

"If it doesn't, this whole trip will be a disaster," Joannides warned.

"I'll do my best," Joe said.

"You'll need to," the assistant said. "Do you realize how much it costs Aloft to keep our CEO away for an entire week? We're paying for pilots to sit around in your little town while we do this. The jet alone uses four hundred and fifty gallons of fuel per hour. Plus, every decision he isn't there to make can mean millions of dollars to our shareholders."

Joe took a deep breath and held it. Then he said, "I sent you a list as well. Did you get all the gear and equipment I wrote down?"

"We did our best," Joannides said. "I'm sure you can imagine that some of the items aren't easily found in downtown San Francisco."

"Got it," Joe said. "So let me know what you brought and what you didn't. I'm sure I can fill in where you're short."

Joannides scrolled to another page on his device. He said,

"We've got tents, sleeping bags and pads, headlamps, rain gear, camo clothing, optics, and personal items. Steve-2 has a knife."

Joe mulled over the items for what was missing. "I'll throw in a couple more knives, a meat saw, and some game bags."

"Yes, we weren't able to locate those. And we wondered about 'alligators'?"

"Not alligators," Joe said, stifling a smile. "*Gaiters*. You buckle them on over your boots and ankles for wet conditions or snow."

"Oh."

"Don't worry—I've got a couple of extra pair."

"Just make sure Steve-2 gets some."

"Of course."

"Anything else?"

"Where we're going, mountain money is important."

After a beat, Joannides said with mild panic, "*Mountain money?* What's that?"

"Toilet paper," Joe said. "It's more valuable than cash. It wasn't on either of our lists, but I brought plenty."

The rough two-track began to level out a mile and a half away from the trailhead. The terrain on the top of the plateau was embedded with football-sized rocks and Joe slowed his truck as he drove over them. Battle Mountain loomed in the foreground and its timbered slopes rose and dissipated into the low-hanging clouds. Tendrils of fog and vapor reached down into the trees like bony fingers.

Joannides scrolled through his iPad with a hint of desperation, as if trying to recall things he'd missed.

Joe recalled tips and techniques he'd been studying—again—for loading the packhorses and panniers. He'd practiced tying diamond hitches for days with rope, and he'd reread both *Horses, Hitches, and Rocky Trails* by Joe Back and *Packin' in on Mules and Horses* by Smoke Elser and Bill Brown to refresh his knowledge. He felt as comfortable as he could be before they set out and he was grateful Brock was accompanying them because of his familiarity with the horses.

"I feel like we're on top of the world," Joannides said. He'd finally looked up from his screen.

"We're not," Joe said. "But you can see it from here."

FOUR

Over two miles away, deep in the cover of a thick stand of spruce trees and several hundred feet higher than the trailhead parking and staging area, Earl Thomas pushed the lens of a spotting scope through a thick growth of mountain juniper. He was prone so there'd be no profile if any member of the hunting party decided to look up in his direction.

With stubby fingers the size of sausages, Earl delicately manipulated the focus knob until he could see sharply.

"It's them," he said in a low baritone. "I recognize the game warden's horse. He rides a paint."

His adult sons, Brad and Kirby, were huddled together near his feet. He'd told them not to stand up, too. They were on the back side of the small rise Earl had shinnied up to place the spotting scope.

Earl said, "One, two, three, four, five of 'em. Eight horses that I can see so far."

"Only five?" Brad said. "That don't seem like a fair fight."

"Shut up, Brad," Kirby said in a whisper. Then to Earl: "Do you see Steve-2?"

Earl didn't respond right away. He slowly panned the scope from right to left.

The two pickups, the big SUV, and the horse trailer were the only vehicles in the clearing. The rancher was backing horses out of the trailer one at a time and tying them nose-first to the side of the unit. The game warden—easily identified by the red sleeves of his uniform shirt, although he was wearing a dark vest—was pulling bag after bag of gear and equipment from the back of the SUV and stacking it in a large pile on the flat, unpaved surface. Three others milled together on the periphery of the staging area, looking on. Earl stopped his lens on them.

"There he is," Earl said to Kirby. "There's that son of a bitch."

Price stood out. He was fairly tall and slim, willowy and pale, and despite his camo hunting clothing he looked like he was wearing a costume, Earl thought. Like he was about to go trick-or-treating on Halloween. His ginger hair was like an ill-fitting skullcap.

The two men with him didn't seem comfortable with each other. One was shorter than Steve-2 and he fidgeted and bounced from foot to foot as he stood there. He kept glancing at the screen of an iPad. The other was thick in the chest with dark hair, dark clothing, and a way of holding his arms out away from his sides that suggested his bulging muscles wouldn't allow him to stand comfortably. He wore a tight parka and his eyes swept the area around them. Earl recognized the big man's actions and demeanor: security.

"Let's see if my plan works," Brad said, almost to himself.

Earl could hear the muffled click of a handheld radio behind him. Then Brad eased the volume up.

For a moment, Earl assumed the signal was bad. After all, there was a considerable distance between the staging area below and their position on the mountainside. Plus, there were other considerations.

"Maybe somebody noticed it and turned it off," Brad said.

"Or maybe it was a fucked-up idea to begin with," Kirby countered.

"Boys," Earl hissed.

Then the radio crackled. Brad turned up the volume.

"I want everyone to grab a canister of bear spray and a PLB," said a distant voice. *"Test your PLB to make sure it's fully charged. Then I'll show you how to use the bear spray."*

"That's Joe Pickett," Brad said. "I recognize his voice."

"I do, too," Kirby said.

"Yeah," Brad agreed. "Too bad he had to do this. I've always gotten along with the guy."

"Ol' Dudley Fucking Do-Right," Kirby said with derision.

"Boys, keep it down," Earl said without looking at them. The reception on the radio wasn't clear. All he could hear was murmuring and men talking over one another.

"Don't worry about using all the battery," someone said. *"We brought a couple of booster chargers and a solar unit."*

"We can't pack it all up there, though." Joe again.

"I'm supposed to wear this thing on my belt?" someone else asked.

"What's this orange thing do?"

"Do you spray it at a bear like a hose or do you, you know, blast a bunch of short bursts?"

Earl could make out what was going on by watching gestures and body language. The game warden was demonstrating how to pull the orange safety clip from the nozzle of the bear spray and trigger it to spray. He stepped away from the three onlookers until he was downwind from them. He extended his arm and Earl could clearly see a big bloom of pepper spray shoot from the canister Joe held. The cloud of red floated away from them until it dissipated near the tree line.

Afterward, Joe walked back to the group of men and personally showed each one how the spray worked. Then he helped to clip a unit of the bear spray onto Steve-2's web belt. The other two watched and did the same.

"Now we need to make some decisions," Joe said to the men. He chinned back toward the big pile of gear and equipment. *"We need to decide what we absolutely need and what we have to leave behind."*

One of the three moaned. Earl didn't think it was Steve-2.

Earl followed while Joe Pickett led the three over to the gear. Unfortunately, it was out of the range of the live radio because their voices trailed off into nothing.

"What's going on now?" Brad asked.

"They're making two piles of gear," Earl said. "Stuff that stays and stuff they'll take with them, is my guess. Jesus, they really brought a shitload of crap."

"What kind of gear are they leaving behind?" Brad asked.

"Who cares?" Kirby hissed. "What are you going to do? Go down there and root through it?"

"It's probably worth a lot of money," Brad said. "We could sell it for a lot. Those boys are richer than hell."

Earl took in a deep breath and sighed. He was getting impatient with their bickering, and both boys knew the signal and shut up.

Earl grunted as he bent around so he could see them both. Brad, the older one, was an ungainly bear of a man. Earl was big himself—over six feet tall and thick through the middle—but Brad was an even larger version of that. He wore a curly black beard and his metal-framed glasses with thick lenses were always smudged. The lenses made his eyes look bigger at certain angles, which gave him the appearance of always being puzzled and a few beats behind whatever was going on. Which, in most cases, was true.

Brad wore a camo Carhartt hunting parka the size of a tent and huge lug-soled black lace-up outfitter boots. He could pack two quarters of elk out of the backcountry with one haunch on each shoulder. His size made it necessary for him to ride a draft horse instead of a mountain quarter horse.

Kirby, meanwhile, was wiry and compact with close-cropped sidewalls and a mop of dark brown hair on top, a recent haircut that made him look like a 1930s mobster or a Nazi party member, Earl thought. Kirby *looked* mean, like his mother, and he was. He was also smart and quick and ruthless.

Earl often told clients Kirby could put the sneak on a bull moose in the willows, leap on its back, and cut its throat from behind. And Brad was there to pack it out.

His younger son favored tight-fitting high-tech KUIU camo clothing. Unlike Brad, Kirby was meticulous in his dress. There were no motor oil stains on his jacket and no mud on his knees. Under his left arm, he wore a shoulder holster with a .44 Magnum revolver, and on his right thigh, an exterior sheath with a twelve-inch bowie knife.

Earl said to both of them, "We're not going down there and looting the crap they leave behind."

Brad instantly looked away. He hated being chastised by his father, and Earl knew it. So did Kirby, who looked smug and triumphant.

"We've got a job to do," Earl said. "We can't be screwing around with things like that."

"My radio trick is working," Brad said, gesturing to his handheld.

"Except we can't hear a goddamned thing," Kirby replied.

"He's right," Earl grunted as he turned back around and positioned himself at the spotting scope. "Hearing them talk to each other doesn't help us at all. Plus, it could backfire on us if even one of them notices there's a radio on in a day bag. I'm just not sure it was worth the risk."

Kirby said, "The tracker we planted on them is good enough." That had been Kirby's idea, of course.

Earl said, "We don't need *any* of that high-tech shit. You

know how I feel about relying on technology. It's like counting on horses. Both will always let you down when you need 'em most. These guys won't be hard to track at all."

The radio in Brad's hand crackled.

"*. . . time to match up horses to riders,*" said a faint voice over the radio. The three Thomases got quiet.

It was Joe Pickett again, moving closer to the horse with the radio in the saddlebag. Earl watched as the game warden spoke to the three Californians and then obviously stepped aside and deferred to the wrangler.

They couldn't hear the wrangler speak, except a word here and there.

"Brock's sizing up each guy," Earl reported quietly to his sons. "He's matching each one to a specific horse. Like they was some kind of dude ranch or something."

"It kind of is," Brad said with derision.

"Where's Pickett in all of this?" Kirby asked.

"Off to the side saddling his horse," Earl said.

"I bet he doesn't want anything to do with these dicks," Kirby said.

Earl chuckled. He was thinking the same thing.

"Now he's putting the panniers on the packhorses," Earl said after a few minutes. "The rancher is helping him. They seem to know what they're doing."

"Can Pickett tie a diamond hitch?" Brad asked.

"Looks like it."

"Well, I'll be damned."

———

An hour later, Earl slid backward from the juniper with his spotting scope. "They're moving out."

Joe Pickett was on the lead horse, followed by Steve-2, the big dark guy, and the nervous weasel. The rancher trailed them, leading a string of three packhorses. The live radio hadn't been discovered and turned off, but the sounds from it were muffled and random.

All that the Thomases could hear over the radio was the sharp punctuation of horseshoes striking rocks and an occasional nervous word or two from the riders.

"Are you sure my saddle is tight enough?"

"Is this how you steer a horse?"

"How can I make this horse pick up the pace?"

"My butt is going to hurt like hell tonight."

Brad extended his hand and helped his father stand up. Earl's joints got stiffer every year. As he pulled Earl to his feet, Brad said, "Sounds like a bunch of guys who have no business coming into our mountains."

"I think we knew that," Kirby responded.

"Do you have to comment on everything I fucking say?" Brad said to him, raising his voice.

"Boys, please," Earl said. "Put all that bullshit aside until we're done."

"Okay, Dad," Brad said, looking down at his big boot tops. "Sorry."

Kirby rolled his eyes and turned away. Earl couldn't recall a time in Kirby's twenty-eight years on earth when he had apologized for anything. It was the way he was.

The three of them walked silently through the forest to where their horses were tied up. They'd learned long ago how to move through the timber without making a sound—stepping deliberately and walking heel-first, heel-first. Avoiding dry twigs and branches. Skirting thick dead leaves that might crackle. Spotting static branches that would make scratching sounds against the fabric of their clothing and ducking away.

As they walked, Brad fitted in an earpiece. He said he'd report anything he heard that seemed significant.

Earl untied his big bay gelding and swung up into the saddle. He tried not to grunt, even though the action was getting more difficult by the year. Once he was deep in the saddle, his knees and back stopped aching. Sometimes he wished he could live out the rest of his life on horseback.

"Brad," Earl said, "you lead the packhorses."

Brad grunted and rode to where they were tied up to trees. There were two of them, their panniers packed with gear and food. He untied the knot of the lead rope and did a quick hitch with it around his saddle horn.

One horse, a black gelding with a single white sock, bristled with rifle butts that made him look like a pincushion. The weapons were in scabbards lashed this way and that to the packsaddle.

Earl said to his boys, "Keep a good distance between us

when we ride. No nose-to-tail bullshit. This ain't no sightseeing trip."

Brad and Kirby acknowledged the order. They knew that if a horse spooked, even if it were for a dumb reason like a flushing grouse or a branch snapping back into their eyes, the trailing horse might do the same if it was close enough. Although Earl's string was well trained and considered bombproof, even the best horse was capable of doing stupid things.

Earl shot out his arm so his coat sleeve hiked up and he could see his wristwatch.

It would be eight and a half more hours until dark.

FIVE

Thirteen miles away to the southwest, twenty-four-year-old Sheridan Pickett stood near the precipice of a vast cliff face and stepped into her climbing harness. The wind whipped her blond hair across her eyes until she pinned it down with a stocking cap and tucked its length into the back of her collar. It also made her eyes tear up, and she used the back of her hand to dry them.

After double-checking the security of the anchor bolt that was wedged tightly between two truck-sized boulders and pinned into the soil by a steel rod, she threaded the climbing rope through the rappel anchor in a figure-eight follow-through knot, grasped the downhill length of it in her right hand, and backed toward the edge of the cliff.

It was at that moment, one step away from leaning back into the void, that her stomach always gripped itself and her head swooned with momentary panic. There was nothing beneath her for three hundred and fifty feet until the pile of sharp scree at the base of the sandstone feature.

If the anchor bolt gave way or her harness or equipment failed or she'd overlooked procedural safety steps on her checklist—it would be over for her.

But the rope held and pulled taut and it reassured her that she'd prepared well. The belay device on her harness held her in place, her feet in her climbing shoes were splayed wide on the vertical face of the rock, and her back was parallel to the ground below. The light blue sky filled her scope of vision and the wind had been cut, now that she'd dropped over the rim.

She took several deep breaths to calm herself.

She could feel her heart race. Although she'd had dozens of hours of instruction from Nate, from a climbing wall to windmills and the sides of local barns, she'd only rappelled down half a dozen cliffs in the past few months. She still wasn't comfortable doing it. According to Nate, he hoped she never would be.

Two hours earlier, before Sheridan had arrived at his place, Nate Romanowski had been sipping coffee at the dining room table at his compound in the sagebrush foothills when he'd heard a chirp from a speaker on the counter. Instantly, he'd narrowed his eyes and done a quick mental inventory of where his weapons were located within the house in case he needed to grab them.

The chirp meant a vehicle had entered through the distant gate.

Nate was tall and rangy with sharp blue eyes, and his blond ponytail cascaded down the yoke of his thick flannel work shirt. He'd gotten up before dawn to feed his falcons and had gotten distracted by two coyotes passing through the field who seemed to be doing surveillance on his birds in their mews. The coyotes had a sneaky way about them, how they loped along tossing their heads from side to side as if looking for rodents when they were actually scoping out the birds with sidelong glances. Nate was well aware of that particular tactic, and he'd stood up and flapped his arms to make his presence known to them.

Nate had a way with wildlife and his message had been received. The two coyotes had quickened their pace and kept going until they vanished over a hillside.

Kestrel, his thirteen-month-old daughter, had toddled into the kitchen from the hallway. He loved to watch her figure out the act of walking, the way she held her arms out at her sides for balance and took small mincing steps. When she saw him there, her face lit up and she cried, "Da!" and broke into a gallop until she tripped over her feet and crashed to her hands and knees.

Before she could realize she was hurt and start to cry, Nate scooped her up and held her out away from him at arm's length and said, "How's my little angel?"

"Da!"

"She's fine now," Liv said. "She found her daddy." Liv had followed Kestrel down the hall from the baby's bedroom.

Liv had accomplished something no woman had ever been

able to do before: she'd convinced Nate to come back on the grid, open a legitimate business, and remove his shoulder holster while eating.

"Did I hear the trespass alarm?" Liv asked.

The arrival of his daughter had pushed everything else out of his thoughts, he realized.

"Yes," he said, and handed Kestrel to Liv.

Nate parted the curtain on the dining room window and looked out. Their property was wide and treeless, and his view of the road was unencumbered. He liked it that way, especially since they rarely got visitors and those who found the place usually brought bad news of some kind, like the ex-FBI agent the year before who'd informed Nate there was a Sinaloa cartel hit out on him. Not long after that, Nate had installed the alarm at the front gate so he'd at least have some warning that someone was coming.

But there was no vehicle on the road.

Instead, a liquid herd of twenty pronghorn antelope slid in an undulating line up a hillside to the right of the gate. They'd obviously passed through and triggered the alarm. The herd trailed a spoor of dust as they ran.

"All clear," he said.

"I thought it might be Sheridan," Liv said. "She's coming this morning, right?"

"Yes."

Sheridan Pickett was Yarak, Inc.'s lone full-time employee, Nate's apprentice in falconry, and Joe's oldest daughter. She had been with them for nearly a year.

"Are you sure you want to get her involved in all of this?" Liv asked Nate. "I mean, *everything*?"

"I do," he said. "She's really coming along. She's smart and she has bird-sense. It's time she learned every aspect of the job."

"I worry about her," Liv said, bouncing Kestrel on her hip while pouring a cup of coffee.

"What about?"

"Put aside the fact that she's your best friend's daughter," Liv said. "I get worried that she's isolated out here and on her own. I know she used to have a pretty steady boyfriend back on that ranch she worked at, but pickings are pretty slim in these parts. I think about her all by herself in that little cabin, with no friends or social circle. Women need people, Nate. Even if you don't."

"I've never heard her complain," he said.

"It's not something she'd bring up to you. You aren't exactly a sympathetic ear."

"I thought I was," he said.

Liv laughed and smiled at him. "Don't forget she's a twenty-four-year-old single girl who has barely seen the world. She may want a lot more in her life than a bunch of falcons to take care of."

Nate didn't know how to respond.

"My question is," Liv continued, "are we holding her back? Is she staying with us because she feels obligated, because all of the things you and Joe have been through together? I don't want her to get to a point where she resents us."

"I don't either," he said.

"And when you say she has a lot more to learn, I hope you're talking about falconry in particular and the business in general. You're not having, you know, philosophical discussions with her, are you?"

"What's wrong with my philosophy?" he asked.

"In the past it got a lot of people killed," Liv said, deadpan. "Sheridan doesn't need to know what led to all that . . . mayhem."

"If it weren't for that, I never would have met you," Nate said.

"No," Liv said, waving a finger back and forth, but unable to completely stifle her grin. "You don't want to go there with me right now."

"Even though it's true," he said.

As he did, the trespass alert chimed again. Nate turned back to the window.

"Here she comes now."

Once you get cocky about rock climbing," Nate had lectured Sheridan, "your chances of doing something sloppy or stupid go way up. That's how you fall and die, and then I have to find another apprentice falconer."

His bedside manner left a lot to be desired, she'd thought at the time, but his words stuck with her.

Nate had been an important player in Sheridan's life—and her family's—since she was ten years old. He'd always simply *been around*—despite long absences that were whispered about by her parents and kept from their daughters, and then showing up at odd times. But when he did show up, he was larger than life and he filled the room with a kind of smoldering charisma that she'd never encountered in a man before.

Nate was a self-described "outlaw falconer" with a Special Forces background. He was proficient with large-caliber five-shot revolvers, especially the .454 Casull and the .500 Wyoming Express, both manufactured by Freedom Arms in Freedom, Wyoming. He was also a master falconer, and that had captured Sheridan's imagination to a greater degree than his shadowy past or weaponry.

She could recall the first time, in her early teens, when she'd accompanied him to a small series of willow-choked beaver ponds in the foothills of the Bighorn Mountains. After releasing his peregrine to the sky, he'd waded into one of the ponds, gathering up paddling ducks who were too scared to go airborne. She'd never seen anything like it and it had opened her eyes to a natural order of things she thought long bypassed by the twenty-first century. And it had made her want to become a falconer herself.

Over the years, despite both of their individual journeys, they'd tracked each other. He'd presented her with a tiny kestrel and taught her how to feed, nurture, and fly the smallest of falcons. When it had flown away and never come back, he took her aside and explained that it happened to the best of them. A falconer could "train" a bird to always return, but only at the cost of breaking its wild and predatory instincts. It was better to watch a bird fly away than to turn it into a parakeet. It was a hard lesson.

Nate's relationship with her dad was contentious, yet devoted. It was also very complicated, since her father operated by the letter of the law and Nate operated under his own. She knew they'd had serious disagreements, and she'd witnessed some of them. It was only after she'd gotten older, after graduating from college, working as the head wrangler on an exclusive dude ranch, and returning back to Twelve Sleep County, that she'd realized in a moment of revelation that the bond between her dad and Nate was very much like the bond between Nate and his falcons.

That bond was deep, but predicated on achieving the same goal in the end. With a falcon, it was delivering its next meal. With her dad, it was achieving an end, even if he didn't necessarily approve of every step taken to get there.

Her mother's relationship with Nate was even more complicated. Sheridan couldn't help but notice how her mother lit up when Nate came into the room. Despite some of the crimes Nate had been accused of—several of which Sheridan had no doubt he'd committed—her mother was absolutely loyal to the falconer. She'd once overheard her mother telling her best friend after one too many glasses of wine that if anything ever happened to Joe she'd know where to turn. Sheridan tried hard not to think about that very much.

And, of course, Nate had found Olivia Brannan.

———

For the past year, Sheridan had shadowed Nate on bird abatement calls throughout Wyoming, Montana, Idaho, Utah, Colorado, and South Dakota. She'd also spent the long winter reading through Nate's library of ancient Scottish falconry tomes and modern techniques. It was her job to feed Yarak's Air Force, which consisted of nine mature falcons and two "trainers." Feeding them was easy because they were voracious, but keeping a supply of their food—pigeons, rabbits, mice, gophers, sometimes ducks—was an elemental and bloody business. She'd finally learned to think of prey species as exactly that, although she still found herself turning away when a bird ripped a living creature limb from limb and ate everything: bones, hide, guts, and head.

"Circle of Life" from *The Lion King* was a fine song and she'd loved it growing up, but seeing *nature, red in tooth and claw*, as Tennyson wrote, up close was gritty and difficult. Although she revered the birds of prey for their capabilities and grace in flight, she had come to be wary of them for their ruthlessness and cold-blooded disposition.

The cliff face Sheridan was negotiating now, above the meandering Twelve Sleep River, was remarkable in that four of the six species Nate used in his bird abatement business (red-tailed hawks, prairie falcons, peregrines, and the occasional gyrfalcon) maintained nests there. Since he preferred to use birds he caught himself, it was an amazing resource. No one but Liv and now Sheridan knew about the location, and it told Sheridan a lot that he trusted her enough to show it to her and ask her to rappel down its face.

She rotated her shoulders so she could turn her head and look down. His Jeep was just arriving at the base of the cliff after dropping her off twenty minutes before. The road he'd used was rocky and washed out and it had taken him a while. The top of the fabric roof was a square far below her. Once the Jeep stopped, Nate got out and looked up.

He flashed her a thumbs-up, and she extended her left hand and reciprocated. Her right hand gripped the rope beneath the rappel anchor.

Before descending farther, she checked to make sure the carabiners were screwed down tight where the rope would thread. She knew they were—she'd checked everything twice as instructed—but a third time was always a good idea.

Sheridan relaxed the tight muscles of her legs, bent slightly at the knees, and pushed off while letting the rope slide through her right hand until she dropped four feet. Then she did it again. She wasn't yet ready to fly down a mountainside in a single graceful swoop.

Her thin-soled climbing shoes gripped the texture of the sandstone and she could feel the cold of the rock on her feet. It was still a couple of hours until the sun would warm the surface of it.

She wore tight climbing pants over a thin wool inner layer

and a windproof shell on her upper body. Baggy clothing was dangerous, as folds of it could snag on brush or roots that stuck out from the cliff. A chest pack was cinched tightly against her breasts, containing the gear she'd need.

The first falcon nest, which belonged to a family of redtails, was ten feet below her and slightly to her right. It was tucked in a wind-hollowed alcove and it consisted of a two-foot-wide tangled bed of branches and twigs festooned with the small pinfeathers of consumed prey, almost like macabre decoration.

Sheridan stepped a few feet to the right and then carefully lowered herself to the side of the nest. Although it was unlikely there was anyone home, she'd been cautioned by Nate never to approach a nest straight-on until she could see it clearly and assess if it was occupied.

If there was a resting falcon on the nest and she surprised it, the bird might react in a panic and slash her face with its talons, trying to escape. More than a few falconers had been blinded that way, and some years back a couple had plunged to their deaths.

So she secured the rope to the side of the alcove and carefully peered in.

The nest, as she suspected, was empty. In the hollowed-out bed were more stray feathers, tiny white bones from prey that had been eaten within it, and slivers of eggshells that looked like weathered costume jewelry that had been smashed with a hammer.

Being as close as she was to a falcon nest, so close she could reach inside and pluck a bone from the twigs, made her feel like a voyeur, as if she were walking through the empty bedroom of an unsuspecting stranger.

Her purpose for checking out the redtail nest was to ascertain if it was viable or abandoned, even though any hatchlings would have been born in the spring and since flown away. Not all nests were used annually, and different species of raptors sometimes took them over and made them their own. Occasionally, snakes would move in and make the nest uninhabitable, until the snakes themselves left or died.

This nest, Sheridan thought, looked viable. The remnants of eggshells proved that it had been used just that previous spring to raise little ones. The bones of the prey delivered to the nest looked just a few months old.

But since she was new at judging the condition of existing nests, Nate had told her to photograph the location so he could study it and make a final determination. Sheridan unzipped the chest pack and dug into it for her cell phone.

As she powered it up and punched in the passcode, something about the nest struck her as odd. At first, she couldn't figure out what it was—maybe she simply hadn't studied enough wild nests.

There was something off about the edge of the nest itself, she decided. It was positioned within the alcove on a natural shelf and it didn't completely fill the space as an eagle's nest would have. There was exposed shelf on both sides, and on the right side of the nest, beneath a film of dust, was what looked like a symmetric dark *C* shape. The opening of the *C* arched around the nest. It was smooth and without a flaw. Nothing in nature was perfect like that. She took several pictures.

It wasn't until she shifted her position that she noted something else: a glint from a long thread extending across the mouth of the nest. It stretched from the left side of the nest across the top of the structure and vanished in the twigs and debris of the nest edge near the opening of the *C*.

"A spider's web?" she said out loud. But it was too straight. Too perfect. A single strand of spider's web would have dislodged in the wind, wouldn't it?

After dropping her cell phone back in the pack and zipping it closed, Sheridan continued to study the *C* and the line. It made no sense to her.

When she turned and looked down at Nate, he gestured up to her with both hands out, as if to say, *What are you doing up there?* After all, there were three other nests for her to check out before she could get firm footing on the ground. One had been occupied by prairie falcons, another by peregrines, and the last and biggest by gyrfalcons. Nate obviously thought she was taking too much time with this one.

There was no way to communicate with him—her cell phone had no signal and they hadn't brought radios. To try and indicate what she'd found, she locked the rope anchor to hold her in place and formed a *C* with her arms and gestured into the alcove.

Nate shook his head, not understanding.

"I don't know what I found," she yelled. But the distance between Sheridan and Nate was too far and the wind at the base didn't help. He couldn't understand her.

She sighed and decided to simply show him the photos when she got down. Maybe Nate would know what it was.

Before she unlocked the anchor and rappelled to the next nest, though, Sheridan's curiosity got the best of her and she reached out with her hand and tapped the string to free it.

The result was instant. There was a metallic *snap* and a flash of movement and her entire head, shoulder, and arm were suddenly engulfed within the jaws of some kind of large trap. Her vision blurred and she could taste grit in her mouth.

She pushed away from the cliff involuntarily while she screamed and found herself twisting slowly in the air, looking out from inside the mouth of the device.

It took her a few moments to get her breath back and realize that she wasn't actually maimed—the pressure of the trap was firm but not tight, the jaws of the device were made of fiberglass tubing connected by springs, and the mouth of it enveloping her consisted only of light mesh.

Sheridan locked her rope tight and used both hands to pry the device open and duck underneath it, where it hung in the air. When she realized the trap was secured to the sandstone beneath the ledge, she reached up and pulled the stake free. Then she watched as the trap floated slowly to the ground like a damaged parachute until Nate reached out and snagged it.

———

There were two other set traps hidden on the sides of nests on her way down and she dismantled them both and dropped them to the ground.

At the fourth nest, she paused and cringed and cursed. A prairie falcon had been caught days before. Its body was a hard ball of feathers and its eyes had been eaten out by insects.

She was instantly enraged. Not only had someone set falcon traps on every viable nest on the cliffside of Nate's secret falcon location, they'd failed to check the traps in a timely fashion. The bird had either starved to death or had been so frightened that its heart had given out.

Nate stood at the base of the cliff as still as she had ever seen him. The dismantled mesh traps surrounded him in a pile.

"All of them?" he asked Sheridan through clenched teeth.

"Yes."

"These are bownet traps," he said evenly. "Someone is tres-passing on my cliff. And someone is going to die."

Falconers, she'd come to learn, had a strict code about en-croaching on other falconer's territory. It wasn't done, and the penalty for it was fierce.

"Maybe we should tell my dad," she said. Game wardens were empowered to sign off on falconry permits in their area after the applicant had passed the California Hawking Club's written test. Maybe her dad would have an idea of who else was operating in the district.

"Any scumbag who would set up traps on another man's honey hole isn't the type who would apply for a license," Nate said.

"But we should try that first, right?"

He glared at her. "That sounds like something Joe would say. No. Falconers take care of their own business. Haven't you learned that yet?"

SIX

While Nate and Sheridan headed back to his place, Marybeth Pickett sat across a table in the Burg-O-Pardner restaurant from interim county prosecutor AnnaBelle Griffith, who seemed nervous and a little agitated. It was midafternoon and the lunch crowd had dispersed, so the two women were the only customers in the place, which smelled of faint cigarette smoke and grease from the kitchen, where the specialty, deep-fried Rocky Mountain oysters, had been served for twenty-seven years.

The interior of the restaurant was dated; its light-colored paneling buckled near the ceiling and its deer and elk mounts were interspersed with fading Gordon Snidow Coors Beer prints between them. There were no menus. Breakfast, lunch, and dinner items were written on a whiteboard in quivering script.

Marybeth had suggested they meet at a coffee shop on Main Street, but Griffith had insisted on the Burg-O-Pardner. Since they'd both ordered coffee, Marybeth wasn't sure what Griffith was thinking.

"I've heard of the Burg-O-Pardner since I moved here," Griffith said as the coffee was served. "I wanted to see it for myself. I was kind of expecting more."

"It doesn't look like much," Marybeth said. "But for whatever reason it's the place where all the city fathers meet every morning to discuss local issues. It's our shadow city hall."

"Are any of the city fathers women?"

"Rarely."

Griffith nodded. "I understand that the decision to reach out to me for the job was made here."

"I wouldn't doubt it."

AnnaBelle Griffith, dressed in a dark business suit over a white top and wearing a thin strand of pearls, was in her early thirties, trim, and tightly wrapped, Marybeth thought. She'd recently been asked by the Twelve Sleep County commissioners to fill in as county prosecutor until the next local election, after the last county prosecutor, Duane Patterson, had met his sudden demise. Prior to that, Griffith had been an assistant district attorney in Natrona County.

The commissioners had been busy, and Marybeth understood the pressure they'd been under the past year. Not only had Patterson been gunned down by an associate in the street, but the newly elected sheriff, Brendan Kapelow, had simply packed his belongings and moved away before the state's Division of Criminal Investigation could open a review of his past actions. Although there were some concerns that Kapelow would file suit against the county for the injuries he'd sustained while on the job, he hadn't done so yet.

The commissioners had also asked former Niobrara County sheriff Scott Tibbs to come out of retirement and fill the role in Twelve Sleep County on a temporary basis. Tibbs was older, folksy, slow-moving, and, most of all, clean when it came to scandal. He had a huge white mustache and jowls, and enjoyed the Christmas season because he looked forward to playing Santa whenever he was asked. Thus far, Tibbs had been blessed with a quiet year, with no major crimes or controversies. His easygoing manner was at odds with that kind of thing, and he'd apparently been rewarded for it. His deputies and clerical staff seemed to like him, and he made a point of telling the Saddlestring *Roundup* that he was "button-poppin' proud" of his team.

Marybeth reserved judgment on both new officials. Anna-Belle seemed competent if hard-charging, and Tibbs seemed anything but. It had been Marybeth's experience that political entities always hired the exact opposite of whoever was being replaced, and it seemed to be the case here. Joe had proceeded cautiously with them both as well, saying, "Every time I get to know and like these folks, something bad seems to happen to them."

Do you have any ties to our valley?" Marybeth asked Griffith.

"Not really anymore," Griffith said. "I used to come up here in the summer and stay at my grandparents' cabin in the Bighorns. I always liked it. But no, I don't know many people here yet."

"I'll help with that," Marybeth said. "In fact, there's a Chamber of Commerce social tomorrow night at Rex's Taxidermy on Main Street. You should come. I'll introduce you around to the business community."

Griffith nodded, but didn't commit. She seemed suspicious of Marybeth and not quite comfortable with her. Marybeth empathized. After all, she was about to ask something very sensitive of the new county prosecutor.

"Do you plan to put down roots here?" Marybeth asked.

"I haven't made that decision yet. I'm operating one day at a time. I know how fortunate I am to get a position like this, given my age and gender. I want to make the most of it and we'll go from there."

"Good for you," Marybeth said. "It won't be as hard as you think. This place is filled with strong women. The county attorney before Duane Patterson was Dulcie Schalk. She is my best friend."

"And you're the director of the library," Griffith said. "I haven't been in there yet."

"I know."

Griffith looked startled.

"I didn't mean to sound judgmental," Marybeth said. "I'm not chastising you. But it's an old Carnegie building and very small. I usually know who's there and who's not."

Griffith sipped her coffee and winced. "This is quite strong."

Then: "Is there really a purpose to libraries anymore, with the Internet and all?"

Marybeth tried not to react. She said, "Small-town libraries are often community centers as well. Ours is. It's a place where you can meet a good cross section of locals and learn more about them. I find out more about what's going on in the valley by talking with locals than any other means."

"Interesting."

Marybeth didn't want to say how much Joe relied on her for inside information and intel when it came to his own job and the cases he worked. Not only did she use library resources to do research and access law enforcement databases, she was also his behind-the-scenes partner and adviser. Her position at the library provided him with background and insight he'd never have by himself.

Marybeth took a sip of coffee as well. It was bitter and she guessed the pot had likely stayed on the warmer since lunchtime.

"You asked me to meet you," Griffith said.

"I guess there's no reason to beat around the bush. May I call you AnnaBelle?"

"Sure."

"AnnaBelle, I know you inherited a caseload of work when you took over here. In particular, there are potential charges against a man named Nate Romanowski."

"Ah," Griffith said with a self-satisfied smile. "Now I know why we're here."

"Nate is an old family friend," Marybeth said. "There's no

doubt he's a different kind of person and he's very rough around the edges. But he's a good man."

"A good man?" Griffith said. "Are we talking about the guy who is accused of assaulting the last sheriff and literally ripping his ear off of his head? That good man?"

"Yes," Marybeth said. "As I'm sure you've seen from the case notes, his wife and baby had been kidnapped, he needed to get out of jail to save them, and the sheriff refused to help or cooperate. And Nate never should have been jailed in the first place. That's in the notes, too."

Griffith took in Marybeth and looked her over carefully. Marybeth tried not to crack.

"We probably shouldn't be having this conversation. You're asking me to make a determination on an ongoing case."

"I guess I am," Marybeth said.

"I can't do that."

"I get that. I do. But I thought it important that you know the background. Nate is . . . unique."

"Are you saying he should be judged by a different set of rules than everyone else?"

Marybeth realized that was *exactly* what she was asking, although hearing it in so many words unsettled her for a moment.

"Let me put it this way," Marybeth said. "You're new here. You're obviously smart and ambitious."

"Thank you, I guess."

"In your job, you'll likely make enemies."

Griffith didn't reply.

Marybeth said, "If somebody decided to hurt you, you'd want someone like Nate around."

Griffith looked at Marybeth quizzically. "What would he do?"

"Whatever he had to. Nate has been looking after our family for a long time. I don't always condone his methods, but it's very reassuring to know he's out there."

"Isn't that why we have law enforcement?" Griffith asked.

"It should be," Marybeth conceded. "But it doesn't always work out that way."

At that moment, Marybeth felt her phone burr in her purse on her lap. She glanced down to check the screen.

"I'm really sorry," she said. "I have to take this."

Joe?" Marybeth said. She stood in the vestibule of the Burg-O-Pardner. "How is it going so far?"

"Let's just say there's tension in the air," he said. "But I'll tell you more later."

"I'm surprised you called."

"Yeah, me too. But there's only one place on the face of the mountain that I can get an actual cell signal and I didn't want to waste it. We're way ahead of schedule, so I have the time. After this, I'll have to call you on the satellite phone at night."

"Thank you. I'm glad you took it with you."

"Oh, we've got loads of gear," Joe said wearily. "Sat phones,

GPS units, PLBs, solar chargers, portable satellite broadband transmitters and receivers, and stuff I've never even heard of before. It's quite a wilderness adventure."

She laughed and could picture Joe grimacing at the sight of all that electronic equipment.

"That's so Mr. Price can post everything you do on the trip," Marybeth said. "But let me caution you. Don't let him take photos of you or mention you by name. I looked on ConFab earlier and there's already a lot of backlash."

"Backlash?"

"Anonymous people say all sorts of horrible things on social media. You know that."

"That's why I avoid it."

"I know, and it's the right way to go."

"What are they saying?" Joe asked.

"You can imagine, I think. People who are anti-hunters, vegans, people who call themselves humanists. They're all flaming Steve-2 about going on this trip. They can get really vicious."

"So there's some bad stuff, huh?"

"It's hard to remember sometimes that the people who comment are a really small percentage of the people on ConFab," she said. "Only the worst ones actually post things, and they're anonymous, of course. They'd never use their real names or say those things directly to Steve-2. But there are some good posts, too."

Marybeth chose not to tell Joe about a few of the comments she'd read at lunch. One in particular suggested it would be a good outcome if Steve-2 and all of the people with him were murdered, beheaded, and their heads mounted on the wall as if they were the game animals they were hunting.

"Joe?" Marybeth said.

"Yes?"

"Do you think you could convince Steve-2 just to stay off-line for a while?"

"I really doubt if that's possible," Joe said. "These people are glued to their devices at all times. It's like their phones are part of them."

"Please try. I don't want you to be the target of all these people. And I don't want your daughters to see what people are saying about you."

She could hear Joe take a long breath. "I'll try," he said.

"Take his phone away from him," Marybeth said. "Tell him it's for his own good."

"You haven't met him," Joe said. "He thinks he's doing something noble."

"He might be, but try to convince him to keep it to himself until he's done with the hunting trip."

"It's not that easy," Joe said. "He wants people to get a clue where their food comes from through this trip. It's important to him, or so he says. I have trouble arguing with that."

Marybeth glanced inside the restaurant and saw Griffith reach out and call for the check. She was ready to leave.

"I've got to go," she said. "Call me tonight."

"I will."

"And try to convince Steve-2 to go dark. The world doesn't

need to know everything he experiences. There's value in solitude. Tell him that."

"I kind of like that one," Joe said.

"Love you."

"Love you."

Marybeth slipped her phone back into her purse and sat down at the table before the proprietor could deliver the bill to Anna-Belle Griffith.

"That was my husband. He's high in the mountains where there's no phone signal, so when he gets the chance to call, I need to take it."

"Oh, I know all about that," Griffith said with a loopy grin Marybeth hadn't anticipated. "I saw his photo on my ConFab feed this morning. He's up there guiding Steve-2 himself."

Marybeth knew she'd recoiled. "You saw him?"

"*Everybody* saw him," Griffith said. "I got texts from friends in Casper and all over asking if I knew Joe or about the hunt with Steve-2."

"What did you tell them?"

Griffith said, "I told them I'd met him in passing, but I was actually having coffee with his wife just this very afternoon."

"I don't think Joe has any idea what he's gotten himself into," Marybeth said. "Social media is a cesspool."

"Maybe he'll go viral."

Marybeth briefly closed her eyes and tried to regroup.

"Where were we?" she asked when she opened them.

"You were trying to convince me to look the other way in regard to Nate Romanowski," Griffith said, putting her game face back on.

"That is what I was trying to do."

"Do you realize how inappropriate that is?"

"I do."

Griffith sat back in her chair and looked at Marybeth coolly. "I've heard through the grapevine that Judge Hewitt is quite fond of Romanowski, for reasons I don't yet understand. I've also heard that your friend is represented by Spencer Rulon, your former governor. I'm new here, but I can see when a case is stacked against me from the start. We should probably forget that we had this conversation."

"I've already forgotten it," Marybeth said.

"Me too."

SEVEN

The hunting party established their elk camp on the edge of a mountain meadow as long thin shadows from lodgepole pine trees turned the grass into jail bars. Joe and Brock Boedecker did all of the work. Four tents had been set up: three dome tents for sleeping and one outfitter wall tent with a small stove inside for cooking meals and providing heat.

The dark bank of storm clouds Joe had noted earlier in the day had scudded across the mountains and they were now hunkered down on the north summit, as if curled up and parked there for the night. He was grateful there had been no snow on the ride up, but snow would be just fine. It was easier to track elk in snow than on the dry pine needle forest they would be going into.

Joe filled two five-gallon plastic water bags in a small stream and carried them back to the campsite with one in each hand. They were heavy. He raised each and looped the upper handle around broken-off tree joints to suspend them, then fitted water filter assemblies to the bottom of the bags and attached plastic tubing to each. He was tired from the ride and his inner thighs were already rubbed raw from the saddle. It was early, but he knew he'd be ready to crawl into his sleeping bag.

When the water supply was secure, he looked around the camp and went through a mental checklist. Tents were up and ready. Joannides and Zsolt would be in one, Steve-2 by himself in another, Brock and him in the third. A camp table and chairs were unfolded and set up in the cook tent as well as lanterns. A small supply of firewood was stacked near the little potbellied outfitter stove. Their bags of food were a hundred yards from the camp itself and hung high in trees to prevent marauding bears from rooting through them. A pop-up latrine was set up a hundred and fifty yards away in the other direction, hole already dug.

Brock Boedecker was at the far end of the meadow, unsaddling, grooming, and picketing the horses. Joe could hear him singing a cowboy song to himself: Marty Robbins, "Streets of Laredo."

As the sun dropped, so did the temperature. A stillness enveloped the meadow, amplifying every sound. The cooling air smelled of pine, sweaty horses, and woodsmoke. It was the very best time of the day in the high mountains, Joe thought. They'd gone as far as they could go, much farther than he'd thought they'd progress the first day, camp was set up, and dinner was to come. He didn't think he'd ever grow weary of it.

He placed his hands on his hips and took it all in.

Tim Joannides sat on a stump near the campfire, scrolling

through something on his phone. One of the portable satellite broadband units was on another stump next to him. While Joe set up the camp, Joannides had volunteered to keep the fire going. But he'd apparently gotten distracted because it was burned down to ashes and nearly out.

Zsolt Rumy had spent his time circumnavigating the location they'd chosen, checking for high ground, trails, and sight lines, he'd said. The ride up had warmed him and he strode around with his coat open. Joe noted Rumy had two shoulder holsters under his parka with black straps that criss-crossed over his chest.

Neither man, Joe noted, had offered to help set up the camp or shown any interest in the location. Rumy had placed his bear spray somewhere, although Joannides had his canister near his feet.

Steve-2 had shadowed Joe the entire time. He kept a respectful distance, but he was never very far away.

"Here," Joe said to him. "I'll show you how to get water."

Price came over, his expression curious. Joe snatched a tin cup from a bag of cooking utensils and walked over to the water bags. He raised one of the lengths of tubing and released the pinch valve on the end so that a thin stream of water flowed out. Joe filled the cup, handed it to Price, and tightened the valve so no water would be wasted.

"We filter it to prevent giardia," Joe said. "The creek looks pure, but you never know what might be upstream. Once, I found a decomposing moose fifty yards upstream from where I drank."

Price made a sour face and the cup hesitated near his mouth.

"It's okay," Joe assured him.

Price gulped it down and held out the cup. "I didn't realize how thirsty I was."

"You do it," Joe said, stepping aside. "And remember to drink twice as much water as you think you'd ever want. The elevation and the dry air will turn you into jerky if you don't."

Price nodded and filled the cup two more times.

"I noticed you've got quite a limp," he said to Joe. "Are you sure you can get around?"

"I'm fine."

"What happened?"

"Got shot."

Price looked up, his eyes wide. "Seriously?"

"Seriously. But that was a year ago. I put away my cane four months ago. If I hadn't been in that saddle all day stiffening up, you wouldn't even notice."

"Who shot you?"

Joe shook his head. Then: "Our doctor."

"Your *doctor* shot you?"

"Long story," Joe said. "I'll tell you about it one of these days."

He nodded toward Boedecker on the far side of the pasture. "Right now, I'm going to help Brock take care of our horses before it gets dark. The horses come first."

"Mind if I come along?" Price seemed eager, almost childlike.

"As long as you don't bring your phone."

"My phone is an extension of me," Price said, chuckling. "That would be like asking me to cut off my arm and leave it here in the grass."

Joe rolled his eyes. "Just please don't post any more photos of me, then. It distresses my wife and daughters."

"They're ConFab users? Excellent."

Joe grunted in response.

"ConFab is an agent of good," Price said. "It's not like those other toilets on the Internet. ConFab exists to bring like-minded people together in worthwhile conversations, not to tear people down."

Joe thought Price sounded defensive—and well-rehearsed.

As they crossed the meadow the shadows deepened.

"So is this going to be our camp for the duration of the hunting trip?" Price asked Joe.

"Maybe. I was up here two weeks ago to scout and I saw a lot of healthy elk. We made great progress today to get here. I thought it would take a day and a half, but our early start really helped. The elk up here don't get a lot of hunting pressure be-cause most guys are road hunters and they don't venture this far into the mountains. It's real work to pack an elk out," Joe said. "I figure tomorrow we'll get up real early and glass the meadows about a mile away. We might catch them grazing or about to bed down."

"What if they aren't there?" Price asked.

"Then we'll go farther to the east. We might move the camp

if we need to. Elk are wily. They never seem to be where you expect them to be."

"It's amazing how fast it gets dark and cools down up here," Price said. "It's so still."

"It'll get chilly tonight, but it looks like you brought good sleeping bags."

"I can't remember the last time I saw the stars," Price said. "I mean, *really* saw the stars. It was probably in the Galápagos or a week I spent in Tibet."

"We've got good stars," Joe said. "I recommend our stars."

"What's that pistol you're wearing?"

"It's a Colt Python .357 Magnum. They used to be standard issue for game wardens until the department went to .40 Glocks like everybody else in law enforcement. I kept mine."

"Will it kill a bear? I assume that's why you've got it."

Joe said, "A larger caliber is preferred, like a .44 Mag or a .454 Casull. But yes, it could kill a bear with a well-placed shot. I've loaded it with hot loads that really pack a punch."

"Are you a good shot?"

"I am not a good shot," Joe confessed. "That's why I carry bear spray and keep my shotgun within reach when I'm in the field. But if given a choice in a split second, I'll reach for the spray first. It usually works."

"Usually?" Price said with alarm.

"Yup."

Joe didn't want to tell Price about the grizzly attack that had killed a guide from Dubois the year before. After the Predator Attack Team had located the bear and killed it, they found that the carcass reeked of bear spray. Meaning that on that one instance, it hadn't worked at all to deter the predator. But that was rare.

"I don't know anything about guns except that I don't like them," Price said.

"They're just tools," Joe said with a shrug. "They all have different capabilities and purposes. It would be like going through life with just a screwdriver. If you live out here, you need a complete toolbox."

"Tools that can kill innocent people," Price said.

Joe sighed.

"Everybody out here is armed to the teeth, aren't they?" Price asked.

"Yup."

"The gun culture is so strong out here," Price said. "I just don't get it."

"Most everybody hunts," Joe said. "But those that don't have guns, too."

"The murder rate must be really high."

"It isn't."

"Really?"

"Really. You can look it up. Folks are less likely to threaten somebody with a gun if that somebody is likely armed themselves." Joe paused and asked, "Do we really want to have this conversation?"

"Probably not," Price said. "I don't think either of us is likely to change our mind. We just live in different worlds."

"Yup."

They walked in silence for a minute, then Price said, "You can blame Steve Rinella for me being here."

"Steve Rinella? Really?"

"Have you heard of him?"

"We've got one of his wild-game cookbooks at home," Joe said.

"Ah, I should have guessed. I've read a lot of his work, and a year ago I binge-watched *MeatEater* on Netflix. I became absolutely fascinated with the idea of harvesting my own protein. It seems so pure and primal. It takes the thoughtless cruelty and inhumanity of the mega-corporations out of the equation, it seems to me."

Joe nodded. Price was going on in a way that didn't really invite a response or comment.

"When you see what happens on factory farms," Price continued, "it's just an assembly line of soulless slaughter. Those animals never get to live the experience of being animals. They're just organisms. Some of them never see the sky or eat a blade of grass. They're pumped full of hormones, fed chemically enhanced pellets, and grow until they're killed and butchered. All so we can buy the meat in a sterile package at a supermarket and never even think of where it comes from or how it got there.

"I tried to go vegan, I really did," he said. "I did it for nine months, but I found my brain getting fuzzy. I couldn't focus and I lost my sharpness. I knew I was hardwired to eat meat, but I knew there had to be a better way to get it, a way to earn it with dignity shared between me and the animal who sacrificed and gave up its life so I could eat. I needed skin in the game."

"Got it," Joe said. He picked up one of the saddles Boedecker had placed upside down in the grass to air out and carried it into the trees, where he placed it near the base of a pine tree. If it rained or snowed during the night, the saddle would likely stay dry. Toby was picketed a few yards away from the tree and he was greedily eating meadow grass.

"My board doesn't really understand where I'm coming from," Price said, still trailing Joe. "Nobody does. But I need to experience this on a basic level. I need to get blood on my hands. This is why I'm here. This is why *we're* here."

"Since you're here, why don't you grab one of those saddles?" Boedecker said to Price from where he was brushing down one of the packhorses. "Put it over in the trees with Joe's. Then we can get started on dinner before it's completely dark."

"Excuse me?" Price said in alarm. It was as if Boedecker had rudely derailed his train of thought.

"I've got it," Joe said to Boedecker, picking up another saddle. He'd been slightly mesmerized by Price's reverie.

"I think I'll head back and get some water," Price said. Then he turned on his heel and walked toward the camp and the fire.

"Take it easy on him," Joe said softly to Boedecker when Price was out of hearing range.

"Why? Did I offend him? We're busting our asses getting this camp set up and those dudes are either sitting around or yapping too much. Kind of what I expected when I saw 'em get out of the plane. They like to be catered to."

"Yup," Joe said. "That's the job."

"It don't mean I have to enjoy it."

"I find Steve-2 kind of interesting," Joe said. "I didn't expect that."

"He talks more than my wife," Boedecker said sourly.

Joe started to respond but decided not to. Silence, he'd found, was often the best argument. Tension was natural between members of a hunting party when you're thrown together into close quarters with people you've met just hours before. It was a complicated and delicate dynamic, all those strong personalities in what was almost a closed room. So unless the disagreement was about safety or security, Joe preferred to stay out of it.

He was a little surprised Brock voiced such hostility, though. Brock took inexperienced clients into the mountains all summer long on multiday pack trips. Maybe Boedecker was just a little burned out. It happened often in the guide and outfitter business. Bitterness toward clients brought down as many wilderness enterprises as the economy or loss of access.

"Looks like we'll need to gather more wood," Boedecker said after a long glance at the campsite. "That Joannides guy nearly let the fire die out, and now he's building a bonfire."

Joe looked over his shoulder. Boedecker had a point. The fire was enormous and throwing showers of sparks in the direction of the tent.

"It's like taking little boys camping," Boedecker said.

EIGHT

I don't know what they're doing down there," Aidan Jacketta said aloud to himself as he leaned into his spotting scope and zeroed in on the large campfire. "It looks like they're trying to burn down the whole forest."

Jacketta was long and lean with a pointy blond beard and tiny-lens, horn-rimmed glasses. He was on his belly beneath a canopy of low-hanging pine boughs to observe the hunting party's camp far below. A small white-gas camp stove hissed near his feet, but the water in the pot hadn't yet begun to boil. His simple one-man tent was set up at the base of a massive ponderosa pine and his sleeping bag and pad were unfurled inside it. His soiled camo cap was tilted back on his head so the brim wouldn't interfere with the eyepiece.

"Fucking idiots," a deep voice said from the trees to his right.

Jacketta scrambled to his feet, startled. He was camping

alone and hadn't seen any sign of other hunters, hadn't even heard anyone approaching.

"I guess you're watching that group of idiots down there," the voice said.

Jacketta glanced toward his custom recurve hunting bow, which was strung tight and hanging from a peg on a tree trunk next to his tent. His quiver of ten homemade arrows hung next to it.

The man who'd spoken moved out of the shadows until his bearded face glowed with the reflection of Jacketta's small stove flame. He glided into the camp as if sliding on a track, without making an audible footfall.

"Brad Thomas?" Jacketta said when he got a good look at the visitor. "Is that you?"

"Aidan Jacketta, right?" Brad said. "I didn't expect to find you here. I didn't expect to find *anybody* up here."

Jacketta let out a long breath and relaxed his shoulders. He no longer felt the need to snatch up his bow.

"I didn't hear you coming," Jacketta said.

"That's the idea. I didn't mean to startle you."

"Well, you did."

"You weren't thinking of pulling a weapon, were you?" Brad said. "Because I hope not."

Jacketta could now see that Brad held a short carbine of some kind with the muzzle down. It could be swung up and fired in less than a second.

"I'm not rifle hunting," Jacketta said. "Here, I'll show you."

Jacketta pulled a headlamp from the pocket of his cargo pants and strapped it over his cap. He turned it on to the lowest light. Since the beam went wherever he turned his head, Jacketta deliberately avoided staring at Brad full-on. Blinding someone temporarily with a headlamp was rude camp etiquette.

Instead, he shined the beam on his recurve bow and quiver.

"See?" he said.

Brad moved over into the light and reached out and fingered the leather-wrapped grip of the bow and tapped on the extended stabilizer.

"Nice bow," Brad said. "Did you make it yourself?"

"I did," Jacketta said with some pride in his voice. "That was my winter project. I made the arrows, too."

Brad *hmmm*ed his appreciation. "Looks like a piece of art. I didn't know you had that in you. Can you hit anything with it?"

"I can hit a target. It's got a sixty-five-pound pull."

Brad *hmmm*ed again. "Seeing anything?" he asked.

"I passed on a spike this morning," Jacketta said. "He walked up to me at twenty feet and just stood there staring for a while. It would have been a fairly easy shot."

"But you want something bigger," Brad said.

"I'd like a big bull, but I could live with a big lead cow. This is about meat, for me."

"Yeah, I know."

Jacketta had tangled with the Thomas clan at a Game and Fish Department public meeting the year before. Jacketta was a software engineer who'd moved from Boulder to the Twelve Sleep Valley to, as he put it, live a more basic existence. He was a low-impact kind of guy: light packs, no footprint, pack out everything he packed in. The Thomas operation was big and old-school: wall tents, stoves, ATVs, rifles. They prided themselves on delivering trophy elk for out-of-state hunters. Meat was a long way down on their list, Jacketta thought.

Jacketta was new to the area, but he considered the Thomases to be the last of a dying breed. They were second- or third-generation guides and outfitters who seemed to have the impression that the Bighorn Mountains belonged to them, even though most of the terrain was public national forest land. The family had well-established camps in the mountains in choice locations and they were known for scaring off and intimidating anyone who dared to use the locations without their permission.

Earl, the patriarch, was cantankerous and loud and he didn't seem to care who he offended. After Jacketta had stood up at the meeting and said he lived in the valley and appreciated the mountain resource as much as the old-timers did, Earl had said to him, "You millennials with your beards and flannel will come and go. And when you're gone, we'll still be here."

Jacketta wanted no trouble with the Thomases. He wanted no trouble with anyone. He just wanted to hunt for his own food and stay above the fray when it came to disputes about territory or tradition. He'd never attended another public meeting, nor had he spoken out after Earl had dressed him down. He'd done his best to avoid all of the Thomas clan.

Which reminded him of something he'd heard about the family, something about a sister . . .

"I see you've got a little camp stove," Brad said, nodding toward the hissing unit. "I suppose it works okay if you're cheap and needy. Our camp is about a half mile away. Do you want to come and eat with us? We've got steaks instead of the freeze-dried crap you've got."

"Thank you for the offer," Jacketta said. "But I'm fine. I want to go to sleep early tonight so I can get up at three-thirty and go find an elk."

"What are you planning for dinner?"

"Ramen noodles," Jacketta said. He wished he'd said the name with more authority, like he was proud of it.

"Really?" Brad said. "You'd pass on a steak?"

Jacketta shrugged. "And the whiskey that comes with it, I would guess. I want to be clearheaded."

"Very sporting of you," Brad said. Jacketta detected a half sneer in the dark. That was something he'd learned about the Thomas clan: they were arrogant. He didn't know Brad well, but he could hear Earl's voice talking through the bearded mouth hole of his big son.

It was then that Jacketta realized Brad had casually swung the muzzle of the carbine up a little, even though he still held it one-handed. It wasn't pointed at him exactly, but it was just a flick away.

"Let's go get a steak," Brad said.

"I can't tell if that's an offer or a threat," Jacketta said.

"You've got a lot to learn if you can't tell the difference. Come on," Brad said while he stepped aside. "Follow me. I know you've met my old man, but I don't think you've met my brother."

"Maybe I'll come along and say hello," Jacketta said, as much to himself as to Brad. "Since we're all in the same area and you're locals and all."

Brad nodded his agreement. "This way," he said.

The first thing Jacketta noticed was that the Thomas men weren't set up in one of their more established camps like the ones they used when guiding hunters. Instead of cleared trees, decades-old fire rings, and elevated cross-poles in the trees to hang game, this camp looked temporary, as if set up to be torn down at any time.

The second was that they didn't appear to be grilling any steaks.

There was one medium-sized canvas wall tent, a small campfire shrouded on four sides by gnarled root pans as if to hide the flame, and various gear bags and panniers scattered on the pine needle forest floor. He could smell the musky odor of pack animals as they got closer and he sensed their big bodies within the trees, but he couldn't see them in the dark.

Jacketta squinted and said to Brad, "I thought you said your brother was with you."

"He is."

"I don't see anyone."

As if that were a signal in itself, two men stepped out from behind trees on either side of the camp. Earl was armed with a rifle, but the other, smaller man didn't appear to have a weapon.

"What the fuck, Brad?" the smaller man said.

"Look what I found about a half mile away," Brad said to Earl.

Earl approached Jacketta and looked him over carefully. "I know you," he said.

"Aidan Jacketta," Brad said. "We met him at that meeting last year. He's one of those millennials, like Kirby."

"Fuck you, Brad," Kirby said.

Jacketta nodded to Kirby as if trying to establish a kind of bond. Kirby didn't reciprocate.

"What are you doing up here?" Earl asked Jacketta.

"Bowhunting for elk."

"By yourself?"

"Yes."

Earl narrowed his eyes. "Didn't nobody ever tell you it isn't a good idea to hunt alone? Does anyone know where you are in case something happened to you?"

It was a loaded question, Jacketta thought. Why was he asking?

"My wife knows I'm up here," Jacketta said. It wasn't a total lie. Erin knew he was going hunting for a few days, but he hadn't said specifically where he'd be because it was important for him to have flexibility. If the elk were on one mountain, he didn't want to be stuck on another. Plus, Erin wasn't a worrier.

She trusted him and she was used to absences of a couple of nights here and there.

Earl seemed to weigh his answer, but said nothing. Finally, he asked, "Did you ever know my daughter, Sophia?"

The question had come out of nowhere, Jacketta thought. Was Earl implying something?

"No, I don't believe so," he said.

Jacketta noticed that Brad and Kirby were exchanging looks and expressions without actually speaking. Kirby seemed agitated that Brad had brought Jacketta into camp. Brad seemed to be defending what he'd done at first and then doubting it a second later.

"Look," Jacketta said. "I don't want to screw up your hunt. I didn't know you guys were up here, either. I just want to get along."

Earl said, "It's just that we know you and you know us."

"So?" Jacketta said. "Why does that make any difference?"

Earl looked to both of his sons and said something to them with his eyes. Jacketta couldn't interpret it.

"We both know I have as much right to hunt on public land as you do," Jacketta said, "but I don't want any trouble. There's three of you and one of me. I'll break camp first thing in the morning and hike eight miles or so to the east. I'll give you guys this whole mountain and stay out of your way."

Jacketta hated giving up so easily. He'd scouted the area for months before the season opened and he knew there were elk here. He wasn't so sure that would be the case eight miles east.

Brad said to Earl, "He was glassing the hunting party when I found him."

Earl turned his gaze on Jacketta again. "Do they know you're up here spying on them?"

"I wasn't spying. They built a gigantic fire and it got my attention."

"Do they know you're here?" Earl asked.

Jacketta shrugged. "I don't think so."

"Do you know who is in that hunting party?"

"How would I know that?"

Jacketta looked to Brad and Kirby and made a *What's this all about?* gesture with his hands.

"He don't know," Brad said.

"Don't know what?" Jacketta asked the three of them.

Earl slowly shook his head and mouthed something to his sons. Jacketta thought it was "No guts," which he took as an insult.

"Brad offered me dinner, but I'd like to take a rain check," he said. He started to walk back in the direction they'd come, but Brad blocked him.

"Really," Jacketta said. "I'll break camp tonight and move on. I really don't want to run into you guys tomorrow, either."

Then it hit him. The words Earl had mouthed weren't "No guts." They were "No *guns*."

Jacketta broke for it, shouldering himself around Brad and running as fast and as hard as he could for the dark trees in the direction of his camp.

"Shit," Earl said from behind him. "The prick is fast."

———

Jacketta ran blind, and it was terrifying. Tree trunks zipped past him on both sides and he couldn't see well enough to know if he was about to slam into one. Once he got deep enough into the lodgepoles, he thought, he'd put his headlamp on for the rest of the way. But he wasn't far enough from the Thomas camp yet.

Jacketta had no idea what had just happened and he hoped he hadn't misread it. But he didn't think so. He thought he'd made the right decision to bolt. His heart whumped in his chest and he could feel the rise of goose bumps on his forearms.

Brad knew where his camp was, but Jacketta thought he could reach it and pack up before Brad could catch up. Brad was stealthy, but he wasn't quick on his feet. Earl didn't seem spry, either. Then instead of east where he'd mentioned, he'd go west. Throw them off his trail. And when he got back to town the next day, he'd go to the new sheriff and file charges. Enough was enough with these people, no matter how long they'd been in the county.

That's when he heard footfalls on the forest floor just behind him.

Jacketta stopped and listened. He recalled how Brad had approached him without making a sound. Whoever was chasing him wasn't taking those precautions.

Jacketta threw his arms up in front of his face and took off again. He pushed through pine boughs and bounced off tree trunks and he could see nothing. He was getting winded from running and his lungs burned, but he tried to control his exhalations.

He ran across a small open meadow that was half-lit by starlight, then into another wall of tight lodgepole pines on the other side. Although he knew he shouldn't take the chance, he paused and looked behind him.

It was Kirby, Brad's brother. Kirby was just twenty yards behind as he crossed the meadow. A glint of starlight reflected off the blade of a large knife in Kirby's hand.

There was no point in standing his ground, Jacketta thought. He'd left all his weapons at his camp. So he plunged forward. Jacketta couldn't believe what was happening and he didn't know why it was.

Footfalls. Kirby was getting closer.

Then Jacketta ran headlong into a tree trunk and smashed into it so hard the only thing he could see were orange orbs exploding in front of his eyes. He knew he'd opened up a gash on his forehead and he wiped the blood away and tried to get his bearings. For a few seconds, he lost his sense of direction.

As Kirby closed in, Jacketta bolted away, stumbling eastward.

The slice of the blade through the back of his leg felt cold, as if he'd been raked by an icicle. The cut itself wasn't painful—yet—but he was sickened by the feeling of his untethered hamstring retracting up into his thigh.

Jacketta went down. When he turned over and looked up, he saw Kirby standing over him with the big knife in his hand.

No guns, Jacketta thought. Earl didn't want anyone in the

mountains—the hunting party—to hear a shot and know they were up there.

"*Damn*," Kirby said after taking gulps of air, "you can run like a motherfucker. I didn't think I'd catch you."

"I can't believe you did that," Jacketta said. "Don't let me bleed out."

"Naw. I just had to stop you."

"I won't say anything to anybody," Jacketta said. "Just let me go to my camp and pack up."

Kirby seemed to be considering it for a moment. Then: "No dice. I'll help you up and we'll go back and get you patched up. We'll talk to Dad and see what we can figure out. You just ran away so damned quick we were afraid you got the wrong impression about us. You didn't give us a chance to explain why we're up here."

Jacketta didn't think he had a choice. He reached down and could feel hot blood pulsing from the wound. He knew his femoral artery had been cut.

"Maybe we could put on a tourniquet," he said. "You could use my belt."

"We'll do that when we can see what we're doing," Kirby said, extending his left hand. "Here, grab on."

Jacketta reached out and Kirby pulled him to his feet. He couldn't feel his right leg or foot, so he balanced on his left boot. Kirby stepped under Jacketta's extended arm and folded it at the elbow around his neck to support him.

"Can you walk?"

"Barely."

They stumbled out of the trees into the starlit meadow. Kirby was surprisingly strong, Jacketta thought. He could lean all of his weight on the man.

"Too bad you saw our faces," Kirby said. "Too bad you knew Brad and Dad. That's where things went off the track."

"I don't know why," Jacketta said. "What in the hell is going on?"

"You don't know, do you?"

"No."

"Family business, I guess you could say."

Jacketta looked over to try and get a better understanding. The last thing he saw was Kirby flattening the blade of the bowie knife and positioning the point of it under his armpit. Before Jacketta could react, Kirby thrust it to the hilt between two ribs and into his heart.

Aidan Jacketta died on his back, looking up at the wash of stars. There were a lot of them.

Monday

Green / Red Day

For a successful technology,
reality must take precedence over
public relations, for Nature cannot be fooled.

—Richard P. Feynman

NINE

At four-thirty the next morning, Joe shouldered on his pack in the dark and left Price and Rumy in a tangle of downed timber at the head of a dry wash. They were hunkered down. Rumy had kept completely silent all morning as if he weren't yet awake and alert, and Price was just the opposite: anxious, excited, curious about what might happen next.

Joe had explained it to him in a hushed tone before leaving. The only illumination in the tangle was from the muted beam on Joe's headlamp. The light from it was altered by a red filter, and the pink glow on both men created an eerie, otherworldly atmosphere, with deep shadows and discolored eyes. Price had placed his compound bow in the crook of an overturned pine root pan and lined up his high-tech arrows next to it. He was ready.

"You can't see it right now," Joe had said, "but facing us to the west is a large meadow on the side of the slope. The meadow gets blown free of snow in the winter, but it grows good grass

101

in the summer and fall. The elk—if they're there—graze on it during the night and then move into the timber to bed down for the day as soon as it's light. My plan is to leave you two and circumnavigate the meadow so I can come up behind them. I'll stay deep in the trees and try not to make any sound. The wind is with me right now, so I shouldn't startle them before dawn."

Like all hunting plans, or plans in general, Joe knew it would be a crapshoot. The wind could shift on him while he was making his way there, he could stumble in the undergrowth and snap a branch, or the elk could simply not be present at all.

"Why the red light?" Price had asked, gesturing toward Joe's headlamp.

"So I can see where I'm going but the elk can't see me," Joe explained. "These animals have a wide field of vision and they can see very well in the dark. But unlike humans, they have what's called dichromatic vision. They only see blue and yellow, and the rest is black and white and shades of both. In the dark, red light is invisible to them."

"Fascinating," Price said.

"I've still got to be really stealthy and slow getting around them. They know it's hunting season."

Rumy scoffed at that, but Joe ignored him.

"Give me at least an hour and a half," Joe said to Price. He described how the clearing went all the way to the top of the slope summit and a little over to the far side. His plan was to work his way through the timber until he was on the other side of that rise. Then he'd crawl or crabwalk to the top until he could look over at the meadow from the opposite side.

"If the elk are in there, they'll eventually see or sense me up there," Joe said. "I'll try not to panic them. I want them to walk away from me rather than run."

"You think they'll come to us?" Price asked.

Joe gestured toward the shallow wash that was below them. "They could come up right here in front of you," he said. "I can't guarantee it, because the herd might decide to bolt off to the north or south into the timber instead of coming your way. But the wash you're looking over serves as a kind of funnel. They might appear right in front of you."

"How far is the wash?" Price asked. "I obviously can't see it yet."

"The edge of it is thirty yards away. The opposite rim is about fifty yards away. Your shooting zone should be right in the middle."

Price nodded and grinned. His teeth shone pink in the light. "It's a good plan," he said.

"As far as plans go," Joe conceded. "Elk have minds of their own. I've seen them do all kinds of things that don't make any sense, like turn and run right over you. Or in this case, over me. The only thing that's pretty certain is that, whatever they do, they'll stick together in a herd."

"What do we do if that happens?" Price asked. "If they go out through the side or run over your position?"

"Sit tight," Joe said. "Don't chase them. You'll never catch them. If they move on us, we'll get back together, regroup, and make another plan.

"If the herd does come up here," Joe continued, "you'll likely see a big dry cow first. She's the lead cow. Think of her as their scout. If she senses you up here, she'll turn or reverse direction. But if she thinks the coast is clear, she'll lead them in a line right in front of you."

"Should I try for the lead cow?" Price asked.

"It's your call," Joe said. "But if you want a bull, you'll have to wait. Bulls will come up at the end of the string."

"And if I decide to shoot?" Price asked.

"Aim for the chest just in back of the front shoulder," Joe said. "That's your best chance of hitting the vital area and making a kill shot. Don't aim at the head, neck, or shoulder. And if you hit the elk, grab another arrow. Keep shooting. Stick it with arrows until it goes down."

Price shook his head. "Brutal," he said.

"This is brutal business," Joe agreed. "But what's even worse is wounding an animal. We don't want to spend the rest of our time tracking a wounded elk and we don't want that creature to suffer."

"I'm with you on that," Price said.

Joe cast a quick glance to Rumy, who appeared bored with the conversation. He also looked to be very cold.

"It's gonna get colder before the sun comes up," Joe said. "If you need to get some circulation going, one of you at a time can get up and walk around back there in the trees. Be careful where you step and keep silent. You don't want to scare them off before they get here.

"Whatever happens, don't leave this spot," Joe said, emphasizing his point by jabbing his index finger earthward several times. "Since we aren't using radios, you'll just have to wait for me to come back. I *will* come back here, whatever happens. And then we can plan our next move." He looked at Rumy as he said it. Rumy struck him as the kind of guy who might decide to pursue fleeing elk or just want to go back to the camp for breakfast.

"We'll do what we want to keep Mr. Price safe and comfortable," Rumy said.

"We'll stay," Price said, cutting off his man. "We'll do this right."

"Good," Joe said.

It had been Price's decision to hunt without radio communication to better ensure a classic fair-chase hunt. Joe was fine with that. It bothered him when he encountered hunters in the field who operated as if big-game hunting was a military spot-and-kill maneuver. Radios weren't necessary as long as everyone involved understood the strategy and contingencies.

Then he pulled his pack on and left them.

It was a surprisingly cold morning, Joe thought. There had been a dusting of snow during the night from the storm clouds he'd seen, but not even an inch of accumulation. The kind of snow that would likely melt off during a sunny day. He hoped Price and Rumy could stay loose and warm.

The light snow was a plus, he knew. It made it much easier to see tracks and gauge movement across the forest floor and in the meadow if the elk weren't where he guessed they'd be.

The forest was dense with downed timber and tangled limbs. He had to make several detours to get around impenetrable brush so that his path, if mapped from the air, zigzagged all the way down the mountain and up the other side. Joe was grateful he was the one on the move because his activity warmed him up. It wasn't long before he could feel the prickle of sweat beneath his armpits and in his crotch beneath his light wool underlayer.

In addition to the pack filled with extra clothing, optics, gear, a first-aid kit, and a knife and saw for field dressing, Joe wore both his .357 Magnum and a canister of bear spray on his belt. He'd laced gaiters over his boots to keep out the moisture from the snow.

In a perfect world, he thought, his plan would work at least as far as presenting the shooter with an opportunity. But anything could happen. Price might miss or wound his target, and they'd deal with either result. Panicking at the sight of elk happened often to many first-time hunters, Joe knew. It had happened to him the first time when he was fourteen and he'd let a lead cow walk by him so closely he could see the dew sparkle in her thick hide. He'd been frozen to his spot and never taken a shot. Joe planned to be very forgiving of Price if the same thing happened to him the first time.

He might not be as forgiving if it happened repeatedly.

As he picked his way through the trees, Joe couldn't push away the feeling of being oddly disconcerted. Part of it, he knew, was leading an elk hunt for people he didn't know. Another part of it was that he hadn't been able to talk to Marybeth the night before because his satellite phone wouldn't work. Talking to his wife was a ritual and it helped them both. It bothered him that he'd been unsuccessful and he felt like there was a hole in his heart that needed filling.

He also knew that when he didn't call her—and it was rare when he couldn't—her mind began to conjure up all kinds of worst-case scenarios. Especially when he was in the field. He was hurt, he'd been abducted, he'd been killed. And he couldn't really assure her that none of those things were possible because of the many close calls he'd had in the past, *including* from his own doctor.

The sat phone had been reliable in the past and he'd tested it before they'd ridden away from the base camp. But although it'd powered up like it should, the device somehow couldn't fix on a signal. He'd watched it search for twenty minutes. And since there was no cell phone signal this far away from civilization, he'd been left with no options.

When he mentioned to Boedecker that morning that he'd been unable to use the device, Brock nodded conspiratorially and had taken Joe aside.

"I saw that Joannides guy going through your gear bag," he told Joe in a whisper. "He looked like he was looking for something."

"Tim?" Joe asked. "Are you sure?"

"I thought maybe he just got the bags confused," Boedecker said. "Lord knows he's got enough equipment along with him and we had to repack, so he might not know where everything was. But he looked kind of suspicious to me while he was doing it."

"When did this happen?" Joe asked.

"While we were making dinner. I came outside the tent to take a pee and I saw him over by your stuff. I didn't say anything at the time."

Joe nodded and filed it away. Boedecker had made no secret of how much he disliked the hunting party members, so maybe his take on what he'd seen had been colored by that. And he hadn't mentioned it to Joe any further during the evening.

But it was odd that his sat phone didn't work. And if anybody knew their way around electronic devices and how to disable them, it was probably Joannides. But why would he do such a thing?

Joe planned to confront the man about it once the morning hunt was over and they were back at camp. He decided not to accuse Joannides of anything outright, but to bring him the sat phone and ask him to take a look at it to see if he could figure out what was wrong with it. Joannides's reaction to that request might give Joe the answer he sought. And if nothing else, if Boedecker's distrust was misplaced, Joe could ask Joannides to lend him *his* sat phone so he could check in with Marybeth.

And all would be right with the world.

Until he talked with her and got right, he would simply proceed, he thought. Elk-hunting trips had a certain rhythm to them from day to day.

Elk were most active at daybreak and dusk. During the day they bedded down and hid in thick timber and were hard to locate. Joe's intention was to hunt hard very early in the morning and late in the afternoon until dark and take a long break—and a nap—in between.

Hunters got their elk less than half the time, he knew. Some years the success ratio was less than that overall. On average, it took about eighteen days in the field for every elk taken.

Their odds for a five-day hunt weren't in favor of Steve-2. Which meant the odds of Wyoming landing the server farm project Governor Allen desired weren't really very good, either.

Nor were the prospects for his continued employment.

It was about a half hour before sunrise, when the eastern sky began to take on the vague cream color that would erase the stars, that Joe saw something in his peripheral vision. Something on the forest floor had struck him as incongruous.

He paused long enough for his breath to return to normal, then slowly rotated his headlamp beam to the right. He wasn't sure what he'd seen other than it didn't fit within the powdery snow cover.

Joe placed one hand on the grip of his Colt and with the other he pushed a gloved index finger through the trigger loop of his bear spray canister. He backtracked a few feet and aimed the red beam down.

At first, he thought it was a disturbance made by a very large elk hoof or by a moose moving through the timber minutes before him. Both could do so without making a sound. The soil was churned and pine needles stuck out of the depression, and when he bent down to get a closer look, he realized it was a fresh boot track.

Cleated Vibram sole, maybe size eleven or twelve. From a big man. Who appeared to be alone.

Joe could hear the beat of his heart in his own ears. A chill that had nothing to do with the cold morning crawled down his spine.

From his low angle, he could see the single tracks continue on and he was surprised he hadn't noticed the trail sooner, since he'd obviously crossed it a few yards before. He guessed that the boot prints had been made within the hour.

The first likely person he thought of was Zsolt Rumy. Rumy was a big man who wore brand-new hunting boots straight out of the box. But why would Rumy be on the move and out ahead of him instead of back in the brush with his boss? It didn't make sense.

Joe raised his head and studied the forest around him. If it wasn't Rumy who'd made the tracks, he was surprised there was a hunter out before him and he wondered why they hadn't seen anyone or noticed a camp. Since the area was entirely off-road, the lone hunter must have come in on foot or horseback. But they'd seen no one—or any sign—on the trail.

Joe dug his phone out of his breast pocket. He shielded the flash with his left hand and snapped several photos of the track, as well as the others as they proceeded north to south. Whoever it was wasn't headed in the direction of the clearing.

Joe stood and simply listened for several minutes. He closed his eyes to concentrate. But the sound of a footfall, a grunt, or a snapped twig didn't come.

The elk, if they were there, would be through the trees to his left. The lone hunter was somewhere to his right. Joe vowed to himself to keep all of his senses turned up high and to keep his head on a swivel as he proceeded.

The elk were there, all right. Joe smelled their musky odor before he saw them.

On his hands and knees, he crawled up the grassy back side of the hill. He knew he was near the top when a slight cold wind hit him from the east. On the very top he flattened on the ground and inched forward, taking in the clearing below him a few inches at a time. His heart raced and his breath shallowed out as he slowly moved to where he could see the clearing below.

Thirty-five to forty elk grazed in the meadow, just like he'd hoped. They were scattered across the breadth of it, grazing with their heads down. Because it was so cold, their breaths created condensation clouds that dissipated quickly but still made it look like the herd was a single organism puffing like a kind of steam train. Five were bulls, and one of the bulls was a magnificent seven-point royal, with seven tines on each antler. The rest were cows, calves, and two young yearling spikes. Although Joe had seen thousands of the animals throughout his career, he still marveled at how those big bulls could carry their heavy racks around, not to mention running with them full-speed through dense timber.

Joe brought his binoculars up. He focused in on the mouth of the dry wash at the bottom of the clearing and tilted the glasses up into the dark forest. Although he couldn't clearly see where he'd left Price and Rumy, he got a good idea of their location. He wondered if they could see the herd in the clearing from their vantage point.

The situation was as he'd hoped it would be, but he waited another fifteen minutes until it got lighter. It was a risk, he knew. But moving the elk into the dry wash when it was too dark for Price to see clearly in the forest shadows wasn't a good idea, either. That could result in wounded animals.

Finally, Joe rose up slowly from where he lay so his profile was skylighted on the horizon of the top. He didn't climb to his feet, but he knew he could be seen from below.

Several calves reacted first, and they ran around in circles as if they didn't know what to do. Then a cow looked up and blew twin plumes of condensation from her nostrils. Another woofed. The herd was instantly aware of him and they began to mill around.

This was the moment, he knew, where they'd make their decision.

It was the big lead cow—and she was nearly as big in body as the bulls—who wheeled on her back feet and headed down and away from him. Her pale butt flashed and it was joined by a dozen others.

Joe could hear the muffled footfalls of the entire herd as they rumbled away from him. It wasn't a panicked run, but it was steady. The herd coalesced from where it had been spread out across the meadow and flowed like a tan-and-brown stream of liquid straight toward the mouth of the dry wash. He glimpsed their dark heads and heavy shoulders as they moved up the wash until they couldn't be seen in the timber.

He watched them go, estimating how many seconds it would take for the herd to appear before Price and Rumy. Since Price was bowhunting, there would be no sound of a shot.

Joe listened for a whoop that might indicate that Price had hit his target, or a curse that would convey the opposite. But there was no such sound beyond the occasional snap of a twig and the thumping footfalls of the moving elk up into the timber.

After waiting five more minutes, Joe got to his feet and hiked down into the clearing, which was now bereft of elk. He was in clear view, in the open, and there was no reason to walk stealthily as he had earlier. Hard black pellets of elk scat still steamed in piles in the grass. He followed the churned-up track of the herd down to the bottom and up into the dry wash. The heavy odor of the animals still hung in the trees, even ten minutes after they'd been there.

As he climbed up the wash, he kept his eyes open for the steaming body of a downed elk or a blood trail that might lead him to a wounded animal. He saw nothing.

Joe climbed in silence. He didn't want to call out in the

remote possibility that the herd had bunched up ahead of him and Price was waiting for a good shot.

He stopped and listened. Nothing.

When he climbed out of the wash, he realized he'd walked twenty yards past the tangle of brush where he'd left Price and Rumy. Joe walked back to the downed timber cover. They were gone.

Confused, Joe surveyed the location carefully. Perhaps he'd confused it with somewhere else? It had been completely dark when he'd left it, after all.

Then he noticed a football-sized piece of bark propped on the root pan that Price had been stationed behind. Written on the smooth light skin of the underside of the bark, with a felt-tip pen, was:

Joe:
Back to camp. Hurry.
S-2.

Seething, Joe strode back to the camp. He didn't hurry as instructed and he crossed no elk along the way, but he did see Price's and Rumy's fresh prints in the thawing surface of the trail.

He paused to study them. Rumy's were larger than Price's. Joe retrieved the photos he'd taken that morning and compared the shot to Rumy's actual boot print. They weren't the same. The lugs on Rumy's soles were sharper and less worn.

Then he noticed two other sets of prints. They were hoof-prints of shod horses—one on each side of the trail about five feet away.

As if a set of horsemen had followed them back to camp. Or accompanied them. Or had driven them.

Ten minutes later, Joe could smell the pleasant odor of wood-smoke and bacon cooking. Their pack animals whinnied from where they were picketed.

It wasn't until he was nearly upon the camp that he realized there were too many horses tied up in the trees. In fact, twice as many as they'd ridden up there.

They had visitors.

Joe stepped behind the trunk of a tree so he couldn't be seen.

TEN

Joe pressed against the sticky rough bark of the pine tree and carefully peered around the trunk. He wasn't certain why he'd taken the precaution, but something in the air just didn't seem right. The fresh boot tracks he'd discovered, the fact that Price and Rumy had abruptly left their position, the hoofprints along the trail, the arrival of visitors in their camp—things didn't add up.

He couldn't see what was happening because the walled cook tent blocked his view, but he could hear voices and snippets of speech from the other side of it. He heard a bass voice rumble the word "ConFab" and Price raise his own voice with a question: "How can we settle this?"

Joe thought, *Settle what?*

His first thought was that perhaps they'd unwittingly encroached on someone else's hunting camp or area. It was unlikely but possible. Joe knew where the elk outfitter camps were located in the Bighorns because he patrolled them annually, and no one he knew of had used this particular location in years because it was so far from any roads. That was one of the reasons he'd chosen it.

Maybe someone was using the area for something they didn't want discovered? A gang of poachers operating in the mountains wasn't unheard of, but poachers in Joe's experience were opportunists. They'd rather gun down a trophy from their truck and cut off the head and antlers and get away. They rarely devoted themselves to the hard work, planning, and logistics it took to use this remote location.

Whatever was happening on the other side of the tent would have to be dealt with. He wanted to make sure he handled it the correct way. Joe didn't want to alarm anyone or panic them because they'd know from his uniform shirt that he was law enforcement. He also didn't know how many individuals he'd be confronting.

The best method he'd found, since he was always outnumbered and outgunned when he approached a hunting camp, was to be as amiable and friendly as possible. He'd smile and ask about their day while at the same time keeping himself far enough away and to the side so that he wasn't directly challenging them. And he'd keep moving, walking and talking, because a moving target was harder to hit.

It was also possible he was misreading the entire situation and conjuring up a threat when there was none. Maybe the two horsemen had stumbled onto Price and Rumy and the four of them had decided to go get coffee back at the camp. Maybe someone was injured and needed medical attention. It could be anything.

And Joe had to be prepared for anything.

What he wasn't prepared for was when a forearm flashed across his vision and his head was wrenched back by a powerful hand and he felt the cold bite of a knife blade on the skin of his throat.

"We were wondering where you were," said the man who'd come up silently behind him. He spoke softly into his ear. "Don't fucking move."

Joe marveled that he had not heard the man approaching. And he didn't move. He was too startled to be scared.

"I'm going to let go of your head, but the knife stays where it is," the man said to him. "If you move, I'll cut you."

"Mmmmm." Joe didn't want to speak or nod. The grip was released on the crown of his skull.

He felt the man tug at his pack to remove it. Joe rolled his shoulders back to make it easier. Then the man pulled loose the safety strap of his revolver and drew it out of the holster.

"A Colt Python," the man said with admiration. "Nice. I've always wanted one."

Joe expected the man to reach up under the other side of his coat and pull out the canister of bear spray that was velcroed to his belt, and he did. Then his cell phone was removed from his breast pocket and the personal locator beacon was removed from his back pocket. A few seconds later, Joe heard the crunch of glass and components as both devices were crushed underfoot.

"You didn't have to do that," Joe said.

"Do you have any more weapons?" the man asked. As he did, Joe felt the pressure of the blade lessen slightly, which allowed him to talk.

"I've got knives and saws in the pack for field dressing," he said. "No more firearms."

Which was true. He'd left his rifle and shotgun in camp that morning. There was a spare can of bear spray in the side pocket of his daypack and a Leatherman multi-tool in the other, which he assumed the man would find if he searched it.

"What's going on?" Joe asked the man. The harsh nature of the situation was starting to take hold.

"You'll find out soon enough."

"You know I'm a Wyoming game warden, right?"

"Oh, I know who you are."

"Then you know you could be in big trouble. I'd like to avoid that and I'm sure you would as well."

"We'll see," the man said. He took the blade away from his throat and a second later Joe felt the sharp point of it cut through the material of his coat, shirt, and underwear where it pricked the skin between his ribs. Joe flinched in surprise from the pain.

"I'm not fucking around," the man said while applying a little more pressure to the point of the knife. "I'll push it all the way into your heart if you try anything stupid."

"I won't."

"Walk slow."

"Where are we going?"

"The camp, idiot."

As he stepped away from the tree, Joe shot a glance over his shoulder.

"I know you," he said.

"You should," Kirby Thomas said. "You fucking arrested me once."

Joe nodded and continued on. Six or seven years before, he'd been patrolling the breaklands in his pickup when he rounded a corner on a two-track road and saw that another truck was stopped and blocking his path. Joe had pulled around it to find a fatally wounded pronghorn antelope sprawled across the road in front of the truck and a man in the process of viciously kicking it in the head to kill it. The buck's head snapped back with each blow and broken yellow teeth littered the ground. It was sickening, and Joe recalled the scene more clearly than he wanted to.

Kirby had obviously shot the antelope from the window of his truck directly from the road—two violations in one act—and instead of finishing off the wounded creature with a knife or fatal shot, he was manically kicking it with furious blows. That was until he looked up and saw the green Ford F-150 nose around his truck and he recognized who was driving it.

Joe would also never forget the look in Kirby's eyes while he was kicking the pronghorn in the head. The young man looked out of control. Like he was really enjoying himself.

He arrested Kirby on the spot and cited him for the two clear violations as well as for not having a valid hunting license and conservation stamp and for wanton destruction of wildlife. The last charge was the stiffest and could result in jail time as well as the confiscation of Kirby's truck and weapons and a ban on future hunting privileges, but Joe hadn't been sure it would hold up in court. He hadn't cared at the time, because he was both sickened and disgusted by Kirby's acts and he wanted to make a public example of him.

Joe had learned from experience that men who violated hunting and fishing regulations, especially when they did so with sadistic glee, later turned out to be capable of *anything*. Which was why he wanted to throw the book at Kirby Thomas.

But he never found out whether he'd overcharged him or not because days afterward the young man was arrested for beating his live-in girlfriend to a pulp and was later sent to the Wyoming State Penitentiary in Rawlins for domestic assault. Despite pleas from Kirby's outfitter father, Earl, Joe didn't drop his case against his son. Earl maintained that the hunting violations, whenever they were to be adjudicated, would damage his reputation as a prominent guide and outfitter in the area.

Instead, Joe held the charges in reserve for when he could serve them in person. He did it for himself and for that poor pronghorn antelope buck.

Until the moment Joe glanced over his shoulder, he hadn't known Kirby was out. He didn't think it was a good time to remind the man about the pending charges against him that Joe was sitting on.

And now Joe was terrified. He didn't want to see that look in Kirby's eyes ever again.

As Joe rounded the corner of the wall tent with Kirby right behind him, the knife point stinging him, he tried to quickly assess the scene:

Price sat on the log by the fire with his hands on his knees, looking up at Earl Thomas, who towered above him. Earl had a carbine in the crook of his arm.

Zsolt Rumy was sprawled on his side near the smoldering campfire. He had a head wound under his scalp that bled in rivulets across his face and pooled in the grass beneath his head. His wrists were bound together behind his back with nylon rope.

Brad Thomas, Earl's massive other son and his partner in the outfitting business, straddled Rumy and grasped a shotgun butt-down, as if prepared to bludgeon the man yet again if he dared move. Joe noted that Brad's large boots were approximately the same size as the tracks he'd seen earlier that morning.

Tim Joannides stood on the other side of the fire ring with his arms crossed in front of him and his head tilted toward Price, as if trying to solve some kind of puzzle. He wasn't obviously injured and he wasn't constrained.

Brock Boedecker stood just inside the flap of the doorway of the cook tent as if he didn't know where else to go. He wore his big .44 in a holster at his side. So they hadn't disarmed him. He looked at Joe as if pleading for some kind of understanding.

A glittering pile of smashed electronics—sat phones, solar battery chargers, PLBs, digital tablets, cell phones—were on the ground between the firepit and the opening of the wall tent.

Joe tried to make sense of it, but couldn't on the fly. Too many mixed messages.

"Look who I found," Kirby said to Earl.

Earl looked Joe over and nodded a greeting of sorts. Price gestured to Joe with his hands out, as if to say, *What do you make of this?*

Joe said, "What are you doing, Earl?"

"Something that should have been done a year ago, Joe," Earl replied.

Joe shook his head, not understanding.

"Frontier justice, you might call it," Earl said.

"For what?" Joe asked. "What do you think we've done?"

"You haven't done anything," Earl said. "Neither has Brock. You're just with the wrong people at the wrong time."

"What does that even mean?"

Earl raised the carbine out of the crook of his arm and swung it toward Price. Price's eyes got large and he sat farther back on the log as if that would make him harder to hit.

"Your crime is enabling this asshole. This guy here," Earl said. "Mr. Bigshot San Francisco Tech Mogul. He's going to finally get what's coming to him. It's high time."

"High fucking time," Brad said in an echo.

"Shut up, Brad," Kirby whispered from behind Joe, as if embarrassed by his brother.

Earl stepped forward and lowered the rifle so that the muzzle was inches away from Price's nose. He said, "You killed my Sophia."

Price flinched and shook his head. "Who?"

"My Sophia," Earl said. "My Sophia."

"*I* killed her?" Price asked, obviously confused. "I don't even know her. I don't know anyone named Sophia. Jesus—this is insane."

Earl's face got dark and Joe took in a breath, anticipating the rifle fire. He could see Earl's index finger whitening on the trigger.

"No," Earl said to Price, "you *don't* even know her. She's nothing to you. Nothing. And that, you little prick, is a big part of our problem here."

Price looked to Joe and pleaded with his eyes for him to intervene.

"Sophia," Joe said to Earl as calmly as he could. "She was your daughter, right? Brad and Kirby's sister?"

"She was."

"He always liked her best," Brad said without malice.

Price looked from Earl to Joe to Brad, as if watching the most confusing tennis match he'd ever seen.

"I'm sorry to hear that, I really am," Price said. "But what about her? How could I hurt someone I don't even know?"

"Because that's what you fucking do," Earl said to him. "That's how you make millions of dollars."

Joe wanted to talk Earl down, but he wasn't sure what to say. He remembered Marybeth looking up from her laptop the year before and saying how sad it was that a beautiful local girl named Sophia Thomas had taken her own life. It was such a tragedy, Marybeth had said. Sophia had been in Lucy's class at Saddlestring High School. Joe hadn't known her, but he was aware of the Thomas family, especially Kirby.

Earl said to Price, "You let them torture her until it became unbearable. You allowed that to happen."

"I still don't know what you're talking about," Price said.

"You're a liar," Earl said. "I called you. I called your company thirty times to complain. I left messages every time, but I never talked to one living person and no one ever called me back. All I got was automated voicemail. You just sat there in your fucking headquarters and minted money while my Sophia was being hounded to death."

Price slumped forward and placed his head in his hands. "I have no idea what's happening here!" he cried.

Joannides broke in for the first time. "It's company policy to disregard individual user complaints," he said calmly to Earl. "We don't react until there's a groundswell or unless an important influencer has a reaction online. Steve-2 thinks there are too many users to respond to each and every time there's a complaint."

"I wasn't a user," Earl said. "I was Sophia's father and I had to watch her spiral. So *fuck* your company policy."

Joannides didn't argue, but he looked away furtively. Joe noted that he didn't seem scared or frightened by the Thomases, and he wasn't bound. That didn't quite fit with the scenario. Just like the fact that Boedecker still had his weapon.

Just then, Earl gestured to Boedecker in the tent. "You can go now," he said. "Just don't tell anyone what you saw here today."

"I won't," Boedecker replied. "Will you let Joe go with me? That was part of the deal."

"What deal?" Joe asked, stunned.

Boedecker wouldn't meet his gaze. Joe realized the rancher had been in on it from the beginning. *That's* what his early warnings and his antipathy toward the hunting party had been about.

Joe felt sick to his stomach.

"For a year I tried to figure out how to get at this guy," Earl said to Joe about Price. "But God works in mysterious ways. I never could have imagined he'd be *delivered* to me. So for that I have to thank you, Joe Pickett."

"Yeah, thank you, Joe Pickett," Brad echoed.

Joe looked to Price and saw absolute fear in his eyes.

"I had nothing to do with this," he said to him.

"Thank the governor, too," Boedecker said as he stepped out of the tent. "That bastard finally did something right."

Joe sensed Kirby relax behind him. The knife point was withdrawn, but he still stood there, ready. Kirby lowered Joe's pack to the ground at their feet. It seemed as if he were about to be released. He doubted Price and Rumy would get the same deal. He wasn't sure yet about Joannides.

Boedecker grasped his personal gear bag and started to walk in the direction of the horses.

"No," Earl called to him. "You need to hoof it yourself."

Boedecker turned. "They're *my* horses."

"And they'll stay with us," Earl said to him. "It'll take you two or three days to get back down to the trailhead. We need the time in case you change your mind and start yapping."

"I won't change my mind," Boedecker pleaded.

"Start walking before I change mine," Earl threatened.

"My radio is in the pannier of my horse," Boedecker said. "You know that one Brad told me to keep on? I might need it in an emergency."

Joe thought, *A live radio in Brock's gear?* So the Thomases had been listening to them?

"No," Earl said to Boedecker. "You'll need to be radio-silent so we can do what we're here to do."

While the two of them went back and forth, Joe noticed in his peripheral vision that Rumy had regained his wits on the ground. Although he still lay motionless on his side beneath Brad, his eyes darted around and he was carefully working on loosening and stretching out the rope on his wrists so he could get his hands free. Brad was preoccupied watching the exchange between Boedecker and Earl.

Rumy, Joe thought, was preparing to make his move.

"I want to get those horses back from you as soon as I can," Boedecker said to Earl. "I've got clients coming."

"I'll get 'em back to you," Earl said.

"They're my best, you know."

"I know. And leave that handgun. I'll give it back to you when this is over."

Boedecker was alarmed. "You're kidding, right?"

"I am not. I'd prefer it if you weren't armed."

"What about bears?"

"Make plenty of noise."

"Earl, this isn't the arrangement we discussed."

"Seems like you want to argue some more."

Boedecker apparently thought it best to shut up. With a curse, he turned his back on Earl and began to trudge away.

At that moment, Joe saw movement from the camp and he turned his head to see Rumy roll onto his back. He kicked up at Brad with one decisive movement. His boot came up between Brad's legs and hit with an ugly *thump*. Brad gasped and stepped back, doubling over. He still grasped his shotgun.

Rumy continued his roll until he was on his hands and knees. Then he launched himself up and ran through the campsite and toward the trees to the east. He didn't even look over his shoulder as he did so. Not protecting his boss, Joe thought, but saving himself.

"Fucking Brad," Kirby hissed behind Joe.

"Get him," Earl ordered to Brad. "Get him before he reaches the trees."

Brad moaned and then howled. He sounded like a wounded animal.

"*Stop him!*" Earl shouted.

Brad took a raggedy breath and placed his big hands on his knees and pushed himself back up to his six-foot-four height. His face was a twisted red grimace.

All eyes in the camp were on him as he raised the shotgun to his shoulder. Rumy was thirty yards away—nearly out of effective buckshot range. Five or six full strides and he'd be into the timber.

The blast split open the still morning, and Rumy's arms shot out from his body and he tumbled forward. He was obviously wounded but likely not yet dead.

"Go finish him off," Earl ordered. Brad grunted in pain and lumbered in Rumy's direction. He jacked a fresh shell into the receiver of his weapon as he did so.

"Move your ass," Kirby hissed to his brother.

At that second, Joe glanced in Price's direction and they made eye contact. A message was exchanged.

Now.

Joe bent his knees, grasped the shoulder strap of his daypack, and came up with it as he wheeled around, surprising Kirby, who was distracted and watching his brother.

While Joe frantically unzipped the side pocket, Kirby recovered and stabbed at him. Joe raised the pack to intercept the blade, although he saw a flash of the knifepoint emerge through the nylon skin of it inches from his bare hand.

Joe yanked the canister of bear spray out of the side pocket, gripped the red plastic safety mechanism with his teeth, and pulled it free. He let the pack drop a little and he hit Kirby point-blank in the face with a blast from the canister.

Kirby screamed and backpedaled away until he tripped on a tree root and fell to his butt. His eyes were clenched tightly and his face was crimson.

Joe turned quickly toward the camp to see that Earl had heard Kirby and was now raising his carbine away from Price on the log and toward him. Joe raised the nozzle of the bear spray until it covered Earl's upper body and he squeezed the trigger. A huge plume of red spray shot across the distance between them and engulfed Earl's entire face and neck.

Joe didn't let up. He kept the spray going full-blast while Earl spun, cursed, and fired without aiming in the direction where Price had been sitting just seconds before.

Price was no longer there. He was running toward Joe with his arms up over his head to shield it and to avoid the plume.

At the edge of the campsite there was another concussive *boom*. Brad had caught up with Rumy. He turned to check out the commotion near the tent and no doubt saw Joe and Price break for it, going in the other direction. To the west. And both his dad and brother were writhing in the grass.

"Hey!" Brad called out, running back toward the camp with his shotgun. "They're getting away!"

"*Go, go, go, go,*" Joe barked at Price, who sprinted past him. Joe followed.

As they penetrated the tree line, Joe heard another *boom* and the angry whap of buckshot pellets tearing through pine boughs and smacking into tree trunks behind him. He wasn't hit, and Price, who was ahead of him, didn't break stride.

The two of them ran until Joe's lungs were on fire. Price had fallen back, but he stayed with Joe every step of the way. He was in good physical shape, Joe was pleased to find out.

Tree trunks shot by them and Joe made no real attempt at

stealth. They ran generally west, but not in a straight line. All he cared about was putting as much distance as possible from the Thomases. He assumed Brad was back in camp trying to help his dad and brother, and wasn't pursuing them at the moment.

That would come later.

Joe had to finally stop and catch his breath. Price seemed grateful as well for the pause. They again exchanged glances, but no words were said. Too tired, Joe thought.

They'd chosen to rest on the cusp of a vast stand of aspen. The forest floor was colored gold and vermilion with fallen leaves in various stages of death.

Heaving for air and with his hands on his knees, Joe thought:

No horses.

No weapons.

No food.

No way to communicate.

Leaving an easy-to-follow trail in the dirt.

Finally, Price recovered enough to say, "Are we fucked?"

"Yup."

ELEVEN

Marybeth was in a feisty mood and she tried to work her way out of it by concentrating on the budget presentation she'd have to deliver to the county commissioners in two days. She'd started the morning by having a tense exchange with Evelyn Hughes, the front desk librarian, for forgetting to make sure the exit doors had been locked the night before, which they hadn't been. It was Evelyn's responsibility to check them.

"I thought I had," was Evelyn's response.

"Please make sure you do so in the future," Marybeth had snapped.

"I really thought I had," Evelyn said before looking away.

So Marybeth scrolled through the spreadsheets and graphics on the monitor of her library computer and tried to anticipate not only the questions they'd ask her, like, *Do people even go to the library anymore?* and *Do you have porn filters on the computers available to the public?* but what her answers would be.

There were five commissioners. Two were reliably pro–library funding. Two were adamantly against any taxpayer expenditures that weren't devoted solely to infrastructure, although they had pet causes such as funding the county fair and spending money on lawyers to advance a county-wide wolf eradication policy in opposition to the U.S. Fish and Wildlife Service. The fifth commissioner, Laura Beason, could go either way. Beason was the swing vote, and Marybeth had learned to tailor her answers to her. Beason had married into a third-generation ranch family, and although her husband was squarely with the two anti-spending commissioners (except for *his* pet projects, of course), Laura enjoyed defying him when she could. Marybeth would play to Beason's soft spot for culture and the arts in the community. It had worked in previous years.

Satisfied that she could respond to even the most hostile questions from the commissioners in a cheery and informative way, Marybeth saved the presentation to her laptop so she could go over it at home, then cautiously opened the ConFab app on her phone.

Since she hadn't heard anything from Joe the night before, which was the reason she was in such a foul mood to start the day, the only way she could assure herself that he was still alive and well up in the mountains was to monitor Steve-2's posts.

The last post he'd made was from late the night before. Obviously, someone else had taken the shot and had posted it on Steve-2's behalf. It was a photo of him sitting on a log in the firelight looking satisfied and very content as he gazed at the campfire near his feet. The caption simply read:

> *Home, home on the range,*
> *Where the deer and the antelope play.*
> *Where seldom is heard a discouraging word . . .*

What she'd noticed, though, was that to the side of Steve-2, leaning back out of the firelight, was Joe. His head was turned away, but she knew the profile. He obviously didn't know the photo was being taken at the time.

She scrolled through Steve-2's previous posts and photos to find there were many discouraging words aimed at him. There were a number of user threads denouncing Price and threatening to delete the app because he was in the act of hunting. Others defended him, but they were overwhelmed by animal rights activists and others who thought a man of his wealth and intelligence should be spending his time on more beneficial pursuits. Marybeth thought several of the users made very good points.

She wondered if Steve-2 cared either way what some of his users thought. She sensed that he had such supreme self-confidence—and so many millions of users around the world—that their arguments would wash right over him.

But there was Joe, she thought. He looked fine. So why hadn't he called her as promised and filled her in? And why did she have to resort to checking social media to know that he was still alive and well?

Marybeth was mulling this over when Evelyn Hughes stuck her head through the open door and cleared her throat.

"Yes, Evelyn?"

"Your daughter is here and she asked if you had a few minutes."

"Sheridan?"

"Yes."

"Of course."

She gathered herself and placed her phone facedown on her desk. It was rare when Sheridan showed up without texting.

As Evelyn exited her office, Marybeth called out to her. The older woman turned.

"I'm sorry if I seemed snappish to you this morning. I apologize for my tone. I just worry that some derelict will wander in here during the night and wreck the place."

"You have nothing to apologize for," Evelyn said with a blush. But she was obviously relieved. "I've got a lot on my mind. I really thought I'd checked the doors."

That doesn't matter, Marybeth wanted to say while throttling Evelyn. *We all have a lot on our minds. And it doesn't matter what you thought you did. Just take responsibility and apologize and don't mess up again. Why is it that adults—and you're older than me, Evelyn—can't admit an error without offering up an excuse?*

But she didn't say any of it. She knew Evelyn was a long-time library employee who was very quick to complain to HR about any perceived slight. Marybeth knew she couldn't afford a complaint like that on the record prior to her budget presentation before the commissioners.

So instead, she asked, "Where is my daughter?"

"I think she was on her way to the computer room."

"Thank you."

"My pleasure, Marybeth."

She found her oldest daughter perched in front of one of the public monitors in the rear of the old Carnegie library. There was a bank of them separated by partitions and they were largely used by older patrons or unemployed drifters. There was one of each on either side of Sheridan—a disheveled man in a camo parka with a gray ZZ Top–length beard, and a matronly retired postal worker with steel-framed glasses and a permanent scowl—so Sheridan stood out.

"Hey, Mom," Sheridan said. She looked lean, tan, and outdoorsy, Marybeth thought.

"What brings you here?"

"There are a couple of articles I'd like to print out and give to Nate. Is it okay to use your printer?"

Like most kids of Sheridan's age, she didn't have a printer at home.

"Sure, I'll authorize it," Marybeth said. The library charged five cents a page.

Marybeth looked over Sheridan's shoulder to see the results of a Google search for "Falcon Smuggling."

"That's interesting," she said.

"Yeah. I'm trying to do some research to share with him."

Sheridan lowered her voice as Marybeth bent closer to hear. "I'm trying to prevent him from going medieval on whoever has been stealing birds. He takes it personally and I know he's on legal thin ice as it is. I talked to Liv and she agrees: we need to try and intervene before someone gets hurt."

Marybeth looked up to see that the retired postal employee, a notorious local gossip, was peering at them over the partition.

"Let me buy you a cup of coffee across the street," Marybeth said to Sheridan. "You can print out the articles afterward."

I talked with the new county prosecutor," Marybeth said to Sheridan over a mug at the Burg-O-Pardner. "I think she's inclined to let things go. That's just my impression from having met with her. But if Nate draws too much attention to himself or commits another violation, all bets are off."

"That's what I'm trying to prevent," Sheridan said as she winced from her first bitter sip. "I'm trying to learn as much about falcon smuggling and smugglers as I can because stealing eggs and birds and selling them overseas is totally illegal. Maybe I can help locate the guy and we can deal with him legitimately. Did you know that some falcon eggs go for up to twenty thousand dollars in the Middle East? Or that a fledgling peregrine falcon is worth fifty thousand dollars to a falconer in Qatar? This is big business, but from what I've learned there are only a few poachers in the world who can pull it off. I think one of them is in the area."

"And you'd like to find him before Nate does," Marybeth said.

"Yes, but I'd rather Dad found him. I'd rather the guy be arrested than be pulled limb from limb and left for dead. That's what Nate would like to do to him."

"You're like your father," Marybeth said. "Trouble has a way of finding you."

"Speaking of," Sheridan said, "where is he? I texted him this morning and he didn't reply. I thought he might know if there's another falconer around."

Marybeth paused. "You don't know, do you?"

"Know what?"

Marybeth told Sheridan about the assignment from the governor, the hunting expedition, about Steve-2 Price.

Sheridan's eyes got big. "Steve-2 Price? The ConFab guy?"

"Yes."

"He's here and Dad is guiding him?"

"Yes."

"That's absolutely *insane*. Does Dad even know who he is?"

"Not really," Marybeth said.

Sheridan laughed and said, "I mean, us girls had to beg him to even get a cell phone. Do you remember he used to keep his off all the time to, quote, 'save the battery'?"

"He's gotten better about that. He even texts, as you know."

"Yeah, but in complete sentences," she said with a roll of her eyes. "April and Lucy and I laugh about it all the time. We send each other stuff he writes because it's so formal."

Giggling, Sheridan dug her phone out and found the message app. She opened it up and showed the screen to her mother. It read:

Dear Sheridan:
I hope this finds you well. As you know, next week is your mother's birthday and I wonder if you have any ideas on what she might like as a gift? She's mentioned a new saddle but . . .

Marybeth smiled. She was flattered that Joe was aware of her birthday, even if he was flummoxed about what to get her. She opened *her* phone and the ConFab app and handed it to Sheridan.

"This is the most recent post, from last night," she said.

Sheridan shook her head as she scrolled down through the posts. "I can't believe I knew nothing about this."

"It was supposed to be a secret," Marybeth said. "Apparently Steve-2 and his people think otherwise."

"Since I started working at Yarak, I feel so out of it," Sheridan lamented. "I spend a lot of days out of cell phone range and I just don't keep up on what's going on anymore. Nate's like Dad—he doesn't do social media. I used to live on my phone, like everybody else I know. It seemed so important. It seemed vital to be connected at all times. Do you realize that in my lifetime I've never *not* been online?"

Marybeth sat back. "I'd never thought of it like that."

"It's true. I'm not online during the day, and when I get home at night, I'm too tired to check Facebook or Insta for very long. I hardly ever post anything because everyone is so judgmental. It's hard for my old friends to understand what I do, and too many of them feel the need to comment on it. I *never* comment on what my friends are doing unless it's positive and innocuous. I know they aren't as happy and successful as they pretend to be, but I let it go. But not some of these people I'm talking about. They ask, 'Why are you wasting your life?' or 'Whatever happened to you and Lance Romance? Is he still in the picture?' None of it is anyone's business."

"I'm grateful I haven't gotten married and had any kids," Sheridan said without realizing her words were a shiv into her mother's heart, "because if you have a baby, every damn supermom in the world feels entitled to tell you you're doing everything wrong and harming the child. I've seen it. My friends who have kids get beaten up more than anyone. It's no wonder so many of us don't have them."

Sheridan sighed. The topic was obviously very much on her mind. "But it's maybe not so bad," she said. "I imagine it's like quitting drugs cold turkey. It hurts at first, but as time goes by it gets better. You start to feel normal again. But the thing is, Mom, I'm not sure I know what normal *is*. Social media has always been there, you know? Maybe we take it too seriously."

Marybeth said, "I know what you mean. I'm probably overreacting myself. There's probably a really good reason why your dad didn't call or text me last night, and I've let it derail my entire morning. There was a time when men went off to sea or into the frontier and their wives wouldn't hear from them for months, even years. Somehow they survived."

"Yeah," Sheridan said. But she didn't sound convinced.

"So you haven't heard anything from him this morning, either?" Sheridan asked.

"Not yet."

"And Steve-2 hasn't posted anything more?"

"No."

"Maybe they got their elk and they're busy taking care of it."

"That's the only explanation I can think of," Marybeth said. "It's the only one I *want* to consider at the moment, because it means they'll be headed back soon."

"Do you know where he is in the mountains?" Sheridan asked.

Marybeth vaguely gestured toward the east. "Kind of," she said.

"He didn't leave a note?"

"No. He told me, but I didn't write it down. He has a sat phone and he swore he'd take a personal locator beacon. Brock Boedecker is also along with them, so I didn't worry about it this time."

"There are ways of finding him if Steve-2 doesn't post again," Sheridan said. "You know, cell phones can be tracked and things like that."

Marybeth sat back. "A full-fledged search-and-rescue operation could be launched, I know. But that takes time and we've got this new sheriff who hasn't done it here before . . ." She trailed off. Then: "If I don't hear from him by this afternoon, I may need to call him, as well as Director Ewig. I don't want to overreact, though. Lord knows he's been late or out of touch before."

"We grew up with it," Sheridan said. "Dad can handle himself pretty well."

"He can," Marybeth said. "I'm sure there's a good explanation. But right now I want to know he's safe so I can kill him."

Sheridan laughed. Then she got serious. "This could turn out to be a huge social media story, but I don't want to follow it that way. Please keep me in the loop."

"I will."

"And I'll join ConFab to see what Steve-2 posts. I know April and Lucy are on it."

TWELVE

After leading Price through the sprawling aspen grove, Joe turned around and looked with dismay at the tracks they'd left. The thick carpet of dropped leaves acted as a cover to the surface below, so the moist soil hadn't dried out. Their muddy boot prints were as distinct as a popular cattle trail.

Price followed Joe's gaze. "Are they going to come after us?"

"Yup," Joe said. "And we're making it easy."

"So what can we do?"

"Let me think," Joe said.

"You saw what they did to Zsolt," Price said. "They shot him down like a dog. I've never experienced anything like it before."

Joe didn't reply. He carefully studied the terrain and wished he could see through the impenetrable wall of aspen to determine if the Thomases were coming through it from the other side.

"I also can't believe he ran like that," Price said, still focused on Rumy. "He didn't even attempt to save me. He's been at my side for five years. Man, I trusted him. I always kind of thought Tim might turn on me at some point, but I trusted Zsolt."

"Can we talk about this later?" Joe asked.

They'd come through the aspen grove east to west on a slight decline. Although there were natural rises and ridges in front of them, as well as black timber to navigate, the trailhead and his truck were in front of them, but at least a day and a half away on foot. There would be no doubt where they were headed, Joe thought.

He swung his daypack off his shoulder and dropped to one knee. Inside, he found the folded topo map in a ziplock bag that he'd been carrying with him since he first patrolled the mountains. The map was over twenty years old and had started to come apart at the folds, but the features of the Bighorns hadn't changed much. He spread it out on the forest floor.

Price got close so he could see the map over Joe's shoulder.

"They know we've got to keep heading west," Joe said softly. He ran the tip of his index finger over the paper. "There are three drainages to the bottom from where we're at. We're currently here on the top of the middle one. If we follow it down and nothing stops us, we'll eventually reach the trailhead."

"I see."

"But that's exactly what they'll expect us to do. They can move faster on horseback and they've got us outmanned and outgunned. It's just a matter of time before they're on us, especially considering that track we've churned up."

"Shit," Price whispered.

"Do you have anything on you?" Joe asked Price. "Your phone or your PLB?"

"No," Price said. "They made us turn everything over. That big dumb one smashed all of our electronics with the butt of his shotgun."

Joe nodded. They'd been rendered completely dark. "Do you have anything with you that can help us?"

"My amulet," Price said, reaching into his collar and displaying a smooth blue stone the size of a robin's egg mounted on a gold chain. "I got it in Nepal. It's supposed to ward off evil."

"When does it start to work?" Joe asked.

Price smiled bitterly and tucked it back beneath his shirt.

Joe turned back to the map, studied it, then tilted his head up and scanned the skyline of a steep rocky ridge to the north. It was two to three miles away and the granite outcropping rose out of the timber.

He chinned north and said, "I assume the Thomas clan will figure we're taking the most direct route. That's what *I'd* assume. My suggestion is that we turn ninety degrees and climb that outcropping and drop down the other side. The north drainage will take us down out of the mountains a few miles away from the trailhead, but I think we can find it if we don't overrun the location. That route will add a lot of time to get to the trucks, but it's less likely they'll look for us over there."

Price put his hand to his brow to block out the morning sun.

"That looks steep. Are you sure we can climb out of here?"

"No," Joe said. "And we have to be careful we don't rimrock ourselves so we can't climb either up or back down. But it's harder to track a man in the rocks than it is on the forest floor. And one thing I know about Earl Thomas is he's a hell of a tracker."

Price put his hands on his hips and slowly turned around, taking it all in: the mountain ridges on both sides, the sea of trees before them, the aspen grove they'd just hiked through, the cloudless big sky overhead.

"It's beautiful," he said. "It's too bad we have to see it like this."

"Hmmm," Joe said while carefully folding up his map and putting it back in the plastic bag. As he'd guessed, Kirby had removed the Leatherman tool from the side pocket of his daypack.

The morning was cool and sunny at the moment with little wind, but he knew the weather could change at elevation in a heartbeat and they weren't equipped for it.

Price said, "Is it true an aspen grove is one of the largest living organisms on earth? That all of the roots are intercon- nected so that it's all a single entity?"

"Yes, that's true."

"So it's kind of like the Internet," Price said.

That made Joe pause.

"Except right now we can access the aspen grove, of course," Price said with a sour chuckle.

For the first time that morning, Joe smiled. But it wasn't a happy smile.

Joe shouldered his pack and started walking east again. Price dutifully followed. After a half mile, Price said, "I thought this wasn't our plan."

"Just for a while."

"Can you give me a little more than that?"

Within fifty yards Joe could hear the furious rush of a small spring-fed creek coursing down the center of the drainage over and through large rocks. He turned in that direction until he found a wide bed of smooth, tumbled stones. The tiny creek was feisty and the only glimpses he actually had of it were pillows of foam between river rocks and a few droplets spitting into the air between them.

"In the spring, this is a big creek," Joe said. "There's even a waterfall down below. But right now there's not much water to speak of."

"I see that," Price said.

"This is where we cross and go north," Joe said. "They'll be able to track us to here and they'll figure we followed it down. If we do this right, I think it'll take them a long time to realize we didn't."

Price nodded slowly and gave Joe a thumbs-up. "I like it," he said.

"Step from rock to rock," Joe said. "Try not to lose your balance and fall. We don't want any broken bones."

"No, we don't."

Joe dropped to his hands and knees and pushed aside a

dying fern that covered a six-inch-wide opening between the rocks. The stream was clear and no more than three inches deep. He bent down, closed his eyes, and sucked in ice water until his throat hurt.

When he was done, he climbed back to his feet and gestured to Price to do the same.

"Is the quality of the water something we should worry about?" Price asked.

"Maybe," Joe said. "But I think we have more things to worry about right now."

As he said it, he recalled that he had a plastic bottle with a Katadyn water purification filter in his pack. He hadn't used it in years, but he thought the filter would still be okay. Joe dug it out and handed it to Price. "Better use this," he said.

Price reached for it and froze with his hand inches away from the Nalgene bottle. Joe noted that Price's eyes were focused on something over his shoulder.

"What?" Joe asked.

"I saw movement over there in the trees," Price said, his tone rising with panic. "I think they found us already."

Get down," Joe said, placing his hand on Price's shoulder and forcing him to his knees. Joe dropped with him until they were both on their bellies on the edge of the creek. They were low enough that the exposed rocks in the creek bed shielded them from being seen by someone at the same level from the other slope. The ground was cold and his body heat instantly thawed the frost from the bunched-up grass.

Joe mouthed, "Where?" to Price, and Price chinned toward a long finger of aspen on the other side of the water. The finger went down the slope until it petered out as it approached a wall of spruce and mountain juniper.

After removing his hat, Joe raised his head until he could see over the top of the rocks in the creek. It took a few seconds before he saw movement—something in the aspens among the trunks. The form was vertical, unlike the blocky outline of an animal. Dark color strobed between pale tree trunks at a slow but steady pace. It was a man and he was moving from east to west, the same direction they'd come.

As Joe watched, the vertical form became Brock Boedecker as he shouldered around a tree trunk and walked toward them. Boedecker gave no indication he'd seen them yet, and his attention was focused up the slope to the east, where the Thomas clan would no doubt come from, Joe thought. Boedecker had left the shelter of the aspens and was now in the open. It was as if Boedecker had been drawn by the water, just as Joe and Price had been.

"He's coming right at us," Joe whispered to Price over his shoulder.

"Does he know we're here?"

"I don't think so."

"Is he with us or against us?"

"Don't know," Joe said. "Stop talking."

Boedecker was forty feet away, directly across from them on the other side of the stream. He halted at the edge of the rocks and squatted down to fill his water bottle. Joe recalled Earl ordering the man to give up his sidearm, and he couldn't determine if he had any other weapons. Like Joe, Boedecker had a small daypack.

Boedecker stood and drank. He was so close, Joe could hear the glugging. The rancher refilled his bottle and then, as he lowered it to slip it back into the side pocket of his pack, his upper body turned, and their eyes met.

Boedecker froze. "*Joe?*"

Joe reached back and indicated to Price with a hand wave that he wanted him to remain flat on his belly and out of Boedecker's sight. Then he rose up until he and Boedecker faced off eye to eye. Boedecker made no threatening movements.

Joe unzipped his parka and slipped his right hand inside his coat to where his empty holster was. It was a ruse, but he hoped it would make Boedecker think twice.

"Don't make me do something I don't want to do," Joe said. "You showed your hand back at the camp. I'd suggest you keep moving."

"It isn't like that, Joe," Boedecker said. "I didn't know how things would go."

"You were in on it," Joe said. "What did you do, tell Earl where we'd be camping?"

Boedecker's eyes darted several times to where Joe's hand was concealed beneath his coat. He obviously wasn't sure that Joe wasn't armed, although the chances of it were unlikely.

"I never told him, Joe. Because I didn't know where we'd camp for sure when we set off. *You* were the guide, remember?"

"He knew when we left. He knew which trailhead. And you allowed them to listen to us through the radio in your gear."

Boedecker didn't deny anything and, to his credit, Joe thought, he didn't try to come up with a lie. Instead, he said, "I never thought it would go the way it did. You might not know it, but Earl has a right to be on the warpath. I knew he'd want to confront Steve-2 in person because he couldn't get near him any other way. But this . . ." Boedecker widened his eyes in disbelief.

He continued. "When Earl sent me away without my horses or my guns, I knew what was going to go down. But I didn't expect it until it happened."

Joe didn't reply. Instead, he gestured for Boedecker to move along.

"I ain't going by myself, Joe. Come on, man."

"You got yourself into this."

Boedecker said, "They'll kill me."

"Why would they kill you now? You helped them."

"Because they can't leave any witnesses," Boedecker said. "There's something you don't know."

"What's that?"

Boedecker pointed toward the east. "After I left camp I ran like a son of a bitch. I heard the shots and it spooked the hell out of me, so I deliberately went in the wrong direction. I figured I'd put as much distance as I could between them and me before I started down the mountain."

Joe nodded for him to go on.

"I found a dead hunter lying facedown in a little meadow," Boedecker said. "Lots of blood, and he wasn't completely stiff, so it happened just last night, I think. I rolled him over and saw the stab wound in his ribs."

Joe shuddered and recalled the knifepoint at his side just a little over an hour ago. Kirby.

"Who was he?" Joe asked.

"Don't know," Boedecker said. "But he looked like one of those millennial types. Long beard, wearing all camo. Young guy. I figured he might have stumbled on the Thomases last night and they took him out. Poor fucker."

"And you left him there?"

"What the hell else could I do?" Boedecker asked. "It came clear to me right then that Earl doesn't want anyone to talk about what happened up here. The only people he trusts are his sons. They'll kill me, and you if they have to. That seems like a good reason for the two of us to stick together. We're not involved in this dispute."

Joe thought about it. Boedecker didn't push him.

Do you have a cell phone on you?" Joe asked.

"Nope. Didn't even bring it with me."

"Any weapons?"

"Earl made me drop my .44. I'm unarmed and defenseless. I've got a skinning knife and fencing pliers in my backpack, but that's it. I don't even have bear spray. I can't remember the last time I was in these mountains with no way to defend myself. How'd you get to keep *your* gun?"

Joe kept his hand where it was. He didn't want to reveal the truth.

"They took your weapon away, didn't they?" the rancher asked. His eyes twinkled.

Joe let his right hand drop away from the empty holster.

"Yup."

"You had me going there for a minute, though," Boedecker said with a chuckle. "Of course, if I would have thought about it more, I'd remember you can't hit a damned thing with a handgun."

It was true.

"They were pretty thorough," Boedecker said. "They had this thing planned out. Earl has been thinking about it for close to a year."

Joe wondered how Thomas had known about it that long.

"Hey," Boedecker said, "where's Steve-2? Did they get him? Was that what all the shooting was about?"

Again, Joe didn't respond. He recalled that Boedecker hadn't been there when he and Price had made their run for it.

"The bodyguard made a break for it," Joe said. "Brad wounded him with his shotgun and finished him off."

"Jesus."

"That created a distraction," Joe said. "I hit Kirby and Earl with bear spray and took off."

"So Steve-2 got away, too?"

"I reckon."

"They want *him*, not us," Boedecker said.

"What's your point?"

"If they have him, they might not come after us for a while. If he somehow got away from them during the confusion, I wouldn't think a guy like that would get very far."

"Again, what's your point?"

"I'm just saying, if you and me stick together, we might be able to get down the mountain in one piece. And if we run into Steve-2, well . . ." He let his thought trail off.

"Are you saying we should turn him over to them?" Joe asked.

Boedecker shrugged. But it meant *Maybe*.

"Do you really think that could happen?" Joe asked. "We've already got them down for two murders. Do you really think they'd let us walk even if we gave them Price?"

"Maybe, but probably not," Boedecker said. "Earl may be inclined to make us a deal—Steve-2 for us. I know I'd make that deal, considering what the guy did to Earl. It would be a good thing for humanity in general, I'd say."

"I didn't do anything to that man!" Price shouted at Boedecker as he scrambled to his feet behind Joe. Joe sighed inwardly to himself. The man just couldn't be silent.

"You had no good reason to betray me," Price said to Boedecker. "I don't even know you."

Boedecker registered his surprise by stepping back a few feet. When he recovered, he said, "I might not have a good reason, but Earl sure as hell does."

Joe, once again, was confused. There seemed to be a lot going on beneath the surface he wasn't privy to. But he didn't want to take the time to litigate it, not with the very real possibility that the Thomas clan could emerge through the aspen at any moment.

He had to think fast.

"You can stay with us for the time being," Joe said to Boedecker. "We were just about to climb that north ridge and drop down into the next drainage. We thought we might be able to shake 'em."

"Harder to track over the rocks. Smart. I'll do my part," Boedecker said with relief. "I know the country over there better than most. I've hunted it all my life."

"I'm aware of that."

To Price, Boedecker said, "I didn't know you were there. I was just spitballing ideas with Joe."

"Fuck you," Price spat.

A half hour later, the trees started to thin as the granite wall punched up through the forest floor. It was marked by fissures and ledges that looked difficult to climb, but not impossible. They'd tried to step from rock to rock on their way north to avoid leaving tracks.

Boedecker announced he'd scout to the west to see if there was an easier route to the top than the one they were looking at.

When he was gone, Price turned to Joe. "Were you really thinking about giving me up?"

"Nope, although I'm not sure why."

Price ignored the caveat. "Can we trust your friend?"

"Nope."

Price was angry. "Then why are we bringing him along?"

"He knows the country over there, like he said," Joe whispered. "And I'd rather know exactly where he is at all times."

Price looked puzzled at first. Then he said, "You don't want him hooking up with the Thomases and showing them where we went."

Joe nodded.

"Thank you," Price said.

"Thank me if we get out of this," Joe said. "Until then, stick close to me. Don't engage with Brock. Sound carries up here, so try not to talk—or argue—unless it's important."

"That'll be tough for me."

"I know."

THIRTEEN

For the next hour, they climbed up the north ridge. Boedecker led and Price brought up the rear. Joe chose to stay in the middle to keep them apart from each other and to prevent another loud argument. And he didn't want Boedecker behind Price on the ascent. It would be too easy, Joe thought, for Boedecker to give Price a shove and send him tumbling down the mountain when Joe wasn't looking. Since Boedecker had already stated his willingness to sacrifice Price to the Thomases to save himself, Joe couldn't give him the opportunity.

Much of the climb was hand over hand, grasping exposed tree roots and granite outcroppings for balance. The pitch was steeper than Joe had guessed it would be when he'd surveyed the wall from a distance. He also realized as he struggled upward that for the last third of the route the three of them would be in the open. There were very few trees above them all the way to the summit and those that clung to the wall were stunted and sparse. The three of them, he thought, would be easy pickings for a marksman. Joe was well aware of the lethal capability of ultramodern long-range rifle technology. He knew that even from the distance of the valley floor they were vulnerable.

Brock Boedecker chose the route to the top well, Joe thought. He moved steadily and knew how to avoid dead ends and side trips that might be physically less taxing than straight up, but would threaten to rimrock them or make them backtrack. It was a skill born of guiding hunters in rough terrain for years.

Boedecker looked over his shoulder at Joe from time to time to make sure he was still with him. When Boedecker shifted his gaze to Price, Joe could see the contempt in his face. He didn't seem to really care if Price made it or not.

I need a break," Price wheezed to Joe. "I can't get air. The altitude is really getting to me."

"I know it's tough, but we've got to keep climbing," Joe said in response. His legs hurt as well, especially the left one, where he'd been shot. The muscles in his wounded thigh were overwhelmed and he felt at times that he was more swinging his leg up behind him than using it to climb. He could feel a sheen of sweat beneath his clothing.

The sky darkened into overcast and it was getting colder the higher they went. Their breaths had turned into cloudy puffs of condensation.

"My thighs are burning," Price said.

"Shhhh."

Price cursed at Joe, but he chose not to stop and rest. Joe was thankful for that.

Almost there," Boedecker said with a voice hoarse from exertion. "I can see the top of the ridge."

"It's about time," Price said.

Joe wasn't sure how much longer he could go on without a breather. His lungs ached and his knees screamed with sharp pain. He was getting to the point where his hands were trembling and his climbing technique was getting sloppy and imprecise. It was like the end of a long day of fly-fishing, he thought, when he would cast with tired arms and the line would bunch up in the air and fall around his head and shoulders. When that happened, it was time to quit.

But he couldn't quit now.

Ahead of him, Boedecker cursed.

"What is it?" Joe asked.

"False summit," Boedecker groused. "I thought we were there, but there's another fifty yards to go."

Joe took a deep breath and kept climbing. As he did so, he looked over his shoulder to see that Price had stopped. The man was pressed against the rough granite wall with his eyes closed and his mouth agape. He was heaving in an attempt to get more air.

"Steve-2?" Joe said.

Price waved at him to indicate he was still alive. Barely.

"You've got to keep climbing," Joe said. "It isn't far now."

He noted that Boedecker had scrambled ahead. Maybe, Joe thought, the rancher would get to the top and take off running on his own and they wouldn't see him again. Joe could deal with that, and it might even make the situation more manageable. But the rancher could also choose to use his advantage of being on higher ground to make a stand. He could prevent Joe from getting on top of the ridge or kick Price in the head and send him falling down the mountain. All of those scenarios seemed possible. Boedecker was a wild card in every regard.

A moment later, Boedecker appeared above them. He'd reached the top and stood facing them on the lip of the rim, his hands on his knees to recover.

"What's going on?" the rancher called down to Joe.

"Giving him a minute," Joe said.

"Fuck him," Boedecker advised as he shook his head with disgust. Suddenly, he locked in place, his gaze hard on the huge aspen grove below them.

"They're *coming*," he whispered. Then he backed out of view.

As hard as it was, as much as it hurt, Joe shinnied back down the ridge until Price was within reach. He extended his hand and said, "Grab it. Let's go. *Now.*"

When Price reached up, his hand was shaking. Joe grasped it. "Come on."

Joe half climbed and half pulled Price along with him. He gave it so much effort that his vision blurred and blood pounded within his ears until he couldn't hear anything else. Price's weight threatened to pull Joe's shoulder out of its socket.

He crawled up over the lip of the ridge and pulled Price along behind him. Then he rolled onto his back and lay there until he could breathe again and his heart slowed back to almost normal. Price gasped for air next to him. Their shoulders touched. Joe thought it uncomfortably intimate.

Finally, Joe opened his eyes and turned his head. They were on the very top of the barren ridge and the wind was cold and strong. He'd sweated so much on the climb up that as he dried out, he felt even colder.

Boedecker was nowhere to be seen. Where the man should have been was a tremendous vista leading down to the adjacent drainage. The way down looked to be a much gentler grade than on the way up. Between where they were on top and where thick black timber carpeted the slope, the rest of the way to the bottom of the drainage was a vast gray scree field of broken rock plates.

As he watched, snow clouds like white smoke rolled over the top of the opposite ridge and rushed across the valley. The storm came fast, softening the sharp views of timber and granite. Within a minute, snowflakes swirled around them.

Joe had recovered enough that he could move again, although he grunted when he rolled from his back to his belly. He crawled back toward the lip of the ridge and slowly raised his head so he could see where they'd come from before the snow obscured everything.

"Where did your friend go?" Price asked.

"I don't know."

"Is he leading the way or running from us?"

"I don't know."

In the distance on the floor of the drainage where the rocky creek bed halved the meadow, four distant horsemen emerged from the aspen. Three rode parallel to the stream, one on the south side and two on the north. Trailing them was the last rider, whom Joe could identify as Brad by his size and the bulk of his horse. Brad led a long string of packhorses behind him. The pack animals were loaded with bulging panniers and gear bags and Joe guessed they were a combination of Thomas and Boedecker stock.

The riders, Earl, Kirby, Joannides, and Brad, grouped up in the middle of the meadow not far from where Joe and Boedecker had squared off an hour before. They seemed to be having a discussion.

Joe lowered his head, even though he was a long way from them. He didn't want his silhouette to be skylighted against the snow clouds.

Why did they stop at that particular spot? he wondered. Could the Thomases, who were legendary trackers, see signs in the grass? Or, Joe thought with a chill, had Boedecker secretly dropped an item there to be found by them?

Joe expected the riders to all turn in unison in their saddles and look up at him. But they didn't.

The last thing he saw, before swirling snow blocked out

everything, was the four riders continue down the drainage adjacent to the creek bed.

His plan to cut away from the trail and confuse the pursuers had worked, he thought. At least for now.

What happened back there this morning at the top of the dry wash?" Joe asked Price after they'd scrambled over and through the sharp edges of the snow-slicked scree and had finally entered the spruce forest. The canopy was thick and oppressive and it allowed only a few stray snowflakes to filter through to the pine needle floor.

"We'd been there about twenty minutes," Price said. "Zsolt had to get up to piss, which made me kind of angry. I thought he should have taken care of that before we left to go hunting. But he went and did it anyway.

"When he came back and got down into the brush with me, he said he thought he'd heard something out there. My first thought was the elk were coming, just like you said they might. So I strung an arrow and got ready. I hoped it would get light really fast so I could see better. Zsolt was right behind me looking over my shoulder to help me spot a bull. It was a pretty cool moment. It was like when you're coding and you start to realize something huge—a breakthrough—is about to happen."

Price cursed as he tripped on a rock and pirouetted into a nice recovery, Joe thought. It barely broke his concentration, though.

"That big one, Brad, snuck up on us and was standing right

over the top of me before I even realized he was there," Price said. "He scared the shit out of me and he took Zsolt by complete surprise, which until that second I didn't think possible. It's like he was *transported* right on top of us."

"They know how to walk quietly in the woods," Joe said. "They were watching us set up the whole time. I found their tracks, but I didn't know who it was."

Price said, "No shit about walking quietly. He was just there and I saw he was holding a shotgun on us. Since he was only a few feet away, I didn't think there was much we could do. Then I realized the smaller one, Kirby, had also come up behind us. He had a gun in one hand, a pistol, and a big knife in the other. For some reason, I was more scared of the knife."

Joe grunted. He understood.

"Brad ordered us to stand up, which we did. Then he said, 'All of your electronic shit. All of it—give it to me.' So we dug everything out of our pockets and handed it over. I'll tell you, Joe, it was a really weird feeling. It was like being stripped naked in front of strangers."

"So just the two of them?" Joe asked.

"Yeah. I didn't meet Earl until we got to the camp. Anyway, they gathered up all of our phones and devices and Zsolt's weapons. He had three pistols on him and two knives. I never knew he had that much hardware on him. I kept thinking he'd make a cool move like in the movies, you know? Like he'd be in the act of handing his gun over but he'd spin the pistol around upside down on his index finger and start blasting those guys. But he *didn't*. He didn't make a move to protect me. He just handed everything over, just like I did."

"Rumy wasn't in on it, was he?" Joe asked.

"No," Price said with a sigh. "He just wasn't as tough or loyal as I thought he was. What a disappointment he turned out to be." Then, after a few seconds, Price said, "May he rest in peace."

Joe asked, "Did you have any idea at the time why they were there?"

"Not at all," Price said. "I mean, I asked them. I thought maybe we'd trespassed on their space, you know? In fact, I sort of threw you under the bus. I told them Joe Pickett had stationed us there while he went out to look for elk. I told them if they had a problem with us being there, they should take it up with you."

"Wish they would have," Joe said.

"Not that it mattered," Price said. "They took my bow and arrows and all the stuff they made us hand over before they told us to start walking back to camp. They had their horses tied up about a quarter mile away and mounted up and herded us back to the camp like we were a couple of stray cows. Again, I kept thinking Zsolt would do something, like whip around and spook the horses or jump on those guys. But he just walked alongside with his head down.

"I kept thinking, 'What do these rubes want with us?' I thought about all kinds of *Deliverance* shit. 'Squeal like a pig, Steve-2,' I thought."

Price said it in a faux southern accent that Joe thought offensive.

"What about Tim Joannides?" Joe asked. "You acted like you weren't very surprised he turned on you."

"No," Price said, "I *was* surprised when I saw him standing there with Earl. But when I thought about it, well, I should have known better. I should have been more ruthless with him. I let sentiment overtake me, and that's one thing that will kill you in Silicon Valley."

"Meaning what?" Joe asked. He was mildly curious, but he was also cognizant of the very dire situation they were in. It continued to snow, and the temperature had dropped into the mid-twenties. It would only get colder as the day went on, and the night might be brutal. They had no food and no weapons. They had very little survival gear and few tools to make a shelter. Their heavy winter gear was back in the camp or stuffed into gear bags on Brad's string of horses.

If he could keep Price distracted and talking—not a tough thing to do, he'd learned—he might be able to stave off the inevitable disorientation and panic. To have any chance of getting away, Joe thought, he had to keep Price engaged and moving forward. Not doing so might slow them down or get them killed.

"Do you know anything about Aloft, my holding company?" Price asked.

"Nope."

"Everybody knows me for ConFab, which is a division of Aloft. But ConFab came later. I founded Aloft with Tim back in our dorm room at Stanford. We were fifty-fifty partners and our brilliant idea was to write software that would lift people up—hence the name—and that would help end users to create networks of friends and relatives that everybody involved could access easily on their phones . . ."

For twenty-five minutes, even as they crawled over and through downed and twisted trees that had been destroyed by a microburst and left a landscape that looked bombed, Price kept talking.

Joe understood parts of it and the rest wafted away over his head. When Price finally paused to grimace at a bloody scratch on the back of his hand from a sharp branch, Joe broke in.

"So the idea was that on a single screen on your phone you could see the exact locations of all members of your group wherever they were at the same time."

"As long as they had their phones with them, yes," Price said.

"It sounds intrusive," Joe said.

Price's face reddened. "*No,*" he said with force. "It wasn't designed to be intrusive. It was designed to create a richer community among friends and family members. Everyone in each circle had to opt in, after all.

"You know, there was a time when we knew where everybody was—our siblings, our parents, our neighbors. That's because we *talked* to each other. Actually talked. We knew when someone was going to the store or to the movies. But that was before everybody spent their lives staring at their phones. The idea behind our app was to re-create that simple idea of a community of people who cared about each other."

"Okay," Joe said. "I didn't mean to anger you."

"You have kids, right?" Price asked.

"Three daughters," Joe said.

"Wouldn't you like to be able to open an app on your phone and know where all of them are and that they're safe?"

Joe winced. He thought of several scenarios concerning his adult daughters that he absolutely didn't want to know about. He said, "No, but my wife might like that."

"*Exactly*," Price said.

As they wound through a crowded copse of lodgepole pines, Joe said, "So what happened to the app? Why haven't I heard of it?"

"It still exists, but it isn't public," Price said cryptically. For once, he didn't say more.

"Did you sell it?"

"That's what one does in my industry," Price said. "You invent a unique technology, and if you're lucky, someone bigger wants to buy it for hundreds of millions. Remember, Tim and I were sharing a dorm room at the time. We weren't wealthy. By then I had the majority of the shares by just enough to make the decision on behalf of the company."

"Who bought it? The government? The military?" Joe asked.

After a long break, Price said, "Something like that." Then he moved on quickly. Joe noted it. "Anyway," he said, "Tim and I didn't agree on the sale or the terms. I was able to borrow a few million from a VC and buy him out except for five percent of the parent company. He was really happy with the deal at the time and, frankly, we were sick of each other. Tim thought he'd use the money to go and invent other great products, but he didn't and he hasn't. He had one failure after another, unfortunately. Have you ever heard of WarmGlow?"

"No."

"No one has," Price said. "That's my point. It was supposed to measure the rise in thermal temperature of a potential partner when he or she was near you. Somehow, it was supposed to reveal attraction. That was one of Tim's great ideas. But it was a spectacular flop. It turns out the app couldn't tell the difference between someone who heated up because they wanted to be *with* you and someone who was angry and wanted to punch you in the mouth."

"Hmmm."

"Tim was in debt when he came to me, and his investors wanted to string him up," Price said. "This was just around the time we launched ConFab. He pulled at my heartstrings and reminded me of all those hundreds of hours we'd spent coding together in our dorm room. How we were such good friends. I let my feelings get in the way of my business sense, so I hired him back."

"To be your assistant," Joe said.

"He said he wanted to be partners again," Price said defensively. "It was his idea, and that was the only position I had open in my inner circle. He might have thought he'd step right back into his role as my Steve Wozniak or something. Or that he'd be given a division or a big-shot title someday, but Tim, deep down, is a fuckup. I couldn't just hand him a new venture knowing he'd shit the bed.

"He suggested once that I buy out his remaining five percent.

I said I'd do it, but only at the value of what his shares were worth at the time we split up, so maybe a few million. Tim thought it should be for the current value, say eighty to ninety million. But he'd signed a document when we split up, freezing the value where it was at the time. That was his signature on the deal, not mine. Nobody held a gun to his head and made him sign it. So he'd fucked himself once again. That wasn't my fault. The lawyers said, 'Cut him loose,' but I kept him around. I kept him close. I treated him like a brother."

"I saw how you treated him at the airport," Joe said.

Price waved that away.

"When I think about it, the signs were there that he'd betray me," Price said. "I wanted to bring my wife, Marissa, along. She's a real adventurer, maybe even more than me. She's also three months pregnant . . ."

"Congratulations," Joe said.

Price was on a roll. "I guess Tim didn't want to kill off an innocent woman and our child. That probably would have been too much. But me? I had no idea how much he resented me. I should have listened to the lawyers a long time ago."

Joe and Price trudged across a rockslide that had cleared a steep slope of trees several years before. In the open, Joe noted that the volume of snow had increased and was now accumulating on the ground. That wasn't good, because leaving a trail in the snow was unavoidable if the Thomases figured out they'd been ditched in the southern drainage.

The trees opened up and Joe saw movement ahead and stopped. Price did the same.

"Look," Joe said. He pointed out a small herd of elk grazing on the edge of the rockslide. Four cows, two calves, and two bulls.

"Are those our elk?" Price asked in a whisper.

"Nope. This is a much smaller herd."

As he spoke, the lead cow raised her head and sniffed the air.

"She sensed us," Joe whispered.

The cow turned and rumbled into the timber with the rest of the herd following behind her.

"That was cool to see them," Price said. "I meant to ask you: Did the elk come by our position this morning after we had left?"

"Yup."

"Well, damn. That was probably the only chance I'll ever have to harvest one in the wild."

As they worked their way across the rockslide, Price said, "Earl said he'd contacted ConFab a bunch of times, but I never heard about it. Maybe his complaints worked their way up through the hierarchy until they got to my office and Tim saw them. Maybe Tim fielded them and kept it secret—whatever it was—from me. He's a schemer, and I wouldn't put it past him. Maybe Tim knew about Earl being out here, and he certainly knew about my desire to go elk hunting. He must have put two and two together."

171

"It was Tim who contacted our governor on your behalf," Joe said, nodding to himself.

"Well, there you go."

Joe checked his wristwatch. It was midafternoon and snowing hard. They had three hours before it would start to get dark. He tried to estimate the time it would take on foot to hike down out of the mountains and locate the trailhead. He estimated twelve to fifteen hours at least, since they'd ventured so far away from the most direct route.

"I believe in forgiveness," Price declared. "Tim doesn't."

Then: "We're going to die out here, aren't we?"

"Maybe."

"I was kind of hoping you'd say something else."

"Sorry."

"It'll go viral," Price said. "I'd kind of like to see it blow up."

Joe noted a flicker in the lower branches of the spruce trees just ahead of them, so he stopped and squinted. Price bumped into him before backing off.

Through the tangle of boughs there was a flap of wings and a chicken-sized bird landed heavily on the ground and began strutting between the tree trunks. There were maybe a dozen others, Joe guessed, half in the trees and half on the ground.

"What are they?" Price asked.

"Pine grouse," Joe said. "Some people call them fool hens."

"Why?"

Joe backed up and Price followed.

Joe searched through a tangle of downed branches until he found two that were about three feet long and still green enough to be solid and heavy with sap. He trimmed the dried shooters off the bark and handed one to Price.

"They're called fool hens because sometimes they'll stay in one place long enough that you can whack their head off with a stick."

"Why would we do that?" Price asked incredulously.

"They're good to eat," Joe said. "Pine grouse have saved me before."

Joe cleared some space and demonstrated to Price how to swing the stick like a baseball bat. Price did a practice swing.

The two of them walked abreast back into the trees where they'd seen the birds. Joe stepped up behind the nearest one and took aim. The swing resulted in a *thunk* sound and the grouse bounced up and down on its back in its death throes. Joe stepped over it and targeted another that launched into flight as he neared it. The bird flew so close to his head that he felt the tips of feathers on his neck.

Price took a wild swing at the bird in flight and whiffed. His stick hit a tree branch, which blew up a shower of snow. The birds spooked, but not before Joe thumped another one on the ground. The rest of the flock vanished into heavier timber.

"Shit," Price said. "I missed."

"We got two," Joe said, picking up the warm carcasses off the ground. "They'll keep us alive."

He was standing there, a bird in each hand, when Brock Boedecker stepped out from behind a thick pine tree.

"Good hunting," he said to Joe. "I was sneaking up on them from the other side. I got one myself."

To demonstrate, he held up the pine grouse by its feet. It had been beaten bloody.

Joe glared at Boedecker. "Why did you take off back there? Where did you go?"

"To make sure I could find the cabin where we can stay the night and get out of this damned snow," Boedecker said. "And if you'll come with me, I'll show you where it is."

Joe and Price exchanged a worried look, but they followed him.

FOURTEEN

Thousands of feet below on the valley floor, Nate Romanowski downshifted and grabbed a gear so he could muscle the old truck up a steep embankment on a slick dirt road that climbed west into the foothills. He was driving on County Road 189, which was also known as Spring Creek Road because it hugged the contours of the creek to where it originated in the mountains. The snow had started an hour before and the Bighorns behind him were encased in dark clouds. It looked like a serious storm up there, he thought. Snow had just begun to stick within the gnarled twists of sagebrush around him, making the landscape look like a cotton field.

He'd traded the Yarak, Inc. van for a vintage 1948 Dodge Power Wagon that he'd purchased at an estate auction the previous spring. He'd always wanted one because ranchers he'd grown up around extolled its virtues and they considered it the greatest working vehicle ever made. A version of the three-quarter-ton 4×4 had been first used in World War II, and afterward rural ex-GIs wanted a truck at home in the mountains as tough as the one they'd had in Europe. That original 94-horse, 230-cubic-inch flathead six wouldn't win any races, but it could grind through the snow and mud, over logs, through the brush and willows. This one had been lovingly restored and included big knobby tires, high clearance, and a winch welded on the front. It had a toothy front grille and a split windshield with two headlamps mounted on high, wide fenders. In low light, they looked like dead eyes. Blooms of black smoke huffed through the tailpipe. From a distance, he thought, he'd be mistaken for some ancient set-in-his-ways rancher puttering up the road to the Twelve Sleep Senior Center before the afternoon lunch buffet closed down.

His .454 Casull was coiled in its holster on the cracked leather seat next to him.

It was the perfect vehicle, he thought, for making a personal call on a falcon smuggler and rearranging the man's face and his future plans in the area.

Sheridan's research had helped narrow down the focus of their investigation, and both Liv and Marybeth Pickett had chipped in with their computer skills. For the first time, Nate realized the advantage Joe had possessed these many years. His secret weapon was Marybeth and her ability to find information from both public and private sources. It had taken only a few hours for the three of them combing through records and websites to narrow down his target.

Simply put, there were very few prominent falcon smugglers in the world. Although extremely lucrative, because the primarily Middle Eastern buyers were willing to pay tens of thousands of dollars for wild-caught falcons, the skills, equipment, contacts, and subterfuge required to make it all work quickly weeded out amateurs looking for a fast score. Nate knew this because he'd once been involved in the illegal trade himself, but that had been years before. He had no idea who was still active.

As far as Sheridan, Marybeth, and Liv could determine, there were only three big-time falcon smugglers whose names popped up time and time again on the watch lists of the National Wildlife Crime Unit in the UK, the U.S. Fish and Wildlife Service, and the Rhodesian Ornithological Society, as well as on the website of the Convention on International Trade in Endangered Species. They'd also searched through falconry blogs with threads and comments about missing birds and speculation on who might have taken them.

Frank Szofran, from South Africa, was being held by Welsh authorities after being arrested for taking peregrine eggs from cliff ledges in the Rhondda Valley in southern Wales. His travel records revealed that he'd made dozens of trips to Dubai, presumably where he sold the eggs to Middle Eastern falconers. A rental cottage he'd used was filled with incubators and other equipment designed to keep the eggs alive.

Keith Geis, from Canada, had been arrested the previous year at O'Hare International Airport in Chicago after a bathroom janitor found thin shards of eggshells in a bathroom sink and identified the man who had just exited the lavatory in a hurry. Geis had been pulled out of line in the departure lounge and a search of his body revealed that he had fourteen peregrine and two red-tailed hawk eggs stuffed in thick socks and taped to his torso to keep them warm. Thirteen of the sixteen eggs were shown to be viable. The eggs, along with a ticket to the United Arab Emirates, had been confiscated and Geis was charged with federal crimes. If sold individually, the eggs were estimated to be worth over $650,000 on the illicit Arab falconry market. As far as they could tell, Geis was in custody awaiting trial.

It was possible, Nate thought, that he was up against a falcon thief who was so clever and so diabolical that he'd never been suspected or named. That seemed unlikely, though. The falconry world was small and specialized, and although practitioners often didn't all like each other, they knew each other. For someone to glide through that world without raising a red flag seemed unrealistic.

Which left Axel Soledad, a thirty-five-year-old Utahan and former special operator who had recently moved to Colorado. Soledad was suspected of not only stealing falcon eggs but sending raptor chicks to international buyers via FedEx and private courier. Soledad was a political activist. Background searches revealed that he purportedly used much of the money he made smuggling birds to finance growing antifa movements in Denver, Portland, and Seattle. A warrant was out for his arrest for the beating of a photographer during a Denver antifa rally, and there was a photo attached.

The image showed Axel Soledad to be tall, rangy, and lean with a hawklike nose and piercing dark eyes. He had a shaved head with black stubble on his face. His military background suggested he might have contacts in the target countries. He looked like trouble, Nate thought.

"He looks like *you*," Liv observed while cradling Kestrel. "Same stare. Same intensity."

"And he's a former special operator," Sheridan had added. "What is it with you guys?"

"There is no *you guys*," Nate had said, offended by the implication.

Colorado shared a border with Wyoming, and north-south traffic was significant. Coloradans, with their distinctive green-and-white mountain license plates, were ubiquitous throughout Wyoming and wouldn't draw a second look. Intuitively, Nate knew they'd identified the man who had looted his bluffs. The man who would pay for it in bruised flesh, broken bones, and possibly his life, if he got chippy.

So where is he?" Nate had asked.

He knew that successful falcon smuggling required certain resources. It couldn't be done by an itinerant in a rental car. In addition to the climbing equipment and the bownet traps used to capture birds, a semipermanent place had to be secured with room, electricity, and most of all privacy. Eggs couldn't be kept alive or young birds fed and housed for long in a motel room or vehicle without arousing suspicion. The smuggler would need to secure the young birds while he built his inventory. Falcons needed to be hooded, fed, and watered.

The captured birds could be held anywhere—an out-building, garage, workshop—as long as they were kept out of view from locals or passersby. Trying to figure out who might have recently rented such a space seemed all but impossible, the three of them decided.

But falcon food was a different story. Young raptors needed to eat prey on a schedule, as Nate could attest. Buyers didn't like it if the wild falcons they wanted to purchase had subsisted on commercial feed. Rabbits, pigeons, ducks, grouse, and other wild species had to be available in quantity to keep the birds healthy. Nate spent more than half of his hours hunting and trapping to keep his Air Force maintained. Sheridan had taken on a big chunk of that burden.

And it was Sheridan who asked the question aloud that put Nate on the trail of Axel Soledad.

"If you just showed up in Saddlestring with a dozen hungry birds," she asked, "where would you go to find food for all of them in a hurry?"

He'd taken Sheridan with him to town in the Yarak, Inc. van and parked it in front of Rex's Taxidermy on Main Street. Nate had stayed in the van while Sheridan went inside to see Dusty Tuckness, the owner.

Tuckness was small, plump, odd, and very energetic. He'd purchased the shop from Matt Sandvick a few years before, and his obvious goal was not only to run the busiest taxidermy facility in a thriving hunting community, but to create a destination for visitors. He had a loading dock in the back for receiving big-game carcasses and a showroom in front with local mounts, as well as exotic animals that hunters had sent him from all over the country, including tigers, lions, and Cape buffalo.

Tuckness was preparing his shop to host a Chamber of Commerce social later that night. He wanted to show off the changes he'd made in the facility and urge locals to send tourists his way.

His newest and most lucrative venture was selling "prairie dog skin rugs" that looked like miniature versions of bearskin rugs and were meant to be used as place mats at the dinner table. The tanned rodent skin had all four paws splayed out and an intact head with beady plastic eyes and an open mouth to show its yellow teeth. Tuckness sold them in sets of four for two hundred dollars a set or individually for seventy-five. He didn't care that most of the tourists who bought them intended them as gag gifts.

But because Tuckness couldn't rely on a steady flow of dead prairie dogs from local varmint hunters—or the carcasses he received from them were too blown up by gunfire to be salvaged—he'd built an add-on facility next to his shop to raise the creatures himself. Nate had purchased a few of the prairie dogs to feed to his falcons when the valley was buried by snow or when he hadn't been able to trap or hunt himself. He'd also sent Sheridan to pick up a few of the rodents from time to time.

That's how he found out that Tuckness had a crush on the girl. The taxidermist not only gave her significant discounts on her purchases, but he also called Liv every few weeks to say that he had excess rodents if Sheridan wanted to stop by and procure them.

Nate knew that Tuckness would do just about anything to keep Sheridan in the shop and talking to him, which was why he'd ask her to go inside while he waited in the van.

Twenty minutes later, Sheridan emerged on the street carrying a small box in her arms. She climbed into the van and placed it at her feet.

"He only had four he could spare," she said with a triumphant grin.

"Only four?"

"That's because somebody bought two dozen of them earlier this week. Wiped him out, he said."

Nate raised his eyebrows, waiting for more.

"Dusty said he'd never seen the man around here before. He described him as a fidgety tweaker type wearing all black. Dusty charged the guy more than double per prairie dog, fifty bucks each, and the guy paid it."

Nate narrowed his eyes, thinking. The photo and description they'd found for Axel Soledad didn't fit the man Tuckness had described.

"The guy didn't have enough cash on him," Sheridan said, "so he had to pay the balance with a credit card."

Before Nate could ask, Sheridan drew out her phone and

showed him a photo of the credit card receipt. "Raylan Wagy is his name," she said.

"Never heard of him," Nate said.

"Neither had Dusty before then. He said Wagy left the shop pretty agitated, like he was under pressure to buy the prairie dogs, but he didn't want to have to use his card."

"Interesting."

"I looked up his name on my phone. A Raylan H. Wagy was arrested in Denver for assault at an antifa rally three months ago. This has to be him."

Sheridan said, "So when Wagy drove away from here, he burned rubber on the street and got picked up by one of the local cops for reckless drivng or something. Dusty said he watched the whole thing go down. Which means I now need to call my mom."

Nate pulled away from the curb in a reasonable manner, looking both ways for local police cruisers. He had to be very careful these days, he knew.

"Why your mom?" he asked.

"She knows everybody at town hall," Sheridan said. "She can get Raylan Wagy's address from the citation."

Nate whistled and shook his head. The investigative skills of Sheridan, Liv, and Marybeth continued to amaze him.

They were nearly back to his compound when a text chimed on Sheridan's phone. She read it and said, "It's a temporary address, but it's an address: Raylan Wagy, 114 County Road 189."

"Spring Creek Road," Nate said. "There are a bunch of old ranches out there with plenty of empty buildings."

———

While Nate checked the oil on the Power Wagon in preparation for taking it out, both Sheridan and Liv had asked him not to go out there alone. He'd assured them it was strictly a reconnaissance run, which might or might not turn out to be true.

The snow continued to fall harder as he drove. The ancient heater beneath the dashboard howled as if injured and it filled the cab with an acrid burned-dust smell. The wipers smeared the windshield but kept up.

As he'd mentioned to Sheridan, there were a series of old ranches and homesteads on Spring Creek Road. In an area where cattle companies comprised thousands of acres each, these properties seemed tightly spaced. They'd been founded by some of the first settlers in the valley, who'd been drawn by the water, which was sparse everywhere else. Some of the ranches were still in operation with cattle grazing in meadows or penned in corrals, but most of the properties had been abandoned and bought up by bigger operations.

Fourteen miles up Spring Creek Road, he passed a battered wooden sign mounted on a leaning T-post with *114* hand-lettered on it. The exit was a deeply rutted two-track that plunged off the roadbed. Beyond it on the bank of the creek was a smattering of structures that were dark but ill-defined in the snowfall. It was also hard to tell where the buildings ended and the tall willow brush that lined both banks of the creek began.

Rather than make the turn into the property and announce his arrival, Nate continued over a rise a half mile beyond it. On the other side, he pulled over out of view from the old ranch and slipped his arms through his shoulder holster and got out.

Nate kept to the heavy willows of the creek as he approached the buildings from upstream. The snowfall hushed all sound and muffled his footsteps. He followed a cow path that conformed to the S-curves of the stream and led him under low overhanging branches that were starting to droop with accumulation.

He froze in place about two hundred yards from the ranch when the hairs on the back of his neck and on his forearms pricked up. He knew instinctively he was being observed. Nate slipped his weapon out of the holster and smoothly thumbed the hammer back.

Then the cow moose stepped out from her shelter of brush, snorted, and pushed her way into the heavier willows ahead of her. He gave it a full minute to see if there was a calf with her. If so, he didn't want to get between them. When there wasn't, he lowered the gun alongside his thigh and continued on.

The buildings of the ranch appeared in the snow as he got closer. There was a two-story house that might have served as a residence at one time and it was flanked on both sides by two rows of small cabins, three to a side. By the look of the identical construction of the cabins, Nate guessed the facility had once been a rustic dude ranch or a hunting lodge. There were gaping holes in some of the cabin roofs, as well as collapsed porches and broken windows. None looked occupied, and he could see no parked vehicles anywhere.

He ducked behind a large sagging barn that blocked him from the main lodge and the cabins. The slats covering the barn were silver with age and there were gaps between the planks. Nate shadowed his eyes and peered through one of the gaps in the siding.

Inside the barn on a mat of old hay were small portable wire dog crates. He could smell the sharp presence of falcons from the spatters of white excrement beneath the cages.

"Bastard," he whispered.

Nate found an open side door and slipped inside. Snow hung in the air like powdered sugar. He squatted down in front of the row of cages: a yearling peregrine, a red-tailed hawk, two prairie falcons, and, alone in the largest crate, a pure-white gyrfalcon. All were blinded with leather masks. Leather jesses had been attached to the talons of all of the birds and tied to the wire mesh of the cages so there was no way they could escape. To Nate's eye, the gyr looked either sickly or injured. He confirmed that suspicion by leaning down close to the cage and noting horizontal stress lines on its tail feathers.

Gyrs were notoriously fragile and emotional, he knew. Especially after they'd been captured.

He could see by the tufts of brown hair and bone slivers on the hay beneath the crates that the birds had eaten recently. The falcons' gullets bulged from the meal, except for the gyr.

Nate noted several boxes stacked near the horse stalls. He

recognized the boxes as being similar to what Dusty Tuckness used to crate up his prairie dogs. Sheridan had returned to the van with one earlier.

Next to the falcons were six empty crates. Wagy was still in the act of gathering up more birds, Nate thought.

He took a deep breath and let it out slowly in a cold rage. He wondered how many young birds had been injured or had died and had not been transported to the barn. He was looking at the entire generation from his bluff. All of them were caged and in the possession of the worst kind of outlaw.

The falcons and hawks were destined, no doubt, for buyers employed by Middle Eastern royalty.

On his way to the back door of the house, Nate snatched a pitchfork from where it leaned against the doorframe. The handle was cracked and weathered. The three thin prongs looked rusted but sharp.

He stepped onto the broken concrete porch and tried the doorknob. It turned and he eased it open. He was met with a wash of warm air and marijuana smoke from inside. Of course, he thought, they were from *Colorado*.

With his cocked revolver in his right hand and the pitchfork in the other, he paused and looked and listened. The kitchen was from the 1970s: linoleum floor, rounded white appliances, pink cabinets. The sink was stacked with dirty dishes and the counters littered with fast-food bags, empty beer bottles, and a nearly empty half gallon of Jim Beam. He wondered if the lodge was rented from the owner or simply occupied by a squatter. The latter, he guessed.

Nate padded through the kitchen into a narrow hallway. The walls were covered with faded and crooked sporting prints that looked like they'd been torn from hunting magazines and cheaply framed. So, he thought, it *had* been a hunting lodge at one time.

He could hear murmuring ahead and moved slowly with his gun at his side, ready to swing up and take aim.

The living room was separated from the hallway by a cheap beaded curtain. He hoped it wouldn't rattle when he pushed his way through, so he did it in slow motion.

The murmuring was coming from the screen of an ancient television mounted in a console. There was a snowy picture on it and the audio was tinny. Cartoons were playing.

A man with shaggy hair sat with his back to Nate in an overstuffed sofa, watching the set. Sharp-smelling weed wafted up from where he sat. Next to a saucer filled with cigarette butts on the end table under the arm of the sofa was a semi-automatic handgun. The weapon was an arm's length away from the man on the couch.

Nate stopped still just a few feet behind the sofa, listening. If there was anyone else inside, they were away in another room and completely quiet. Because there hadn't been a vehicle outside, he guessed that the shaggy-haired man was the only person inside.

As he moved close to the back of the couch, the man apparently heard him and turned around and looked over his shoulder. His eyes got big.

"Don't move," Nate said.

The man ignored him and prepared to lurch for the handgun.

Nate raised the pitchfork like a spear and bent over and thrust it down hard in front of the man's face. The middle tine drove through the man's boot deep into the wood floor and he screamed. His joint flew out of his mouth and the sparks from the cherry cascaded down his shirt.

The wounded man lunged for the pistol, but the pitchfork held him in place. His fingers stopped six inches short of the handle of the weapon.

Nate wheeled around the sofa and kicked the end table with the weapon away. The pistol skittered across the floor and thumped into the baseboard on the opposite wall. Then he reached out and grasped the man's ear with his left hand and fitted the hole of the huge muzzle of his .454 onto the tip of the man's nose.

Tuckness had provided Sheridan with a good description. He wore rumpled black clothing and a black bandana around his neck. His cheeks were sunken and his eyes were glassy from smoking weed. His mouth twisted with pain and anger and he looked like he was trying hard to be defiant.

"Raylan Wagy?" Nate asked.

Wagy's eyes got big and he tried to jerk his head away. It was held in place by a rough twist of the man's ear.

"Raylan Wagy?"

"I ain't done nothing," Wagy cried.

"Incorrect. You and your partner have broken the falconer's creed. You've fucked with another man's birds."

"My foot . . . Oh man, it hurts."

"Good," Nate said, releasing Wagy's ear. "Where's Axel Soledad?"

At the mention of the name, Wagy's face turned pale. He was obviously scared of Soledad.

"Where is he?"

When Wagy didn't answer, Nate reached back down and gave Wagy's right ear a full half twist. He could hear tendons pop.

Wagy closed his eyes and made a cry that sounded like "*Skeeee*." It was otherworldly and birdlike, Nate thought.

"I'll take it completely off if you don't answer me," Nate said softly. "That's what I do. Do you understand me?"

Wagy nodded emphatically.

"Will he be back soon?" Nate asked.

Wagy shook his head. "I don't know for sure. He doesn't always tell me. It depends on whether he finds . . . what he's looking for."

"Falcons, you mean," Nate said.

Wagy nodded.

"Then I'll wait for him right here," Nate said. He settled into an armchair across from Wagy and placed his long handgun across his thighs. "You stay right where you are."

Wagy grunted and chinned toward the pitchfork that held him fast. "It's rusty. My foot will get infected."

"Yeah, I know," Nate said with a cruel grin. "Don't pull it out. I like it there."

An hour later, Nate asked Wagy, "What's antifa?"

"We're anti-fascists," Wagy replied. "We fight against racism and capitalism. We fight for social justice against the oppressors."

"In *Denver*?" Nate asked.

"Everywhere we find it," Wagy sniffed.

Nate snorted and said, "Maybe you should get a job. It might take your mind off all the unfairness going on out there."

Then he felt a series of vibrations, one after the other, from his cell phone in his pocket. Without taking his eyes off Wagy, who was now mumbling to himself with his head in his hands, Nate drew out his device. He hated being a slave to cell phones, but his business and the baby demanded that he have one with him at all times.

There were three texts lined up. One was from Sheridan, one from Marybeth, and one from Liv. They'd obviously conspired, he thought. He could envision the three of them standing shoulder to shoulder, tapping out letters.

Sheridan wrote: My Dad is missing and we can't reach him. We're getting worried. Can you please come back?

Before reading further, Nate glanced at Wagy. The man was using the distraction to wrap his fingers around the shaft of the pitchfork to pull it out.

In one motion, Nate grasped his .454, thumbed the hammer,

and fired a round next to Wagy's injured ear. The explosion was like a thunderclap and the force of the big round scared Wagy back into the cushions.

"*Oh my God,*" Wagy cried. "You nearly killed me!"

"Behave yourself," Nate said. "Don't even think of stabbing me with that pitchfork. It's rusty, you know."

Wagy groaned.

He read further.

Marybeth wrote: I've called Sheriff Tibbs and left messages for him to assemble a search-and-rescue team, but he hasn't called me back. We can't wait. We need your help.

Liv wrote: Get your ass home.

All three women in his life were telling him what to do, he thought. He wondered how many years it would take for baby Kestrel to join them as the fourth.

Nate sighed and dutifully stood up. When he did, Wagy recoiled. Blood pooled around Wagy's boot where the pitchfork held him in place.

"Believe it or not," Nate said, "it's your lucky day. I've been summoned."

And with that he walked out through the front door and started hiking toward the Power Wagon. He heard a scream from inside the house as Wagy pulled the pitchfork free.

FIFTEEN

Earl Thomas pulled up on the reins to bring his horse to a halt in the trees at the edge of a large clearing. He placed both of his gloved hands on the horn and leaned forward in the saddle to study the grassy meadow before them.

Tim Joannides sidled up next to him on his horse. He'd been complaining just a few minutes before about how uncomfortable he was and was this snow ever going to let up? His horse had taken on the characteristics of its rider, Earl observed. Nervous, jumpy, twitchy, and annoying. When Joannides asked stupid questions, Earl ignored him. He wasn't a weatherman.

"What's going on?" Joannides asked. "Why are we stopping?"

"To take a look ahead."

Joannides's saddle creaked as he shifted in order to try and discern what Earl was looking at. His horse shuffled its feet as well, again taking on the tics of the rider.

"I see snow on top of the grass," Joannides said. "So what?"

Earl gave Joannides a sidewise glance, then turned back to study the clearing. Kirby joined him on the other side, so the three of them were abreast at the edge of the tree line. Brad was behind them, leading the string of packhorses.

"Are you seeing what I'm seeing?" Earl asked Kirby.

"I am," Kirby said.

"What?" Joannides asked impatiently. "What is it you two are seeing? All I see is snow on the top of grass."

"You already said that," Earl replied.

"We've lost the track," Kirby explained to Joannides. He did so in the tone of an adult speaking to a small child.

"*What?* Why do you say that?"

Kirby chinned toward the clearing. "We've been following the creek in the timber for a long time where you couldn't see footprints on account of the hard ground and all the rocks. But anybody can see that no one's crossed that meadow up ahead. If they did, there would be fresh tracks in the snow."

"Maybe they went around?"

"Not likely."

"This is unacceptable," Joannides fumed. "How could you let this happen?"

Earl turned his most withering deadeye stare on Joannides. It didn't have the desired effect. Joannides was miffed and apparently wanted it known to all.

"It's unacceptable, is it?" Earl asked him.

"How could we *possibly* lose them?" Joannides said, his voice rising with anger and panic. "They were ahead of us. We were right behind them, or so you said. Now they've vanished into thin air. I've done my job: I delivered him to you. Now you have to do yours.

"Do you realize that with every hour that goes by, more and more ConFab followers will start to talk and wonder why they haven't heard from Steve-2? The speculation will begin, if it hasn't already. It'll become a really big thing in the online world. It'll be one of the biggest business stories of the fucking year: *ConFab Founder Goes Dark*.

"Do you realize," he continued, "what will happen to me if somehow Steve-2 and that game warden make it down the mountain and start talking to the police?"

"Yeah, I think I know," Earl growled. "But you won't be the only one in the shit."

"Except *I* matter," Joannides said.

The words just hung there for a moment. Earl felt his face get hot. He could sense a certain stillness in his son Kirby that was often the calm before the storm. Joannides seemed to realize he'd said the wrong thing.

"You know what I mean," Joannides said. "I mean I'm in the tech world. They'll crucify me, or at least some of them will. There are people who hate Steve-2 as much as I do, people he's fucked over. But we're kind of in two different worlds, wouldn't you agree? Not that I'm better than you, just that we exist in completely different universes."

"And you matter in yours?" Earl asked quietly.

"Really, man, I didn't mean it to come out that way. I was just upset."

Earl took that in without comment. Inside, he seethed.

"The guy is right about one thing," Kirby said to Earl. "Steve-2 has millions of followers out there. And Price never shuts up—he posts his thoughts constantly. People will start to wonder why he stopped."

Earl turned away from Joannides because he couldn't stand to look at or listen to the man for another second.

"What do you propose we do?" Earl asked Kirby.

"Buy some time," Kirby said. "Then double back and find where those sons of bitches cut away from the creek. As you taught us, everybody leaves tracks behind. We just have to find them."

Then to Joannides, Kirby said, "You know what to do. Maybe you can dig your way out of the shithole you put yourself in."

Joannides nodded his head and dutifully climbed off his horse.

Ten minutes later, after Joannides had made a ConFab post using Steve-2's satellite phone and personal account, he looked up to see that all three Thomases had dismounted and were surrounding him. Earl observed the man carefully.

"What'd you say?" Earl asked.

"I retrieved a selfie from yesterday that Steve-2 took when we were riding up the mountain. He looks really happy in it. I said, 'Enjoying the big sky and the mountain air. It's fun to be off the grid for a while.'"

Earl grunted his approval.

"Now his followers won't get too concerned if they don't see another post from him tonight. They'll figure he doesn't have cell service. They don't know about all the gear we brought along to make sure he'd never be off-line."

Joannides looked expectantly to Earl, then to Kirby and Brad. He obviously wanted someone to validate his actions and forgive him for his slip of the tongue earlier. Earl eyed him with complete contempt.

Earl said, "Show Kirby here how you did that."

"Did what?" Joannides asked. He was in the process of returning the satellite phone to the saddlebag where he'd retrieved it.

"How you sent that message or whatever you just did."

Joannides paused.

"I need his password," Kirby said.

"But why? I'm here. I can handle it."

"You won't give me his password?" Kirby asked.

"I . . . I didn't say I wouldn't," Joannides stammered. "It's just . . ." He let his sentence drop away.

"What?" Kirby asked.

"This is how I can be helpful to you all. It's my contribution. I can't track men in the snow and I don't know the geography here. But I do know how to post as Steve-2. I do it all the time on his behalf."

"You're real close to him, aren't you?" Earl asked Joannides.

"Of course I am. That's how I was able to make all of this happen. That's how I was able to bring him to you."

"You're one hell of a friend," Earl said. "You're a snake in the grass."

Joannides started to defend himself, but thought better of it. Instead, he looked to Kirby to intervene. Joannides seemed to think he had the best rapport with Kirby, Earl thought. Probably because they were about the same age. Kirby knew all about ConFab, and he participated in social media, after all. Brad was oblivious to it, just like Earl had been until all of this.

But Kirby simply glared back at the man. Joannides, Earl thought, seemed to finally realize what a precarious situation he was in. Almost unconsciously, he slipped the phone he'd been holding into his coat pocket.

Earl said, "You were aware of us because we contacted your company. You wouldn't have known about what happened to my angel any other way."

Joannides said, "You're forgetting I'm on your side. We all want to see Steve-2 pay."

"You know," Kirby said, "we're kind of confused. You know why we want Steve-2. We want justice, after all. But why do you want him gone? That's something we just don't understand."

Earl thought Kirby's tone was just right. Reasonable and soft.

"There are a bunch of things," Joannides said. "The guy is brilliant, but he's also a sick fuck without any loyalty to anyone. He'll screw over his friends and he's ruthless to his enemies. He wasn't always like that, but he's completely changed. All his success has gone to his head."

"What did he do to you, anyway?" Kirby asked.

"He personally fucked me out of billions of dollars," Joannides said. "*Billions*. See, we developed this app together. Fifty-one/forty-nine. I was the forty-nine percent. But rather than introduce it to the market and take the time that was necessary to build the brand, Steve-2 shopped it around behind my back and found a buyer. It was practically a done deal by the time he even told me about it. I didn't want to sell, but he was the majority owner and he could outvote me. Then he bought me out for what I thought was a good price. I later learned that it should have been a hundred times as much."

Joannides looked to Kirby with indignation, and Kirby clucked with sympathy. He didn't seem as wary of them as he'd been earlier, Earl thought.

"I helped build Aloft," Joannides continued. "I was there when we had to pool our money to afford a case of ramen noodles to eat in our dorm room so we could spend every minute writing code and dreaming. But when I came back to the company, he pretended all that never happened. He made me his lackey. It's humiliating. People in tech think I'm washed up—that I'm only there because Steve-2 feels sorry for me. Like I'm his charity case. But I'm no one's charity case. I know my own truth, and I know he fucked me. I swore I'd get revenge when the right opportunity came around.

"When we find him," Joannides said, "remember to make it

look like a hunting accident. That's our deal. If I get back and play my cards right, the board may vote to have me assume the role of CEO. I'm the logical successor, after all, since I co-founded the company. I was with Steve-2 at the beginning . . . and at the end. That's how I'll play it."

Earl looked from Kirby to Brad and back to Joannides.

"So you're saying our tragedy is your opportunity," Earl said.

"You're twisting my words."

"Am I?"

"Guess who he sold our app to?" Joannides asked Earl.

Earl shrugged.

"The PRC."

"Huh?"

"The People's Republic of China," Joannides said, his eyes bulging. "The Chinese Communist Party—the CCP. They use it to track their own people. They use it to keep an eye on dissidents or anyone else they think might be a threat to them."

"I do hate the Chi-Coms," Earl conceded.

"Not Steve-2," Joannides said, sensing he'd found an angle Earl could get behind. "He claims he has no idea what they do with the software, that it isn't his business. No, Steve-2 is a fucking heartless tycoon."

"I can't figure out if you're mad at him because of the Chinese or because he screwed you out of money," Earl said.

"Either one," Joannides said. "Either. Both. But that's why we're here today. We're working together to take him down," he said with triumph.

"Are we, now?" Earl asked.

"Of course. Why do you ask?"

Earl rubbed his chin through his beard. "Because I've been thinking about something. You knew about my complaints. You knew about my daughter and the situation she was in. But you didn't tell Price. Instead, you sat on it until it was too late. Then you reached out to us. Do I have that right?"

Joannides's face went white. He seemed to finally realize what Earl was driving at.

Rather than accept it, he said, "It wouldn't have mattered if I told him, Earl. It wouldn't have made a bit of difference, believe me. Steve-2 doesn't think of people as people. He thinks of them as his users. Steve-2 refuses to accept any responsibility at all for what happens because of his technology. He didn't care how the Chinese government was using our app. He just wanted it to work right and have no glitches. There's a complete disconnect in his brain between tech and the real world where people live."

"We're not talking about Price right now," Earl said. "We're talking about *you*."

"I couldn't stop what happened to your daughter," Joannides said.

"Did you try?"

Joannides turned to Kirby and dropped to his knees with his hands out, palms up. "Please," he said. "Tell your dad we're on the same side here."

Instead, Kirby handed the reins of his horse to Earl and approached Joannides.

"What's Price's password?"

Joannides sighed. "It's LISA2. All caps."

"Spell it."

"L-I-S-A and the number two."

"What's it mean?" Kirby asked.

"It's a Steve Jobs thing," Joannides said. "Steve-2 worships the man. Jobs named a computer after his daughter Lisa."

Kirby took the satellite phone from Joannides and clipped it on his belt.

Joannides used the opportunity to lean forward and whisper, "Help me here, will you? Talk to your dad. We're all on the same team. Tell him. There's a lot of money in it for you if you do. I swear it."

Earl couldn't make out what Joannides said to his son. All he could tell, whatever it was, it caused Kirby to hesitate.

"*Tell him,*" Joannides urged.

Kirby thrust the bowie knife beneath Joannides's chin and used both of his hands on the grip of it to jam it upward until the hilt pressed against the man's lower jawbone. Joannides's bloody body flopped over to the side in the snowy grass and convulsed. Kirby pulled the knife out and wiped both sides of the blade on Joannides's high-tech parka.

"He was a snake until the end," Kirby said to Earl. "Tried to offer me money to save his miserable life."

Brad stepped forward with his shotgun over the body and aimed it at Joannides's temple.

"No," Earl commanded. "No gunshots. We don't know how close we are to Price and Joe. I don't want them to hear us."

"She was my sister, too," Brad said to Earl with an adolescent whine.

"Then go get your ax," Earl said. "But hurry. Bring a shovel, too. We've got a lot of ground to cover before it gets dark on us."

SIXTEEN

The tiny one-room log cabin was located deep in the heart of a lodgepole stand that fronted a steep granite wall. The last rays of the sun lit up the face of the rock formation and threw dark shadows into its folds and cracks. A single raven hugged the rim of the wall and flew in lazy, ever-widening circles.

The snow had stopped and the storm clouds had moved on, opening up the sky at dusk. Joe could already see a few stars winking through the dark purple. He could feel the temperature drop as he followed Boedecker across a bench and into the lodgepoles. Cold crept up his pant legs and down the collar of his parka. His knees stiffened, as had the carcasses of the pine grouse he carried, which had been warm and soft when he gathered them up.

"Not much farther," Boedecker said over his shoulder.

"I see it," Joe responded. The cabin was a black square within the spindly trunks of the trees. Next to the cabin was a sagging lean-to.

"It had to be a poacher's cabin at one time," Boedecker said. "My dad told me about it a few years ago, but I wasn't sure where it was. It's too hidden away for a line shack and too far up for lumberjacks."

Joe grunted his agreement. Over the years, he'd stumbled upon dozens of shelters constructed within the national forest he patrolled that weren't supposed to be there. He was always curious who had built them and what they were used for. When he found them, he notified the ranger's office and gave the coordinates. He doubted anything was ever done about them.

"It's sure as hell not much," Boedecker said, "but it'll get us out of the weather for tonight. It's going to be a cold one. When it snows and the clouds go away like that—watch out."

"Yup."

"I'm already freezing," Price grumbled from behind Joe. "I don't know why you people even live here."

"This is where the elk are and the people aren't," Joe said.

"Believe me, I'm *done* with hunting elk," Price said. "I just want to go home."

"We all do," Joe said.

"Back to your mega-mansion overlooking the Pacific?" Boedecker said to Price. "Yeah, I bet that's nice."

"Let's worry about *our* mega-mansion for now," Joe said.

To Boedecker: "Have you been inside?"

"Just long enough to stick my head in. Like I said, it isn't much. No water, no electricity, no generator. Pretty much a one-man cabin. And not exactly built by a craftsman, either."

"Are there three beds inside?" Price asked.

Boedecker just laughed. He seemed to revel in causing Price deprivation, Joe thought.

Joe placed the two grouse he'd killed on top of a three-foot-high stack of cut and split wood protected by the roof of the lean-to, while Boedecker and Price went inside. The firewood was pine, and it had been there for so long the exposed outsides of the lengths had turned dark gray. Probably twenty to thirty years, Joe guessed. But it was firewood, nonetheless, and dry.

He could tell by the nails in the wall at the back of the lean-to that the structure had once been used to stretch hides and pelts. Several rusty leg traps hung from the wall, and the floor was littered with bleached coyote, fox, and beaver skulls. The skulls had been exposed so long they looked paper-thin, like they'd crumble into powder if touched.

He turned to see Price coming back outside from the cabin, followed by Boedecker. The look on Price's face told Joe what to expect inside.

"It's a dump," Price said.

"But it's our dump," Joe replied.

He shouldered around them and stepped inside. It was even colder than it had been out in the trees and he could see his breath.

The interior was simple and crude. There was a small rusty potbellied stove supporting a dented galvanized metal chimney pipe in the middle of the room, a metal washtub on a crude counter near the left wall, a rough table and two chairs, and a single bed with an iron frame covered by a ratty army surplus blanket. In the rear corner was a chest-high pile of garbage and parts: two-by-fours, T-posts, squat steel cylinders, broken chairs, a saddle so worn through the wooden frame stuck out from beneath the leather like exposed ribs. An ancient kerosene lantern hung from a nail over the counter with the tub, and Joe brought it down. There was no fuel in the well and he couldn't see a tin of it anywhere. Although the cardboard corners had been gnawed by rodents, there was a half-full box of wooden matches.

Joe slipped his pack off and dumped it on the table and glanced around the interior. There was only one door to the place and it opened to the side mouth of the lean-to, where Price and Boedecker stood stamping their feet to keep warm. There was a boarded-up window next to the front door and a window on each wall of the cabin. All were covered by pieces of plywood from the inside.

The rafters were exposed above him and he could see cracks of light through the planking on the roof.

The cabin was in miserable condition and it had been neglected for years. But Joe was thrilled they'd found it.

Boedecker stuck his head around the open doorframe. "I'll clean those birds and get 'em ready to roast if you'll get this place in order," he said.

"Are we sure we want to fire up the stove?" Joe said.

"How else are we going to cook them?"

"I'm worried about making woodsmoke," Joe said. "The Thomases probably know we ditched them by now."

"We need to eat something. And we need to warm this place up or we'll freeze to death."

Joe knew it wasn't wise. But he was cold, hungry, and exhausted.

"Okay," Joe said after a long pause.

"What should I do?" Price asked from outside.

"Have you ever plucked a chicken?" Boedecker asked.

"No, but I've seen it done. My chef does it."

"*My chef does it*," Boedecker mocked.

Joe ignored them while he removed the covers from the windows to let in the last remaining light of the day. The cabin was even dirtier than he'd thought at first glance. His boots left distinct tracks in the half inch of dust on the floor and his movement caused dust motes to roll across it like miniature tumbleweeds.

He cranked open the flue on the chimney pipe, and when he did a shower of pine needles and a couple of atrophied bird carcasses dropped into the belly of the stove. There were several copies of the Saddlestring *Roundup* from 1983 in a bucket near the stove that he crumpled up and used to light kindling. He watched in anticipation as the first curls of smoke got sucked upward and he was grateful the chimney pipe wasn't blocked by nests or debris. He waited until the flames launched into a full roar and added several lengths of wood from a stack. Then he closed the stove doors and stepped back. As the metal heated, it ticked furiously. But within a few minutes, he could feel heat start to emanate from the stove.

Outside, Boedecker and Price bickered as they prepared the grouse.

"If it wasn't for you, we'd all be home having a cold beer and watching the game on television," Boedecker said.

Price said, "And if you'd raised your hand early to what was going down, we could have avoided it all."

"It's not like you didn't fucking deserve it."

"I have no clue what you or those hillbillies are talking about."

"The hell you don't . . ."

Joe closed the door on them.

He was heartened to find that within the pile of junk in the corner, the metal cylinder he'd noted was actually a propane tank. He lifted it out and by its weight guessed it was a quarter full. He rooted around in the pile and located a round dented metal dish with a heating coil inside. It was designed to screw onto the valve of the tank. If they could get it lit, they'd have sustained heat inside the cabin. And with no woodsmoke giving away their location.

He attached the heater to the tank, opened the valve, and

could hear the hiss of gas. After three attempts with the wooden matches, the coil caught with a *whoosh* and quickly turned bright red. He adjusted the valve to keep it low and positioned the heater dish toward the center of the room.

Next, Joe peeled back the army blanket on the bed, and when he did, a half dozen mice shot out like sparks and skittered across the floor. The mice had nested in gnawed-out holes of a rolled-up mattress at the foot of the frame. There were still some in there, he thought. The bedroll quivered with them.

It answered the question of who would get the bed that night. *Anybody but me*, Joe thought.

That's when he noticed a long bulge running lengthwise down the middle of the ancient box spring. He lifted it.

Between the frame and the box spring, on top of several cross slats, was a small-caliber rifle. It was old and the stock was rubbed clean of varnish.

He picked it up and walked over to the nearest window to see it better. It was a single-shot .22 bolt-action. The stamp on the barrel identified it as a J. C. Higgins Sears and Roebuck Model 41. There was a knob on the back of the receiver that was used to cock it. He tested the action and the spring still had tension. He guessed the gun was likely sixty years old and it had probably been used for plinking or to rid the place of rodents. It was the kind of rifle once given to twelve-year-old boys as their first gun. Joe had had a similar model, but it hadn't been given to him by his dad. His dad never gave him anything like that. Joe and his brother had found the rifle beneath the floorboards of the rental house his parents lived in. They'd taken it out to kill rabbits, and the single-shot capability made him always cognizant of the importance of not taking foolish shots and of placing each round. The .22 wasn't good for much else. It was too cheap and underpowered for game larger than a rabbit or a bird.

Then he noticed a box of cartridges on a shelf next to the door. The brass of the small rounds were mottled with age and the lead seemed so soft he could crease each round with his thumbnail.

Would they fire? He had no idea. Would the rifle still operate? Again, no idea.

Would he share the news of his discovery with Price or especially Boedecker?

He answered his own question as he turned back with the rifle to the battered mattress on the bed. He unrolled it and more mice scattered. The mattress itself was so damaged as to be useless. Joe placed the weapon on the end of the thin cushion and rolled it back up with the box of cartridges. He checked to make sure the butt of the stock couldn't be seen by Boedecker from the outside.

Just as he finished, the door opened and Boedecker thrust the cleaned and plucked grouse inside, holding all three birds by their naked necks.

"Damn, it's practically cozy in here!" Boedecker said. "Let's eat." Then, over his shoulder to Price: "Don't just stand there being useless. Bring in a load of firewood."

———

While Joe roasted the birds in a griddle on the stovetop, rolling them with a wooden spoon often to brown the skin evenly, Boedecker rooted through the junk pile for anything, he said, that could be useful to them. Joe kept a wary eye on him to make sure he didn't roll out the bedroll. His mouth watered as the aroma from the roasting grouse filled the cabin.

Price sat in a chair with his legs splayed and his arms hung down between them. There was a vacant, almost hopeless look on his face, Joe thought. He got up only to peer over Joe's shoulder at the crude cooking and then sat back down.

"Well, *halle-fucking-lujah*," Boedecker called out. Joe turned as the man hoisted a three-quarters-full fifth of Ancient Age whiskey from a wooden box on the side of the pile. "We just might make it after all."

"I don't drink," Price said sullenly.

"Further proof that you're less than half a man," Boedecker said as he crossed the room. "What makes you think I'd offer you some?"

Next to Joe, he unscrewed the cap and sniffed the open neck of the bottle. "I think it's okay," he said. "Bourbon doesn't go bad over time, does it? I think it just gets better."

He lifted the whiskey and took a long pull. His eyes teared up, and he said, "Damn, that's the best bad whiskey I've ever had. It warms you up inside."

He offered the bottle to Joe, who sipped it. The burn spread throughout his mouth and down his throat.

"We better take it easy on that," Joe said.

"Oh, we will," Boedecker said with a grin saying otherwise.

In addition to the whiskey, Boedecker found two misshapen cans of green beans under the wash table.

"What do you think?" he asked Joe.

Joe shook his head, not sure. The cans had obviously frozen and thawed, frozen and thawed over the winters.

"They haven't burst," Boedecker said. "I say we boil the hell out of 'em."

Which they did. Boedecker wiped the dirt from inside a pot and dumped the contents into it. He drank from the bottle as he watched the pot begin to smoke. Then he wandered back to the junk pile and left Joe to oversee the cooking of the meal.

"What the hell?" he said, and Joe turned around again to see Boedecker displaying a battered eighteen-inch speargun. "Why would they bring this up here?"

"Can't even guess," Joe said.

Boedecker located a single spear in the pile. "It's one of them pneumatic ones," he said while inserting the spear and attaching a hand pump into the back of the receiver. He tried to charge it with compressed air.

"Be careful, for God's sake," Price warned.

"Shut the fuck up," Boedecker replied.

Even across the room, Joe could hear air leak out of the device.

"Shit," Boedecker said. "I bet the O-ring dried out. But maybe I can fix it." He sat down at the table and started disassembling the speargun.

"You do that," Joe said, turning back around to his roasting grouse. He approved of the fact that Boedecker had something to do other than root around the cabin and bait Price.

That was magnificent, Joe," Price said as he licked the tips of his fingers. "You can taste pine nuts in the breast meat. These birds are fantastic."

After a few tentative bites, Price had devoured the grouse on his plate and left a pile of thin bones. Since they couldn't find any utensils, they'd torn the birds apart with their hands and scooped steaming green beans from the pot into their mouths with cupped fingers. There was nothing left to eat.

A single candle provided some light from the center of the table.

"It's amazing how good things taste when you're in the mountains and you've been on the run all day," Joe said. He knew the meat had been slightly underdone, but it had been juicy nevertheless and the skin was browned and crispy. He'd been in a hurry to finish it up on the stove so he could douse the fire within it and eliminate the smoke boiling outside from the chimney.

"It's not just that," Price said, sitting back and wiping his mouth with the back of his hand. "This is as basic as it gets, isn't it? This is what I came here to experience. Those pine grouse gave their lives for us, and I, for one, appreciate it."

Boedecker moaned and rolled his eyes. He'd finished before

Joe and Price and had pushed his plate aside so he could continue to work on the speargun. Joe noted that Boedecker had removed the black rubber O-ring from the receiver and was rubbing it around in the sheen of grease on his plate from the grouse.

"You might not appreciate it the way I do," Price said to Boedecker, "but I consider this meal a small miracle. This is what I thought about last year when the whole world first self-quarantined because of the coronavirus. I thought: What would I have to do to survive if it really came down to it? Could I provide for myself? Now I know the answer—that it's possible. I consider the fact that we're even alive after the day we had to be a small miracle, and I've never been religious."

He turned to Joe. "What about you?"

"I'm a believer," Joe said.

"It must be of some comfort."

Joe said, "Yup," but he knew his face flushed while he said it.

After clearing the dishes, Joe returned to the table. Since Boedecker and Price had taken the only two chairs, Joe sat on an upturned stump he'd found outside near the woodpile. The heater on the propane tank glowed red and cast their faces with a light pink hue. The candle flickered. Although the heat from the unit kept the temperature above freezing in the cabin, it couldn't keep up with the cold that was seeping inside through the cracks and gaps in the logs. Anything in shadow was cold, Joe noticed. They'd all put their coats back on after they'd eaten and the stove was doused.

"Okay," he said to the two of them. "Now that we've finally stopped running and the Thomases could show up at any time, can you tell me what this is all about?"

SEVENTEEN

'd like to find that out myself," Price said. "All I know is that Tim turned on me and Rumy ran away. I've never felt so betrayed in my life. I still can't really wrap my mind around it. We start the day getting set up to hunt elk and end it like refugees in a crappy little cabin."

"Bull*shit*," Boedecker said with a snarl. He reached out and grabbed the whiskey bottle by the neck and took another long pull. The Ancient Age was half gone.

"Really," Price said, appealing to Joe. "I created this platform that has millions of users. All I can guess is that the Thomases took offense to something posted on it. It happens all the time, but people don't start trying to kill the founders because of it."

"You're so full of shit I can't believe it," Boedecker scoffed.

"Brock, what do you know about it?" Joe asked.

"Plenty. And this man is a murderer just as much as anyone who aimed a gun and pulled the trigger."

"That's insane," Price said. "It's just insane. We can't police everything that's said on our platform. That would be impossible. Think of ConFab as a public bulletin board. If someone posts a flyer on it that someone else finds offensive, do you attack the person who hung up the bulletin board? Do you chase them down and try to kill them?"

"Hopefully not," Joe said.

"He's a hypocrite and a fucking liar—" Boedecker said, but Joe held his hand up to silence him.

"Let him say his piece."

"Yeah, okay, this I want to hear. Then I'll tell you the truth after that," Boedecker said as he took another drink.

"Thank you," Price said to Joe. He had a habit of closing his eyes when he spoke that Joe found unnerving. It was as if Price didn't want to witness any doubt or confusion in the person he was addressing.

Price said, "ConFab is a good in the world, not an evil. We bring people closer together—people of all creeds, races, religions. Conversations take place on our platform that don't take place anywhere else. We are the public square of the digital age.

"The novelist Walter Kirn said it best," Price said. "He said, 'Twitter sells conflict. Instagram sells envy. Facebook sells *you*.' I like to think ConFab doesn't sell anything. We facilitate conversation. We've created a platform where everyone's voices can be heard no matter who they are. Now, I'm sorry if someone posted something that led to this. I truly am. But what can we do? We can't censor people. There's such a thing as a First Amendment in this country. There's free speech. We have no desire, nor any right, to silence the voices of the people who use our platform."

Joe nodded. As he did, Price opened his eyes in time to see it.

"So you understand," Price said.

"Kind of. But why does Earl Thomas want to kill you?"

"I have no idea, other than he apparently doesn't tolerate opinions that don't conform with his. At least, that's my guess."

During Price's explanation, Boedecker had stared at him the entire time with his eyes bugged out and his mouth half open. He was obviously enraged. Joe prepared himself to come to Price's defense if Boedecker suddenly lunged across the table to attack him. Joe was grateful for the rancher's restraint, but he thought it was very likely the alcohol he'd consumed had slowed his responses.

"Brock?" Joe said. "You disagree?"

"You're fucking right I disagree," Boedecker said. He jabbed a greasy finger toward Price. "He's smooth, but he's just a West Coast sharpie selling you a bill of goods. Don't buy it, Joe. Steve-2 here has created an evil thing, which means he's evil himself. He just don't see it because he's blinded by millions of people following him and telling him how great he is while the money pours in. Meanwhile, he's gathering up data on every user to sell to advertisers and other companies. He thinks he's God, but he's just a punk little coder without a sense of right and wrong."

Joe sat back. He'd never heard Boedecker talk with such passion about anything before.

"Oh, come on," Price said, waving off the diatribe.

"Since he won't tell you what this is about, I will," Boedecker continued. "I heard it straight from Earl last summer while it happened."

Price turned. "While *what* happened?"

"Earl's wife left him a long time ago, but he had a daughter, Sophia. She was his favorite and he didn't care who knew it, including his sons. He called her 'Princess.' She was a senior in high school when ConFab ruined her life. Sophia put a rope around her neck and committed suicide in her bedroom. Earl found her body, and it absolutely wrecked him. He's never been the same since that day. Steve-2 not only killed Sophia, he killed Earl's soul along with her. And now he sits here telling us how much fucking good in the world he's responsible for. It's bullshit."

Price closed his eyes and turned his head away from Boedecker as if shutting him off.

"Walk me through it," Joe said to the rancher. "Your version of it, anyway."

"It's Earl's version, too. And he may be a cantankerous son of a bitch, but he's not a liar like Steve-2 here.

"Here's how it went down," Boedecker said. "Earl has a website for his outfitting business, like everyone does. He updated it last year because he hadn't made any changes or improvements on it for years. Earl sees the writing on the wall when it comes to hunting—he knows he has to appeal to younger people and women these days. So he got the bright idea to use photos he had of Sophia on his site. You know, to show people even a young girl could come out here and get a trophy."

Joe didn't need to urge the man to go on.

"So Earl posts all these shots on his site of Sophia because she used to go on trips with him. Sophia crouching over a dead elk, Sophia looking through binoculars, Sophia smiling at the camera over a dead buck antelope. She was a beautiful blonde, if you never saw her. Gorgeous, with a great smile. Not especially bright, but she loved her daddy and he loved her."

"What does this have to do with ConFab?" Joe asked. Price continued to look away from Boedecker with his eyes clenched tight.

"Somebody, one of Price's users, saw the photos on Earl's site and started posting them to ConFab," Boedecker said. "Some animal rights nut. You know how it is: some anonymous social justice warrior found the photos on Earl's site and posted them. Those types love to look down at the little people out here and humiliate them, or worse. Anyone who does anything they don't agree with is attacked, and a lot of people don't like or understand hunting. Whoever it was put up all kinds of shitty captions about Sophia, saying she was a mouth-breather, a right-wing gun nut, anything you can imagine. The posts got shared thousands of times by ConFab users, and it wasn't long before they went viral. Pretty soon, she's portrayed as a little rich girl who loves killing Bambi. They didn't care that Sophia was posing with animals killed by Earl's clients, that she didn't pull the trigger herself. It didn't matter by then because the cat was out of the bag. All they knew was that *Princess* liked to take photos with dead big-game animals.

"Does any of this ring a bell?" Boedecker asked Price.

221

"No," Price said.

"He's lying again," Boedecker said. Then to Joe: "It wasn't long before other users found her on Facebook or somewhere else and figured out her name and posted it along with her ConFab handle, her email address, her phone number, Instagram, anything you can think of. Sophia started getting death threats, hate mail, people calling her the vilest names you can imagine. And not just common folks—Hollywood types weighed in, and some politicians. They went after this poor girl like a pack of fucking wolves.

"Earl found out about it because Sophia didn't want to go to school anymore and she just stayed in her room. Totally withdrew. She was being hounded to death and there was nothing she could do about it.

"Earl tried to save her," Boedecker said, "but he's ignorant about social media, like most of us old guys. He sent emails to Price here with no response, and he couldn't get a human being out there in Silicon Valley to talk to him. He didn't know what to do. I think at one point he went to see the new sheriff, but no one there could help him. He told me he must have called ConFab a hundred times and no one would speak to him. Sophia's photos showed up everywhere: Facebook, Instagram, even in some stupid magazines. And this guy," Boedecker said, reaching over to slap the back of Price's head before Joe could intervene, "didn't do a damn thing to stop it. So Sophia Thomas hanged herself rather than take it anymore."

Price didn't react to the blow except to hunch his head into his shoulders a little more.

"Take it easy," Joe said to Boedecker.

"I'm sorry it happened," Price said. "I didn't know, but obviously Tim did. We can't control what our users put up, you know? We can't do a fact-check of tens of millions of posts every day."

"Let me ask you something," Boedecker said to Price. "And try to answer honestly for once."

"What?"

"You claim ConFab is just some innocent bulletin board, right?"

"Yes."

"Do you let white supremacists or Nazis put up posts on ConFab?"

"No, of course not."

"Do you let antiabortion groups post on your site?"

"That's too divisive," Price said.

"What about terrorists? Do you let them recruit for their ranks?"

"We shut them down."

"The Catholic Church?"

"No, because of church and state."

"What about right-wing gun nuts like me?" Boedecker asked. "Do you let us defend the Second Amendment on ConFab?"

Price didn't answer.

Boedecker answered for him. "Fuck no, you don't allow those things. All that crap you said about free speech is a lie. You and the ignorant pack of millennials that work for you shut down anything that isn't politically correct *according to you*."

Price sighed. He said, "I'll admit that most of our team members have their built-in biases, but we're working on that. We've got working groups in place to develop internal processes."

"So you finally admit it," Boedecker said. "You let Sophia get harassed to death."

"I didn't say that."

"You won't take any responsibility at all," Boedecker said, leaning close to Price and shouting. "You're not a bulletin board. You're a *publisher*. You create this online *thing* that's worth billions of dollars to you that allows anonymous people to go after little girls until they kill themselves. But you won't apologize, and you won't accept your guilt. You killed Sophia, you asshole. Earl just wants the justice he deserves."

"I don't have to listen to any more of this," Price said, standing up so abruptly his chair toppled over backward. He turned and strode across the floorboards and slammed the door behind him.

Joe glared at Boedecker, who smiled back.

"He's not used to hearing from the likes of me," Boedecker said. "He lives in his own little bubble like the rest of those Silicon Valley punks."

"You were pretty tough on him," Joe said.

"Oh well."

"It may not be as clear as you think."

"Really?" Boedecker said. "What if this happened to your daughter Lucy? Or April? Or Sheridan?"

Joe thought, *Then I'd want to kill him myself.* But he didn't say it out loud.

Boedecker went back to reassembling the speargun in the light of the propane burner. Joe watched the man as he fitted the greasy O-ring into the receiver.

Boedecker looked up and their eyes met. "Think about what I said earlier, Joe. Price is our ticket out of here. We can turn him over to Earl and his boys and never tell a single soul what happened. As far as anyone else will ever know, you and me met up together and came down the mountain after Steve-2 had a bad hunting accident and the horses ran off."

Joe rubbed his face with his hands.

"What do you think?" Boedecker asked.

"I think I better go out and find him and bring him back before he freezes to death."

Boedecker grunted his disgust at that and turned his attention back to the speargun.

Joe clamped his hat on tight, zipped up his parka to the throat, and went out into the night with his hands stuffed into his pockets to keep them warm. It was still and very cold, and the snow crunched under his boots. Price was easy to follow because he'd left fresh tracks around the lean-to and into the lodgepole stand where they'd come.

He almost walked past Price, who was sitting on a downed log at the edge of a small clearing. He was leaning back, gazing at the creamy wash of stars overhead. The starlight was so bright Joe could see his face glowing with it.

"This is better than I thought," Price said. "There are more stars even than in Tibet. Is that possible?"

"Probably a different set of stars," Joe said, sitting next to him.

"Did you come out to find me?"

"Yup."

They sat in silence. Price stared at the sky and Joe looked out across the meadow. Condensation from their breath hung around their heads and filled up with diffused starlight.

"This is the biggest and darkest sky I've ever seen," Price said. "It makes me feel really small. I feel like a single human heartbeat in the middle of the wilderness."

Joe didn't point out that he had a heartbeat as well. So did Boedecker.

"I keep reaching for my phone," Price said. "I want to share this. I want to share my thoughts. But it isn't there when I pat myself down. I've never felt so alone before."

"Maybe everything doesn't need to be shared," Joe said.

"What he said inside, it makes me think," Price said. "He's a prick, but not everything he says is shit. The fact is, I don't know the solution. We create this technology thinking it will do great things, but we can't predict what people will do with it. He has to understand that."

Joe grunted a nonresponse.

"There might be a lot of people out there who hate me and what I represent," Price said. "If I listen to them and let them go on and on, I won't be able to create. I have to think big, without distractions. Would great men like Thomas Edison or Steve Jobs have been able to do what they did if they listened to all the disgruntled people out there? Anyone can bitch and complain. But only a few of us can invent cool things."

Joe thought he heard something in the distance and he sat up straight. Price began to talk again and Joe reached over and clamped his mouth shut.

"Shhhh," Joe whispered. "Listen."

Price's eyes got wide, as if saying, *Listen to what?*

Joe let go. He closed his eyes and strained to hear. He knew that even on a bitterly cold night without wind the forest could be a noisy place. Trees froze and split open, captured snow dropped from branches to the ground below, wildlife moved restlessly through the trees.

Then he heard it again: a whinny.

"That's a horse," Joe mouthed. He pointed to the south where he thought it had come from.

Price shook his head. He hadn't heard it.

Joe gestured that the two of them should go back inside the cabin. He thought that since the stove had been doused and there were no interior lights, it was very possible the Thomases might simply pass by in the timber. If it *was* the Thomas clan out there, and if what he'd heard was indeed a horse.

He knew for sure that it wouldn't be a good idea to sit any longer and listen to Price talk. Sound carried on cold, still nights.

Because it had been so dark outside, Joe thought the interior of the cabin seemed more lit up from the glow of the heating coil than when he'd left. He ushered Price through the door and closed it behind them.

Boedecker still sat at the table. There was maybe an inch of whiskey left in the bottle. The speargun was reassembled and armed with the short projectile.

"You found him," Boedecker slurred. "Too bad."

Then he raised the speargun and pointed it at Joe and Price. It went off with a metallic *thunk*.

The spear tip embedded in a log over the doorjamb, a foot above Joe's head. He looked over his shoulder at it and saw the shaft quivering.

"Damn," Boedecker said. "It *works*."

Joe growled, "Point that at me again and things are going to get real western, Brock."

Boedecker giggled and waved his left hand around in the air to indicate he meant no harm.

He stopped laughing when Joe said, "I think I heard a horse out there."

EIGHTEEN

Are we safe?" Price whispered an hour later. "Do you think they're gone?"

"For now, maybe," Joe replied.

"Or maybe you didn't hear anything at all in the first place," Boedecker said to Joe.

"That's possible, too," Joe said.

The three of them were huddled together in the dark around the hissing orange glow of the heating coil. Their knees were nearly touching. They'd tamped down the flame so there was just enough heat but not enough light from it to be seen from the outside. It was getting colder by the minute, and Joe feared the propane would run out and leave them with only bad options.

"Maybe we're okay," Price said.

Joe hoped that was true. But if the Thomas clan had passed by the cabin a few hundred yards below in the timber and hadn't cut their tracks, his guess was they'd double back at some point until they found the cabin.

They might wait until morning to do that, he thought. He knew that if it was him on horseback in the dark in a night steadily getting colder, he'd stop, build a fire, and make a camp. But Earl was known for his determination. Joe was aware of a few of Earl's clients who had gone home in the middle of guided hunts they'd paid thousands for because he drove them too hard. Joe didn't think there was much of a possibility that the men would give up and go down the mountain. Joe looked at his watch. It was nearly midnight.

Price said, "We just have to stay alive until morning, right? Then we can hike out of here and get back to civilization. Or at least your version of it."

Boedecker moaned and rolled his eyes. Joe could see the whites of them in the glow of the coil. The rancher had been uncharacteristically silent the past hour, Joe thought. As if he were either drifting away or plotting something.

"That's what we want," Joe answered Price.

"I can only imagine what my execs and followers are thinking right now," Price said. "Not to mention my shareholders. They haven't seen a post from me since last night. If they don't see a sign of life within twenty-four hours, I'd anticipate a *lot* of speculation out there in the online community."

"You do think a lot of yourself, don't you?" Boedecker said to Price.

"My life and my vision are worth billions," Price said. "I'm not bragging. I'm just being realistic."

Boedecker scoffed. "My life is worth thirteen cents on a good day, I reckon. What about yours, Joe?"

Joe didn't answer.

Boedecker leaned into Price and said, "If you're worth so much and we manage to get you out of here, you'll probably want to reward us, right? Maybe give Joe and me a few stray million and some stock options?"

"That's not necessary," Joe said, but Boedecker cut him off.

"A few million is nothing to this guy," he said. "He says his life is worth a lot more than that."

"No," Price said.

Boedecker sat back. "No?"

"No. I don't believe in charity, just like Steve Jobs. Providing income for my thousands of employees and dividends to my shareholders is more than enough for any man to do."

"Are you shitting me?" Boedecker asked.

Price shrugged. He apparently didn't want to discuss it any further. "The people I'm associated with will hire guys to come find me if we can avoid the Thomases long enough. It's in all of their best interests that I'm okay, after all."

Joe didn't know what to say.

"Even if that all happens," Boedecker said, "any effort to rescue us won't just happen in an instant. This isn't downtown San Francisco."

"I know that," Price said defensively.

"They'll need to put together a search-and-rescue effort and that takes time," Boedecker said. "You've got to get people together, plus horses, helicopters, et cetera. It isn't one of those flash-mob things you do online."

Price looked to Joe for confirmation. Joe nodded.

As he did, Joe thought he heard a sound outside the cabin. It was a kind of muffled snap, as if someone had stepped on a dry branch and broken it through a layer of snow.

He sat back, suddenly on high alert. Boedecker did the same. He'd heard it, too. Price did a sharp intake of breath as if preparing to speak and Joe touched his index finger to his lips.

"*Shhhhh.*"

"What?"

Joe chinned toward the front door.

Price questioned Joe by raising his hands, palms up.

Boedecker rose and got to his feet with a slight wobble. The alcohol still dampened his movements. He reached out to the table for his speargun, which he'd re-armed.

Joe stood as well and sidled over to the bed. He didn't want to unfurl the bedroll until he had to. But he wanted to be in position to do so.

He surveyed the interior of the cabin once again. There was only one way out, which was through the front door. The window frames on each wall were too small for a man to fit his shoulders through. They were trapped inside, but it also meant there was only one way *in*.

Boedecker padded over to Joe and gestured toward the door. "Should we rush it?" he whispered.

Joe shook his head. He thought that the sound they'd heard might be a moose or elk outside, or possibly a dry branch breaking because it couldn't hold the weight of the snow on it. But he had to hear another sound in order to confirm the first.

Then he heard the clearing of a throat, and: "Joe? Are you in there?"

It was Earl Thomas. He sounded as if he were fifteen to twenty yards away and directly in front of the cabin. Probably looking out from around a tree trunk, Joe thought.

Joe didn't reply.

"Brock? You in there?"

Boedecker looked to Joe and they exchanged worried glances. Joe tried to calculate the odds. Was it a legitimate strategy to simply wait in silence? Would the Thomases decide the cabin was empty and move on without checking inside?

Not with all the tracks outside in the snow, Joe thought.

"They know we're in here," he mouthed to Boedecker.

Boedecker nodded.

Price still sat in front of the heated coil. There was fear on his face. He looked from Joe to Boedecker and back to Joe.

"*Answer him,*" Boedecker whispered to Joe.

Before he could, Earl said, "We know you're in there, Joe. We don't want any trouble with you. We just want that son of a bitch Price. He has to pay for what he's done."

Joe glanced at Price. His face went slack and he closed his eyes as if to accept the inevitable.

"We know you're not armed," Earl called. "We took all your guns and gear. The best thing for you to do is to come on out and leave Price to us. You don't owe that man anything."

"C'mon, Joe," Brad called out. He sounded closer than Earl, and to his left. "Don't make this any harder than it needs to be. We can start shooting right now. We've got enough firepower to fill you all full of holes. Or we can light this shack on fire and pick you off when you come running out one by one."

Kirby remained silent. Either he was hurt, not with them, or slinking along the outside of the cabin looking for a way in, Joe thought. He guessed the latter.

"*Answer him,*" Boedecker pleaded with Joe.

"I'm a dead man," Price moaned.

Boedecker turned to Price. "You've put us in a bad spot," he hissed. "Give yourself up to them. Be a fucking man."

Price grimaced but he didn't make a move.

Joe ignored both men while he surveyed the interior of the cabin once again. The log walls were old and crumbling but solid. There was no way they could batter their way out through the sides or back. Then he looked up and swept his eyes along the center beam and the sagging trusses that held up the warped sheets of plywood roofing. He could see gaps and exposed nails in the plywood sheets where they'd pulled away from the two-by-fours.

"Fuck it," Boedecker announced.

"Don't—" Joe started to say.

"We've got your boy in here, Earl," Boedecker shouted. "You can have him if you let Joe and me come out the door."

"Is that you, Brock?" Earl asked.

"It's me."

"Is Joe in there with you?"

"He is."

"Why ain't he talking?"

"Who the fuck knows?" Boedecker said, and he plucked the

speargun from the top of the table and held it at the ready. Joe couldn't fathom what the rancher's strategy was.

"Please," Price said to Boedecker as he stood up and backed away until he was pressed against the log wall. "Please don't hand me over to them."

"Shut up," Boedecker said as he raised the speargun at Price. Joe leapt toward Boedecker, but as he did the rancher aimed and pulled the trigger. The speargun made the metallic *thunk* and the projectile flashed across the room and pinned Price to a log just above his clavicle and inside his shoulder. Price screamed out.

"That'll hold him," Boedecker said to Joe.

Joe was beside himself. "Brock, what did you do?"

"I saved our lives, Joe." Then he tossed the speargun receiver to the floor and yelled out, "Come and get him, Earl. He ain't going nowhere now."

"I hope you ain't killed him," Earl called from outside. "That's *my* prerogative."

"You can't do this," Joe said urgently to Boedecker. "*We* can't do this."

"Sure we can," Boedecker said as he strode across the filthy floor and snapped back the bolt on the door to unlock it. While he did, Joe spun on his heel and lunged at the rolled-up bedroll.

In his peripheral vision, Joe could see Boedecker throw open the door and fill the doorframe. He held his hands up to show he didn't have any weapons. Price whimpered and tried to pull the spear out of his body with both hands gripped around the shaft.

Joe slid the .22 rifle out of the bedroll and opened the bolt. His fingers trembled as he tried to fit a small cartridge into the chamber. He dropped the first round to the floor and snatched out a second. He shoved the rest of the loose cartridges into his parka pocket.

As he worked the bolt and pulled back on the knob until it was cocked, Boedecker yelled, "I'm coming out, Earl. I'm unarmed. Joe's right behind me."

Before he stepped out into the gloom, Boedecker looked over his shoulder. When he saw Joe with the rifle, his eyes got big and he said, "What in the hell are you thinking, Joe?"

"Go," Joe said. "Get out of here."

For once, Boedecker didn't seem to have words available. His eyes beseeched Joe to toss the rifle aside and follow him outside.

Then a sloppy bloom of red exploded from between Boedecker's shoulder blades at the same instant there was a massive short-range shotgun blast. It was close enough to the open front door that Joe saw the tip of the tongue of orange flame.

Boedecker spun on his feet until he was facing inside, then dropped to his knees in the doorway. A second blast took off the side of his head and he fell face-first onto the cabin floor.

Joe heard Earl say, "Jesus, Brad. Did you have to do that?"

"You said no witnesses," Brad answered.

"That was fucking Brock," Earl said. "He was one of *us*."

"His name isn't Thomas, Dad."

As Brad talked, his voice got clearer and louder. He was walking heavily through the snow toward the front door.

Price froze and watched Joe as he raised the rifle and aimed it toward the open door. When Brad filled it, he was illuminated only by the glow of the heating coil. He held his shotgun loosely at his side. Joe said a prayer that the old rifle would operate and he placed the front sight on Brad's glowing face just above his beard and pulled the trigger.

Click.

Nothing happened. Brad heard the sound and squinted toward its origin. Apparently, he couldn't see Joe clearly in the gloom.

With shaking hands, Joe ejected the bad round and reached into his pocket for a fresh one. He couldn't see well enough to know if the lead faced the correct direction while he rammed it into the chamber, but he assumed it was okay because the bolt didn't seize up. Joe cocked the rifle again and raised it.

Crack.

Brad staggered and reached up with his free hand and covered his face as if he'd been stung by a bee. He cursed and backpedaled out of the light.

"What the hell happened?" Earl asked.

"Joe shot me," Brad answered with alarm and disbelief. "*He shot me.*"

Joe ejected the casing and fitted another round into the chamber.

"Joe, come on," Earl said plaintively. "You didn't need to do that. I thought you were a bad shot, but you proved me wrong, I guess. But this Price asshole means nothing to you."

Joe took several strides toward Price and kept the muzzle

aimed toward the open door. He thought he had a minute at most before Brad came back or either Earl or Kirby arrived.

He grasped the back end of the spear and pulled hard. Joe could feel the spear tip release from the log. The tip of the spear was barbed for fish, so he didn't pull it back through Price's flesh.

"Come on," Joe said to Price.

"Where?"

"Follow me."

"Follow you where?"

"Out of here."

"How?"

"Here," Joe said, thrusting the .22 into Price's hands. "Keep that aimed at the door and pull the trigger if anyone steps inside."

Carrying the stump he'd used for a chair from where they'd huddled around the heating coil, Joe kicked the bed away from the wall and dropped it onto the floor in its place and mounted it. His back was to the open door and to Price, who asked him if the safety of the rifle was off.

"It's off," Joe said. "It's cocked and ready to fire."

Presuming the cartridge is good, Joe thought but didn't say.

"I've never shot a gun before."

"It's a good time to learn."

From outside, Joe heard Earl lament, "Goddamn it, Joe. You shot Brad in the jaw."

"You ruined his beautiful smile," Kirby chimed in with barely disguised glee. "The girls won't have anything to do with him now."

Kirby's voice came from the left side of the cabin, not the front where Earl and Brad were. Good to know, Joe thought.

He braced himself on top of the stump and reached up and placed both palms against a sheet of plywood that rode down the ridge of the truss and appeared to be nailed directly to the top of the log wall. He grunted as he shoved and he felt it give. But it wasn't yet enough to create an escape route.

"What are you doing?" Price asked.

"Aim toward the door," Joe ordered.

He tried to calm himself. He took a deep breath and pushed up with all of his strength. As he did, he could feel a sharp pang in his thigh where the rifle bullet had damaged tissue and nerves the year before. The strain of the push made the stump rock beneath his feet and nearly topple over.

But the plywood sheet separated from the truss and the wall, leaving a two-foot gap. Joe felt icy cold on his face from the opening. He shoved up until his arms were stretched out and he opened the gap to three feet. The bottom edges of the plywood sheet bristled with exposed nail points.

Joe jumped down and pointed out the space to Price as he retrieved the rifle from him.

"Go," Joe said.

"I don't know if I can reach it."

"I'll help you," Joe said. "Just be careful not to snag your clothes on those nails."

Joe tossed the rifle aside on the bed frame and laced his fingers together and squatted. Price stepped into his cupped hands and Joe grunted again as he lifted the man up. Joe felt charged with unnatural strength, probably due to the adrenaline rushing through his body, he thought.

Price scrambled to get his head and shoulders out through the gap and he crawled through and dropped away. Joe heard him hit the ground hard on the other side of the wall.

He grabbed the rifle and tossed it through the space ahead of him so he wouldn't have to try to climb with it. Then he jammed one of the chairs over the top of the stump to gain another eighteen inches and managed to step up to the seat of the chair. It was a rickety setup and he tried to maintain his cool as well as his balance.

While he struggled, he knew he had his back to the door and to anyone who might look inside. He had no defense. Joe anticipated the shock of being hit in the back at any moment.

He pulled himself up by grasping the top of the log wall and managed to find a foothold on the frame of a window. He was able to propel himself up and through the opening. He landed in a heap on his back in the snow with no more grace than Price had shown.

It took him a few seconds to get his wind back, and Joe sat up and grasped his bent knees with his arms.

"Are you okay?" Price asked. "Where do we go?"

"Don't talk," Joe said, aware that they could probably both be heard by the Thomases on the other side of the cabin.

As he said it, a dark form emerged from the corner of the cabin and separated from the structure. Joe could see him only because his body blocked the starlight on the snow in the immediate distance.

The unidentified man walked silently and with caution. He was no doubt hunting down the source of the noise from the back of the cabin.

Joe searched for the .22 and realized he'd landed on it. He was able to roll his butt cheek and extract the rifle just as the form turned toward them. He hoped the muzzle wasn't jammed with soil from being tossed outside. Joe didn't aim but generally pointed the muzzle of the rifle to center of mass.

The sharp *crack* of the shot illuminated Kirby's surprised face for less than a second. He was just ten feet away.

Kirby said, "*Ow,*" and turned away. But he didn't go down.

"*Go,*" Joe barked to Price. He knew he couldn't see well enough to reload, and he didn't know how badly Kirby was hit.

Joe rolled to his feet and joined Price, who was running wildly ahead of him through the snow toward a dark wall of timber.

"Where are we going?" Price asked over his shoulder.

"Just run," Joe said, trying to keep up.

There was a heavy *boom* from behind them, followed by two more. Joe heard a rifle round smack into a tree trunk to his right. The impact sent a shower of snow cascading down all around him from branches that had been cradling it. Within a few steps, they were in black timber.

241

As he ran, sidling around trees and trying not to trip over downed logs or exposed roots, Joe recalled what his middle daughter, April, had said to him a year before when she came to visit him in his hospital bed:

You need to quit getting shot.

Tuesday

Slippery Son
of a Bitch

A man's dying is more the
survivors' affair than his own.

—Thomas Mann
The Magic Mountain

NINETEEN

At 2:45 in the morning, Marybeth parked her van in front of Sheriff Scott Tibbs's rental home on South Nebraska Street and killed the engine. She was furious.

Sheridan sat in the passenger seat, her face illuminated by the glow of the screen on her phone.

"Do you want to come in?" Marybeth asked.

"No, I'll wait out here unless you need me. Maybe I can get some more intel on Steve-2."

"I shouldn't be long."

Marybeth kept the van running so it would stay warm inside and left Sheridan in it with her device.

While driving there, she'd noted that the digital temperature gauge on the dashboard read twenty degrees. It was unseasonably cold out, and she could only guess how much colder it was in the mountains. She knew Joe had packed winter clothing and gear—he always did, no matter the month in

Wyoming—but he couldn't have fully prepared for this kind of weather. It wasn't even winter yet.

Light snow fell and haloed around the streetlamp on the corner. It was the only light on for the entire block, although there was a dull glow behind the curtains in one of Tibbs's windows.

She strode up the broken walkway and rang the doorbell. It chimed inside, but she couldn't hear any activity. So she banged on the aluminum storm door with her gloved fist and it made an impressive-sounding racket.

"Sheriff Tibbs, I need to talk to you."

A minute later, she saw the curtain shimmy from the room with the light on. Someone had peered out to see who was at the door. Then she heard shuffling inside.

Finally, a bolt was thrown from the inside and the door cracked open a few inches. Tibbs was short and stout and he sported a thick white mustache that obscured his upper lip. He had deep-set brown eyes and his uncombed hair stuck straight out to the side a few inches from over his left ear. He was bald, and she realized she'd never seen him without his comb-over. He was dressed in an oversized white T-shirt and red flannel pajama bottoms. His bare feet were nearly as wide as they were long on the hardwood floor. They looked like paddles.

Tibbs stepped out onto the threshold and eased the door partly shut behind him while he pushed at the storm door with a quizzical expression on his face.

"Mrs. Pickett," he said in a slow western drawl. "What can I do you for?"

"You can answer your phone, for one thing."

"What?"

"I've left half a dozen messages for you at your office today. You didn't call me back. Then your receptionist gave me your county cell phone number, and it went straight to a recording that said you hadn't set up your mailbox yet. I've sent you four texts and two emails. Since you didn't respond to any of them, I didn't have much choice but to come over here and roust you."

Tibbs rubbed his face and then his eyes. "It's pretty late," he said.

"I know that."

"It's a good thing my wife is away," he said. "She doesn't like being awakened in the middle of the night."

"I'm sorry," Marybeth said in an acid tone, "I thought you were the sheriff."

"I *am* the sheriff. Look, I can see that you're upset about something, but I don't neglect my duties. We've got staff on call during the night. I think Deputy Steck is on call tonight, in fact. You didn't need to come straight to my house."

Marybeth noted that he'd stepped farther out onto the porch and had eased the door almost but not quite fully closed behind him as he did so.

"That concrete has to be cold on your bare feet," she said. She leaned to the side so she could get a peek inside his house through the thin opening. "What is it you don't want me to see in there?"

Tibbs looked like he was thinking it over.

"This better be an emergency," he growled as he stepped back and welcomed her in.

"It is."

The house was warm inside and nicely appointed, she thought. There was a single lighted lamp near an overstuffed chair in front of the television set and a bar of light on the floor from an open door down the hallway. She hoped he'd turn on more lights because the setting was a little too intimate.

Tibbs retreated to the chair and settled heavily into it. He looked annoyed, but he gestured toward a hardback chair near the door for her to sit in. She didn't.

"So, what's the big emergency?" he asked.

"My husband, Joe, is guiding elk hunters in the mountains and we haven't heard anything from him in thirty-six hours."

Tibbs paused, then scoffed. "I've been hunting in the back-country before, although it's been a few years now. Thirty-six hours is nothing. I remember not talking to my wife for a week."

"We're not like that," Marybeth said, her voice rising. "Believe me, coming here tonight was the last thing I wanted to do. But you don't understand. Joe checks in every night he can when he's gone. He has a satellite phone even if he has no cell signal. Under no circumstances would he forget two nights in a row. Something has happened up there," she said, nodding her head in the direction of the Bighorns.

"There's a lot more to this," she said. "You know that Steve-2 Price and his ConFab people came here to go hunting?"

"Yeah, the governor gave me a heads-up on that. He said to treat this guy like a big VIP, so we closed the road to the airport to keep people away from him when he flew in. So Joe is the one guiding him, huh?"

"Yes. And another thing: Steve-2 constantly posts his movements and thoughts to all of his followers, and there's millions of them. Other than a weird post last evening, he's gone completely off-line as well."

"What do you mean, a weird post?" Tibbs asked. "I'm not up on this social media hoopla."

"My daughter noticed it," Marybeth said. "The photo in it was taken the day before because there is no snow in the background. Why would Steve-2 post a day-old photo?"

"Beats me," Tibbs said. Then: "Do they have plenty of food and clothing?"

"Yes."

"So we're not worried about them starving and dying of exposure up there."

"No."

"I'm not sure this is enough. Why don't we wait until morning before we run around with our hair on fire?"

"It's more than enough," Marybeth said. "The reason I'm here is, I was told by your office that a search-and-rescue effort has to be approved and signed off personally by you before it can be done. Since you aren't answering your phone, I had to come here and wake you up in person."

Tibbs flinched.

That's when a good-looking middle-aged woman wearing a short dark robe peered around the corner from the hallway.

"Scott, what's going on?"

Marybeth recognized her as Ruthanne Hubbard, one of the longtime dispatchers for the sheriff's department. She had a semi-permanent stool at the Stockman's Bar when she wasn't working for the county. Ruthanne was attractive in a rough-edged way and she had at least two ex-husbands Marybeth knew about.

"Hello, Ruthanne," Marybeth said.

"Hello, Marybeth."

"Three of the books you checked out are long overdue."

"I might have lost them."

"Come in during business hours and we'll get it sorted out."

"I'll do that."

"I hope you don't mind, but I'm having a private conversation with Sheriff Tibbs."

"I don't mind." But she didn't move.

"Go back to the bedroom," Marybeth said to her with a sigh.

"Oh, right. I was just making sure everything was okay out here."

"It isn't, but we don't need your help."

"Is it concerning Joe?" Ruthanne asked.

"Yes."

"Is he okay?"

"I hope so."

"I do, too. I really like him. He's always polite when I talk to him. Not every cop or officer is like that."

"Ruthanne, please," Tibbs said wearily.

"This is kind of part of my job," Ruthanne said to him.

"Not tonight it isn't," he replied.

"Okay, I'll see you later, Marybeth. It was good to see you. I hope Joe's okay."

"I do, too. Come in about those books."

"I will." Then to Tibbs: "See you soon."

Tibbs sighed and looked at the floor. His face was beet red and his bare feet suddenly splotchy.

Marybeth said, "*Caught*. No wonder you weren't picking up."

Tibbs rubbed his face again. "Please don't tell my wife when she gets back."

"I'm not a gossip."

"I don't do this kind of thing. I'm not that kind of guy."

"I'm not here to judge you," Marybeth said, although what little regard she had for the new sheriff had just been hit by a torpedo.

"Thank you."

Marybeth took a deep breath and shook her head. She wanted to grab a blunt object, maybe that ceramic zebra on the mantel, and clobber him.

Instead, she said, "Nate Romanowski and my daughter Sheridan are ready and willing to go try and find Joe and the hunters on their own, but it would be much better if you put together an official search-and-rescue effort. We might need aircraft, horses, and men on ATVs."

Tibbs said, "I'm not comfortable with sending Romanowski up there. I've heard some pretty sketchy things about him."

"It doesn't look like I have a choice," Marybeth said with heat.

Tibbs rubbed his jaw. "We can't get anything going until morning, and then it'll take a lot of time and money to get it underway."

"I know that. But we've already lost too much time because you wouldn't answer your phone."

"I've got to figure out the protocol here," Tibbs said. "I haven't been in charge of one of these S-and-R operations here before. I know how we did it back in my old department, but there's a lot more country around here."

"*Then move your ass*," Marybeth said. "Get up, get dressed, and get to your office and start making calls."

"You don't need to talk to me like that," Tibbs said.

"It's been thirty-six hours and it's probably below zero up there," she said. "It's time to do your job."

Tibbs grasped the arms of his chair and hauled himself to his feet. His face was dark with either anger or humiliation or both, she thought.

"I don't know what I was thinking when I let them talk me into this job at the end of my career," he said. "I was told this place was sleepy."

"It isn't," Marybeth said.

Marybeth slid into the driver's seat of her van and closed the door.

"I'm glad he was home and answered the door," Sheridan said. "Did you get him to do something?"

"Yes, but he's not very enthusiastic about it and it won't be as quick as we want. Some of the delay is legitimate. He probably has no idea who to call to get the search-and-rescue team activated."

"Crap."

"I know. I wish we still had Mike in charge."

Sheriff Mike Reed, who'd been gunned down two years before, had been professional, competent, and a friend of Joe's. The entire county missed him.

"So," Marybeth asked her daughter, "what did *you* find?"

"Not a lot," Sheridan said. "There have been no more posts from Steve-2. Even though it's the middle of the night, his followers on ConFab are starting to ask questions and chatter about him. The hashtag *#WheresSteve2* is trending and there are a few memes where people pasted pictures of Steve-2's face on that 'Where's Waldo?' character. Most of the comments are about how he's done this kind of thing before, kind of jerking his followers around by not posting. There are a few people who think something happened to him, but most of them think he's just a self-absorbed asshole."

"Is he?" Marybeth asked.

"Of course. But I checked his timeline and it's rare for him to be off-line for so long. He usually can't wait to share his observations and philosophy."

"Could it be he just can't get on the Internet?" Marybeth asked.

"I suppose that's possible, but I doubt it. He was online before. So what happened?"

"I'm afraid whatever it was happened to your dad as well."

Sheridan sat back and lowered her phone to her lap as Marybeth drove back toward her house. Then she said, "Nate and Liv are at your place, right?"

"Yes."

"I'll call Nate. We can get going right now to go up there and see if we can find him on our own."

"Honey, is that a good idea?"

"Mom, don't talk to me as if I were a child. Do you have a better idea?"

"No."

"We can't afford to wait until Sheriff Dipshit gets his act together."

"Sheriff Dipshit?"

"Sorry, that's what I think of him right now."

"I can't disagree," Marybeth said.

"Just make sure in the morning that he knows we're up there and ahead of him," Sheridan said. "I don't want him tracking us instead of finding Dad."

TWENTY

Raylan Wagy opened his eyes and thought he might be hallucinating from the pain and shock and loss of blood when he saw two rough-looking females gliding through the living room of the old hunting lodge. They seemed to float at first. One had big blue eyes and a headband made of plastic flowers on her blond head, and the other one shut the television off.

Then the second woman, a sturdy brunette with wide hips, large breasts, and knee-high boots, turned and saw him sprawled out on the couch. She screamed. The blonde jumped back as well and joined her friend, and the two strange hippie women stood shoulder to shoulder in front of the fading television screen. They did matching poses when it came to their reaction: they pointed at him with one hand and covered their mouths with the other and screamed in unison through their outstretched fingers.

Wagy winced and grunted as he sat up. His head swooned

from the movement and he almost pitched headfirst off the couch. As he came back into consciousness, he realized that yes, he wasn't hallucinating, and yes, there were two thirty-something women in the house and he had no idea who they were, how they got there, or what they were doing.

"What's going on?" Axel Soledad asked as he entered the room from the kitchen. He was carrying a grocery sack, which he placed on top of an old stereo cabinet. He wore his usual uniform of all black and his bald head bobbed about in the gloom like an unfocused blob, Wagy thought.

As usual on the days he spent climbing cliffs, Soledad clomped around in heavy lace-up boots, and his tactical pants were dirty with mud and debris. He wore a thick black turtleneck sweater with patches on the elbow. Several loose carabiners clinked from loops on his belt.

"There's a bloody man on the couch," the brunette said to Soledad.

Soledad didn't get excited. He never did. Instead, he removed a twelve-pack of beer from the sack, then a sixer of hard seltzer and a fifth of Jim Beam. He turned after he'd opened a beer and drank more than half of it in a long series of gulps.

Soledad had a presence about him, Wagy thought. Even in this situation, he seemed to radiate both menace and confidence. He had a kind of edgy take-charge charisma that at first glance either repelled people or drew them to him. Hence the two strange women he'd brought back.

"What in the hell happened to you?" he asked Wagy.

"I got attacked by a maniac," Wagy said. "He stuck a pitchfork into my foot and nearly shot my head off."

"So that's why you've got that bath towel on your foot?" Soledad asked.

Wagy nodded painfully. His right leg was elevated and propped on the coffee table. He recalled his last action before he collapsed on the couch. He'd lurched into the bathroom on his injured foot and had pawed through the drawers in the bathroom for a clean towel. When he found one, he wrapped it around the wounds on his foot and secured the towel with an Ace bandage. The towel was now wet and hard with blood.

"Fuckin' right," Wagy said. "To stop the bleeding." He noticed that the room was coming into sharper focus now. He knew he must have passed out, but he had no idea how long he'd been sleeping other than it was dark outside.

"What time is it?" Wagy asked.

Soledad didn't respond. The blond girl struggled to remove the phone wedged into her tight black jeans pocket. When she got it out, she looked at the screen.

"Three-o-five," she said. Then to Soledad: "Time for a hard seltzer, I'd say."

Soledad chinned toward the drinks on the cabinet. "'Ain't no laws when you're drinking Claws.'"

Both women laughed at that. Wagy got the impression the phrase had been used quite a number of times between the three of them before they showed up and came in through the back door.

257

"This is Zenda," Soledad said, pointing the neck of his beer bottle toward the blond woman. Then the other: "That's Cyndy. They're passing through, just like us. They're on their way to protest the killing of buffalo that wander out of Yellowstone Park into Montana."

"*Bison*," Zenda corrected.

"That's Cyndy with two *y*'s," Cyndy said.

"Like he's going to have to spell your name in a blog post or something," Soledad chided. Cyndy didn't look amused at the sarcasm.

As the two women pulled thin cans from the packaging, Wagy made a face and addressed Soledad. "Where in the hell have you been? I've been here bleeding out for hours with no way to get help. You took the car, and it's not like I can call an Uber out here."

"Why didn't you call or text?"

"The maniac crushed my cell phone, and the landline here doesn't work."

Soledad shrugged. He was nothing if not cool and uncaring, Wagy thought.

"I thought you'd be happy I brought us some company," Soledad said. "Zenda and Cyndy like to party. Or so they said."

"Not with that one," Cyndy said to Soledad after gesturing toward Wagy on the couch. "He's a train wreck."

"I'm hurt bad," Wagy said, suddenly serious. "I'm in a really bad way. I'm in no shape for a party." Then, to Soledad: "Where have you been?"

Soledad sat down on the coffee table in front of Wagy and

stared at him, then sipped his beer. Wagy couldn't tell if
Soledad was disappointed or angry with him, or simply
oblivious to the situation. He was a hard man to read.

One thing Wagy had learned about Soledad was the falconer's utter disregard toward life and death. The man was totally amoral. Wagy had witnessed Soledad kill living things
like pigeons and prairie dogs to feed to his captured raptors.
There wasn't even a flinch. There was no difference between
Soledad twisting the cap off a beer bottle or the head off a
pigeon. He'd seen Soledad hold a bunny up by the neck and
punch it so hard in the face it died instantly. He'd also observed as Soledad "culled" weak or injured falcons by lopping
their heads off with a scythe he'd found in the barn.

Soledad had the same attitude when it came to human life,
which was disconcerting. Wagy didn't think much about the
welfare of other people either, especially the one percent. But
Soledad was in an entirely different category.

Although Wagy had heard stories, he hadn't been sure he
believed them until that driver in the luxury car shot by them
on Interstate 25 on their way up from Colorado to Wyoming.
The Mercedes SUV was a mile ahead of them when it swerved
suddenly to avoid a herd of pronghorn antelope and it rolled
two and a half times into the sagebrush on the right side of the
highway and finally came to a stop upside down on its roof in
a cloud of dust.

Soledad was driving, and he stopped at the scene of the
crash. There was no other traffic on the road at the time. The
middle-aged woman behind the wheel was injured but alive,

and she hung suspended upside down by the seat belt she wore. Her arms were pinned tight to her sides beneath the belt. Wagy saw her turn her head and watch them climb out of their Suburban and walk toward her.

"Help me," she begged. "Cut me down. Please help me."

Soledad said, "Who have *you* ever helped, rich lady?"

Then he bent down and reached through the smashed-out driver's-side window with both hands. He told her, "I could cover your mouth and nose so you can't breathe and no one would ever be the wiser."

Her eyes got wide and she struggled, but she couldn't wriggle free from the strap.

Soledad chuckled and left her hanging there.

It wasn't a successful day on the cliff when the snow rolled in," Soledad said. "I had to pack it in early, and then I went to a little town called Winchester to drown my sorrows. That's where I met Cyndy and Zenda and we got to know each other. Time got away from me until they kicked us out when the bar closed.

"So," Soledad said, "tell me how he got the jump on you."

Wagy sighed. "He snuck up on me from behind and pinned my foot to the floor with a pitchfork."

"Were you fried?"

"Maybe a little."

"Describe him."

Wagy grimaced as he recalled what had happened. "Big guy, blond ponytail. He seemed to know all about us and what we've been doing. He said you violated the falconer's creed."

Soledad took that in and a small smile crept across his face. "Did he carry a big revolver?"

"Yes. He shot it and nearly killed me."

"I know him," Soledad said. "Or I should say, I know *of* him. His name is Nate Romanowski. He was a special operator in the same unit I was in before they kicked me out. Five years ahead of me, in fact. The officers who knew him talked about him like he was some kind of phantom, and the falconers in these parts talk about him like he's some kind of god. I think it's all bullshit. I'm not afraid of him."

"You didn't meet him," Wagy said. "He twisted my ear half off. In fact, I can barely hear through it now."

"I did notice it was a bit crooked." Soledad placed the bottle down on the coffee table and sat back. The grin grew wider. "That's him, all right.

"He used to be somebody to fear," Soledad said. "He was a legendary badass. He did a bunch of covert crap for Uncle Sam, and when he got out, he did his own thing. But I hear he's gotten old and soft. He's a corporate sellout now. A 'bird abatement' guy trying to make it rich so he can look down on people like me, even though I'm the kind of rebel he used to be."

Soledad drained the rest of his beer and signaled for a fresh one. Both Cyndy and Zenda looked at each other to see who would obey. Finally, Cyndy rolled her eyes and tossed one to him. Soledad opened it and turned back to Wagy.

"Romanowski is like one of those old-school mafia guys you've heard of. He's got a *code*," Soledad said with derision. "You know, like don't hurt the families of your targets or run narcotics in your own neighborhood, or make sure to take care of your brothers when they're in the can—shit like that. He's from another time.

"You and me," Soledad said, nodding to Wagy, "we're the new breed. We're the Sinaloa cartel, the Zetas, the Jalisco New Generation. We're the fuckin' MS-13 of outlaw falconers. That old shit doesn't apply. There are no rules for us, dude. Romanowski's exactly the kind of guy we hate. So he thinks I'm in his territory, does he?"

Wagy nodded his head. He didn't like how this was shaping up. He wanted a doctor.

"Did he find the birds?" Soledad asked.

"He must have," Wagy said. "He seemed to know all about them."

"Did he take them?"

"I don't know. He had to leave here real fast, like it was an emergency. I've been here bleeding out and getting ready to die alone."

Soledad ignored him. He turned to Cyndy and Zenda. "Do you girls need a ride back into town or do you want to crash here tonight?"

Zenda's eyes flashed. "Is this your idea of a party? One drink and we break it up?"

Soledad didn't answer her. And he didn't feign concern, something Wagy had gotten used to.

"You can walk back for all I care," Soledad said to her. "I've got some urgent business that just came up that I need to attend to."

To Wagy, Soledad said, "We're done here. Romanowski has fucked up our operation and I'm six birds short of my goal. There's no way I'm going to take that flight to Dubai six birds short."

Wagy shook his head. "What are you saying?"

"I'm saying I need six birds to fill my order and I know who has them. It's time this creaky old badass got taken down a peg, you know? He has no idea who he's messing with."

"He should be pretty easy to find," Soledad said. "It's not like the old days when he operated off the grid. Now he's a legitimate American businessman. He pays his taxes to fund the gangster government. Shit, he *advertises*. It'll be like nothing getting the birds I need."

"Will you at least drop me off at the ER on the way there?" Wagy asked.

Soledad said, "No can do. That would give away the game."

Then he seemed to notice that both Cyndy and Zenda were glaring at him. Cyndy had her hands on her extra-wide hips.

"Are you still here?" he asked them. His eyes were so cold Wagy felt a chill just being near him.

"My partner's turned into a liability," Soledad said to them. "Maybe you two can help me load some cargo into my vehicle so we can blow this joint. I'll help him out in a minute and meet you in the barn."

"We didn't come here to work," Cyndy said.

"Then you're a liability, too," Soledad said.

Wagy watched as Cyndy and Zenda looked at each other for a moment, trying to decide what to do. Finally, Cyndy said, "What kind of cargo?"

"Falcons in cages. They're not that heavy and they won't bite."

"I suppose we can," Cyndy said. "But then we want a ride into town. This night has really turned into a bummer."

"I'll meet you in the barn," Soledad said. When they didn't move, he pointed toward the back door through the kitchen. "I'll be right out," he said.

Reluctantly, Cyndy and Zenda shuffled out of the house.

When the back door slammed shut, Soledad turned back to Wagy.

"Can you walk?"

"I can try."

"Here," he said, getting up and putting his beer aside. "I'll help you get to your feet. Then you can lean on me to get out to the car."

Soledad walked around the couch until he was in back of him. Wagy felt Soledad's hands slide behind his shoulders until they were under his armpits.

"Ready?" Soledad asked.

"Ready."

As Wagy took a breath against the inevitable agony of

standing up, Soledad's hands disappeared. They reappeared an instant later, with Soledad cupping Wagy's chin with his right hand and grasping the surface of his forehead with the other.

The *crunch* sounded and felt like a muffled thunderclap and that was it.

Just like a pigeon.

TWENTY-ONE

An hour later, Earl Thomas surveyed a large clearing that glowed light blue on the snow from the moon and stars. He'd paused his horse and grunted as he dismounted and stepped heavily to the ground.

"Got to piss," he said to his sons as they caught up with him. Brad pulled up on his right and Kirby on his left. One of the horses in Brad's string blew its nose and whinnied.

Earl relieved himself between his boots and the odor of warm urine splashing on cold rocks was sharp. He turned his head away.

After burning the cabin to the ground, they'd been riding west down the mountain along a small and intermittent creek bed clogged with round rocks. They'd followed the two sets of tracks left by Joe and Price through the heavy timber and it had been a difficult journey. While the two men they pursued were on foot and could climb over downed timber and dodge through closely packed tree trunks, the caravan of horses weren't as nimble and it had slowed them down.

Finally, though, the timber cleared and the trees became more widely spaced. The tracks they'd followed were clear in the snow until they veered out of the forest to the tiny stream. Then, because the smooth rocks in the creek didn't capture the snow the way the grass and pine needle cover had, the tracks had become harder to follow. Earl assumed Joe would keep to the creek as he went west, and eventually down out of the mountains to the foothills, but for the last fifteen minutes he'd detected no sign that confirmed it.

Earl could also tell that the morning was going to dawn much warmer than the day and night before. He could tell by how it felt on his exposed skin and by the fact that the condensation clouds from the nostrils of his horse were getting harder to see. The sky was clear and the stars were hard. Soon, he knew, the sun would rise and melt the dusting of snow that covered the ground.

Keeping right on the tracks of Joe and Price would get harder by the hour.

Earl zipped up. This wasn't working out as he'd planned it. If everything had fallen into place—if Joe hadn't screwed everything up—he and his sons would have been down the mountain by now and loading their horses into trailers. They'd be back in their homes long before anyone realized Price and his party were missing. It would take days and possibly even weeks or months for investigators to come up with a theory of what happened—if they ever did. All evidence of Price and the hunting party should have been buried or obscured, and the winter weather would bury the terrain in heavy snow within a month. Predators would feed on the bodies and scatter the bones. All the physical evidence that the hunting party had even been up here—the gear and supplies—were all packed away on the string of horses that Brad led.

Eventually, somebody might find some exposed human bones. Or maybe not.

Earl knew he and his sons had only a few hours left to catch Price and take care of him once and for all. Joe didn't know these mountains as well as Earl—no one did—but Joe certainly knew if he kept well ahead and continued to the west that he'd eventually hit a logging road or the trailhead itself.

Kirby moved his horse closer to Earl and said, "You know, we probably ought to do a post from Price. His followers are going to start to wonder what the hell happened to him."

Earl made a face. "I wouldn't have the slightest idea how to do that."

"Well, give me his phone and I'll do it."

"I don't have his phone."

"Shit," Kirby said. "We must have left it with Joannides. That was a dumb move."

Earl said with irritation, "I wish you'd said something back then. It don't help much bringing it up now."

"He put the phone in his pocket just before I cut him." Kirby shrugged. "I just now thought about it."

"Fuck—another complication. We'll have to go back and

find the body later and get that phone back," Earl said. "We can't leave evidence like that around."

Kirby grunted and sighed.

Ａs Earl pulled himself back up into the saddle, Brad moaned. It was a plaintive cry. Earl thought he sounded like an exhausted or severely wounded bird dog.

"*Muh fuggin' mouf huts,*" Brad said.

"What?" Earl asked. "I can't understand you."

"He said his fucking mouth hurts," Kirby said, translating. Kirby had always been able to understand the words his older brother said, especially when they were very young and Brad had a speech impediment that later was improved by therapy. Translating for Brad came naturally to Kirby.

"Ah," Earl said. Then to Brad: "Suck it up. You'll be fine."

Brad moaned again and Kirby said, "He sounds like Chewbacca from the *Star Wars* movies. You know, the Wookiee."

Earl reached into his parka and pulled out his headlamp and turned it on. He kept it in his hand and raised the beam to Brad's face.

His older son winced at the light and painfully turned his head. Earl could see the tiny hole in Brad's face through his dense beard. The bullet had entered two inches below his left cheekbone and obviously shattered his jawbone on that side.

Brad leaned forward in the saddle and spit out a gob into the snow that consisted of dark blood with fragments of shattered teeth or bone.

"*It huts*," he said.

"Well, hang in there," Earl said, clicking off the lamp and dropping it back into his pocket. "I've seen worse."

He turned in his saddle toward Kirby. "How are *you* doing?"

"I'm okay," Kirby said through clenched teeth. He rode hunched over, with his arms tight to his sides and his head bent forward. "It hurts to breathe, though."

"Where'd he hit you?"

"The lungs, I think. Or maybe just short of the lungs. I taste blood every now and then. It's hard to breathe."

"Can you keep going?"

"Do I have a choice?"

"Not really," Earl said. "I've got to say, Joe surprised me. He's feistier than he looks. Where do you suppose he got that gun?"

Kirby shook his head. "I don't know. Probably found it somewhere in that cabin."

"Did you see it?"

"No."

"*I seed id*," Brad slurred. "*Id was a fuckin' siggle-shot dwendy-doo. A piece of shid.*"

"What did he say?" Earl asked Kirby.

"He said it was a fucking single-shot twenty-two. A piece-of-shit gun."

"Ah, well. It did the trick, though," Earl said. "It sounds like the first rifle my daddy—your granddaddy—gave me. It's a good thing he didn't have a real weapon."

Brad moaned something.

Earl said, "You don't need to try to talk, Brad. You sound simple when you do."

"He *is* simple," Kirby said. "He should have let Brock come out on his own. If he had, this would all be over."

"*Fug you*," Brad said.

"That I got," Earl responded. "He's got a point."

Brad looked sharply away. Earl was familiar with the gesture. Brad was angry and hurt.

"*Jus' cuz you cain't fug her no mo'*," Brad said.

Earl froze. "What did you say?"

"*She's god. Your liddle Princess. You're puddin' us frew dis 'cause you cain't fug her no mo'*."

Earl turned to Kirby.

Kirby hesitated a moment. His face was ashen, and Earl was pretty sure it wasn't from his injury.

"Kirby, what did he say?"

"He said, 'Just because you can't fuck her anymore, you're putting us through all of this.'"

Kirby's tone wasn't sarcastic or mocking like it usually was, Earl noted. Kirby said the words cautiously.

"Are you sure he said that?" Earl asked.

"Yes."

Earl wheeled in his saddle and hit Brad with the butt of his rifle in his shattered jaw. Brad cried out and fell to the ground beside his horse with a heavy crash.

Earl was on him in seconds, moving faster than he had in years, and he brought the rifle butt down again and again, even though Brad managed to parry a few of the blows. Brad lay on his back with his knees in the air and his arms out in front of his face. He didn't try to fight back. All Earl could see was the massive form of his son writhing through a curtain of red.

"Dad, stop it," Kirby cried out. "You're killing him."

Earl saw an opening between Brad's forearms and slammed the rifle butt through it and into his chest. Brad wheezed and rolled over to his side, exposing the side of his neck.

Earl took aim and raised the rifle when Kirby shouted, "Dad, stop it!" Kirby sounded panicked, which was unusual for his second son.

Earl hesitated. He was out of breath and the red curtain faded away. Brad groaned beneath his feet and turned his bloody head toward him. His expression reminded Earl of the last look from a severely wounded animal before he cut its throat. The look was dispassionate and almost understanding in regard to what was about to happen.

Instead, Earl spun the rifle around and lowered the muzzle until it was pressed against the flesh of Brad's forehead. His son's eyes were white and wide and they stared stupidly up at him.

"Do not ever say anything like that to me again," Earl said calmly.

"*I won'd,*" Brad replied. He sounded like he was gargling at the same time.

"If you do, I'll kill you. *I'll kill you.*"

Brad blinked his agreement and his understanding.

Earl turned on his heel and walked away to cool down. As he did, he glanced over his shoulder. Kirby had dismounted and was helping Brad get to his feet. Brad staggered and Kirby held him up and tried to steady him. They embraced for a moment and then pulled away so they could look into each other's eyes. Something passed between them, something unsaid.

Earl fought an urge to turn, raise his rifle, and shoot them both down.

For the thousandth time in the last year, he asked himself why Sophia had been taken away from him, leaving these two in her place.

The guilt he felt about Sophia was paralyzing to him at times. It wasn't her fault, it was *his*. He recalled her firmness, her smell, her blond hair, her innocence. The fact that she was the only female in the house after his wife left him. Her realization that what he asked of her was wrong, and his pledge to her to stop, now that she was older.

But before he could follow through on that pledge, Steve-2 Price had intruded, and he'd taken her away from him. Before he could make things right.

After he'd walked it off and wiped tears from his eyes no one would ever see, Earl returned to his sons and the horses. No one said a word.

This was how a Thomas male dealt with things, Earl thought: by not addressing them once the storm had passed. It had served them well over the years.

Earl mounted up and said, "We better get going if we're going to find that asshole."

"What about Joe?" Kirby asked.

"Fuck him," Earl said. "He didn't have to protect that prick or shoot either one of you. What happens, happens. He brought this on himself."

"*Fuggin' ride*," Brad replied.

Brad was back in the fold, Earl thought. Kirby, he wasn't as sure about.

TWENTY-TWO

The Vibram sole of Joe's boot slipped off the icy surface of a perfectly round river rock in the dark and he lost his balance and performed a clumsy dance from rock to rock, his arms windmilling, until he hurtled away from the creek as if launched and hit face-first into the trunk of a spruce tree, where he collapsed in a jumble of arms, legs, and the J. C. Higgins Sears and Roebuck Model 41.

He found himself sitting down with his back to the trunk and his legs spread as bright yellow spangles passed across his vision like so many electric clouds.

"Wow," Price said from where he'd been stepping from rock to rock on the creek bed. "That was quite a spectacular crash."

Then, after a beat: "Are you okay?"

Joe closed his eyes, but the spangles didn't quit. He did a mental assessment of his limbs and torso. Nothing broken, he didn't think. He reached up and touched the growing goose

egg above his right eyebrow with the tips of his fingers. He
didn't feel any blood.

"I'm okay, sort of," he said. "But I need a minute."

"You're not the only one," Price said. The man carefully ne-
gotiated the river rocks and joined Joe beneath the tree. Price
sat down heavily and sighed. Both men simply breathed in and
out, in and out, resting while their lungs stopped burning from
exhaustion.

To avoid leaving tracks in the snow, Joe had led them down
the middle of the small unnamed creek. It was treacherous
footing made worse by the darkness. Joe's left sock was soaked
through from an earlier mishap when his foot had glanced off
a slick rock and plunged into a small pool up to his knee. Icy
water had poured in over the top of his waterproof boot and it
now squished with the sound of a wet kiss when he walked.
Under any other circumstance, Joe would have stopped to dry
out his sock before proceeding. But he couldn't afford to do
that now.

"I can't believe you didn't fall down until you hit that tree,"
Price said. "I wish I'd had my phone to get a video of it."

"I'm glad you didn't."

"How long can we rest before we have to get going again?"

"I'm not resting. I'm waiting for my vision to clear."

"You know what I mean."

"The answer is, not long."

"How far do you think they're behind us?"

"No idea. But I'd guess thirty minutes at most."

Price let his head rock back out of frustration, but he hit it on the trunk and it made a hollow sound.

"Ouch."

Joe was exhausted from running, from trying to see which rocks to step on in the creek bed in the pale light of the stars, from lack of food, and from lack of sleep. The muscles in his legs buzzed warm from the effort at the moment, but he knew they'd stiffen and get cold if he sat too long. His left foot could freeze.

Although he could feel that the morning would dawn warmer than the day before and be more in line with typical fall weather, it was still cold out. The sheen of sweat on his skin beneath his base layer was starting to cool as well.

Hypothermia was curling back its lips and exposing its sharp teeth.

Joe grunted and willed himself to stand up. The constant movement had kept him warm. To pause too long was to freeze and die.

Price did the same, using the tree trunk to stand, but he whimpered as he did so. Joe looked over and saw the glint of the starlight on the shaft of the spear that still protruded from Price's shoulder next to his neck. In all that had transpired, Joe had forgotten about it.

"Does that hurt?" Joe asked. He could see the barbed tip on the front of the shaft sticking out of Price's back and an inch or so of the butt of it in front.

"It does."

"You've been pretty stoic about it," Joe said with admiration.

"Thank you. It's probably because every inch of me hurts," Price said. "This is just another thing."

"I could pull it out, but I left my first-aid kit in my daypack back at the cabin. I'm afraid if I pulled it through, it would bleed and I couldn't stop the flow."

"I've got a first-aid kit," Price said.

"*What?* You do?"

Price patted the front pocket of his high-tech cargo pants. "I've had it with me the whole time."

"What else do you have on you?" Joe asked.

"My headlamp. It's in the other pocket."

Joe whistled, and said, "Give 'em both to me. I'll get it done as quickly and painlessly as I can."

"Maybe we should just leave it in there for now," Price said. "I'll be the only tech guy in the boardroom with a spear sticking out of him. That'll really give me some more cred and grow the legend."

Joe smiled. "What if it snags on a branch while you're trying to get away? That could really screw you up."

"Good point," Price said glumly.

"We need to get it out. Your shoulder is probably still numb, but it'll hurt like hell tomorrow."

"I just hope there is a tomorrow," Price said.

Joe slipped the headlamp over the crown of his hat, turned it on, and focused the beam in tight. The barbs on the point were two spring-loaded bends of steel that curled up from the spear. If he tried to pull it through from the front, they would do an enormous amount of damage.

As Joe studied the wound and tried to figure out the easiest way to extract the spear, Price said, "Do you know what I've been doing while I've been following you in the dark?"

Joe shook his head.

"I've been praying to God to help me get out of this. I've been saying in my head, 'God, if you're up there, please help me get home. Please help Joe and give him wisdom. If I get out of this, I'll devote my life to good works.' I've kind of got a mantra going. I repeat it over and over to myself. My mantra is 'Help me God and I'll never let you down again. Help me God and I'll never let you down again.'"

"Good for you, if it helps," Joe said.

"I think it does. If nothing else, it gets my mind off of this situation we're in. It must be easier for you with your deep well of faith."

"Honestly, it's more like a pail of faith," Joe confessed. "But it's interesting you're thinking that way."

"We'll see," Price said. "The jury is still out on this God thing. It's new to me. This is just the beta version."

"Please turn around," Joe said.

Price winced, then did so. He said, "Just tell me when you—"

With no warning and as swiftly as he could, Joe grasped the shaft just behind the barbed tip and pulled the spear straight through Price's shoulder. Price reacted with a swift intake of breath and his legs wobbled. Joe tossed the spear aside and helped steady Price by holding him up in a bear hug from behind.

"Done," Joe said into Price's ear. "Are you okay?"

"I was about to say, tell me just before you do that so I can get ready. You could have given me some warning."

"I could have," Joe said, stepping back and tearing open the first square-gauze package with his teeth.

"You've done this before," Price said.

"I have a few times."

"I think I can feel it bleeding."

"That's good. You're less likely to get tetanus or any other kind of infection if it bleeds out."

"I hope you know what you're doing."

"I do. I get hurt a lot," Joe replied. "And you have no idea how many hooks and flies I've taken out of fishermen over the years. It's best to do it fast."

Price nodded.

"Now take your shirt off so I can put compresses on the wounds and tape it up."

While Price buttoned up his shirt, Joe retrieved the spear he'd dropped and stuck it into his waistband beneath his belt. He didn't want to leave it behind for the Thomas clan to find. Plus, any potential weapon might be useful.

Before turning it off, he ran the beam of the headlamp over the .22 rifle to make sure the muzzle wasn't blocked by mud and that the bolt action was clean. He ejected the single cartridge and studied it, hoping he could tell by looking at it if it would misfire. He couldn't determine anything and he put the cartridge back in and secured it by working the bolt.

Joe looked up and around him. The eastern sky was beginning to take on a slightly cream-with-coffee hue, but it would still be at least two hours before the sun broke over the top of the mountains.

In the dark behind them, a length of wood snapped. It was a heavy crunch, indicating there was real weight behind it. He couldn't guess how far away it had happened, but it was close.

"Hear that?" he whispered to Price.

"I did. What was it?"

"A horse stepping on a dead branch under the snow."

Price's eyes widened and Joe choked the headlamp out.

"What should we do?" Price asked.

"Run."

"Where?"

"That way," he motioned.

"Straight across the creek?"

"Yup. They're right behind us and getting closer. We need to angle away from the creek."

Joe shouldered around Price and walked stiff-legged to the creek. Price followed.

Joe stepped carefully from rock to rock until he was on the other bank. The far slope was steep, but rocks and brush poked through the light carpet of snow.

"Stay in my footsteps," Joe whispered.

281

He climbed the slope, hopping on top of rocks and in the middle of squat brush. It wasn't easy, but it didn't leave a trail in the snow, he hoped. Price kept up as they climbed.

Joe's heart beat with exertion and terror as he ascended the slope. Behind him and up the mountain, he heard another branch snap and then the unmistakable sound of a metal horseshoe glancing off a rock.

He hated going in the wrong direction when the best and fastest route to a trailhead was straight down the mountain, following the creek. But if they kept going that way, he knew, they would soon be overrun.

Joe clawed his way through a dense mountain juniper bush just below the tree line. When he emerged on the other side, he turned and helped Price. He could smell the sharp scent of juniper berries they'd crushed or dislodged.

Joe hunkered down behind the bush and tried to breathe deeply and normally so he wouldn't make loud panting sounds.

Within minutes, he heard the soft thump of horse hooves making footfalls below where they'd just been. He cursed the stillness and wished there was a breeze to provide some cover and white noise, because it sounded like the horses were just thirty to forty yards away in the stillness.

Joe reached out and pressed his gloved hand on the top of Price's head to urge him to keep down. Then he removed his hat and slowly rose on his haunches to get a better sight angle on the creek.

The ghostly dark shapes of two horsemen passed by below them, parallel to the nameless creek. The man out front was bulkier and Joe guessed it was Earl. The second rider slumped over oddly in his saddle. It was Kirby. Kirby looked as though he was either hurt or fighting sleep. Joe hoped it was the former.

Twenty yards behind them, the unmistakable mass of Brad Thomas appeared, leading a line of packhorses. Toby was second from the last in Brad's string. The gelding walked along dutifully, but Joe could tell Toby wasn't liking it by the way his horse kept his head bowed.

There's our stuff, Joe thought. *There's my horse. I wonder where Joannides went?*

Kirby was upright on his saddle, but Joe thought he could detect a slight wobble in him as he rode, as if his bones had softened. Joe *knew* Brad had been hit in the face by the .22 bullet he'd fired.

For a moment, Joe thought about raising the rifle and taking a shot at Earl. But what if he missed? Or what if the cartridge was another dud? Earl's head was hard to see in the darkness, and as Joe thought about it the man passed out of view behind a snow-covered spruce tree. Kirby followed him and was soon out of clear sight as well.

But there was Brad, just about to ride his big draft horse across a patch of snow glowing with starlight that would frame him perfectly for a second or two. If Joe shot Brad again and Brad fell, the packhorses with their weapons and gear might be available to catch, he thought. Joe didn't know if he could scramble down the slope fast enough to get to his weapons before Earl and Kirby turned and came back, but it just might be worth the risk. Even if he couldn't get down there, thinning the immediate threat from three men to two could change the dynamics of the situation. Earl and Kirby would have to contend with how to deal with the severely wounded or dead body of Brad and the string of horses. That was in addition to hunting down Price and Joe.

Joe weighed the odds, then raised the rifle and cocked it and pressed the stock against his cheek.

"What are you doing?" Price whispered.

Because of the darkness, it was hard to see the blade of the front sight to line it up with the slot in the back site, Joe found. But when aligned, and his aim settled on Brad's head and neck area, he let his breath out slowly and squeezed the trigger.

Snap.

The cartridge was another dud.

Joe peered down the rifle sites at Brad, who'd cocked his head at the sound.

Joe thought, *It's over now.*

But Brad didn't react further. He looked up the slope in Joe's direction and then up the facing slope without spurring his horse or reaching for his shotgun. He wasn't alarmed. And he continued to slowly ride alongside the creek.

Either Brad hadn't heard the sound of the misfire, or he'd heard *something* but had no idea what it was. He rode on.

Joe sat back with his heart beating in his ears. He closed his eyes and was grateful things hadn't gone horribly wrong. Price, to his credit, seemed to realize what had just happened, but he didn't say a word.

After a minute, Joe said, "Okay, that cartridge didn't work.

They're all old. But we're fortunate the Thomases passed right by and we bought some time."

"Where do we go from here?"

Joe chinned toward the timber above them. "Back over the top into the drainage we started out in. They'll figure it out at some point when they don't find any tracks, but at least for a while they won't be breathing down our necks."

Price nodded dutifully and rolled to his feet. He moaned as he did so. "This is like a nightmare that won't end," he said.

"How's your shoulder?"

"It's starting to really hurt."

"There were a few ibuprofen packets in your first-aid kit," Joe said. "Take some of those."

While Price dug in his cargo pants for the pain relievers, Joe ejected the bad cartridge from the .22 and let it drop to the soil. He made a point of grinding it into the dirt with the toe of his boot. Then he grasped a handful of six or seven cartridges from his pocket and stared at them in the palm of his gloved hand.

"You pick," he said to Price.

"Why me?"

"You might be luckier than I am."

Price grimaced. "Look at us. I don't feel very lucky at all."

He touched the rounds with the tip of his finger and rolled them around. He selected one and handed it to Joe.

"Who knows?" Price said.

TWENTY-THREE

Nate and Sheridan drove in the dark into the mountains with Marybeth's horse trailer hitched behind the utility pickup Liv had borrowed from a neighbor. Sheridan had a paper napkin spread over her lap with a crude drawing Joe had left behind indicating which trailhead he'd planned to use to lead the hunting party.

"You're sure this makes sense to you?" she asked Nate at the wheel.

"I think so," Nate said. "I've seen him sketch out his routes before."

"It's a good thing my mom found this."

Nate grunted his agreement. "I think I can find the trailhead, but your guess is as good as mine where they went from there."

Sheridan used the illuminated screen of her phone to study the sketch of the map. It showed a dotted line going east from the trailhead—which was marked with an *X*—up into the Bighorns. There was no indication of where they intended to camp or hunt. She guessed her dad had a plan but didn't feel the need to share it. Sheridan wasn't really a hunter, but she'd heard her dad say more than once, "You hunt where the elk are, not where you think they'll be." Which meant the entire eastern slope of the Bighorns was target-rich.

"I wish Steve-2 would post something on his feed," she said. "I know there's a way to get the exact geographic location of a satellite phone. Mom would know how to find it through her networks of contacts. But if the phone stays off—that doesn't do us any good."

She scrolled through her ConFab feed, hoping there would be a post from its founder since *Enjoying the big sky and the mountain air. It's fun to be off the grid for a while*, but there hadn't been. She found that post to be atypical, illogical, and insipid. As if Steve-2 was off his game.

The *#WheresSteve2* hashtag had now risen in rank and was trending in the top three, she noted. Users had pasted photos of his face on iconic symbols from all over the world: on Mount Rushmore, replacing Roosevelt; on Lady Liberty, beneath her crown; blinking on and off at the top of the Eiffel Tower.

Gin and Rojo, two of Marybeth's horses, were in the horse trailer and their saddles and tack were in the bed of the pickup. Sheridan and Nate had packed light with no camping gear because they didn't anticipate being in the mountains overnight.

"Tell me about the personality of your horses," Nate said as they left the paved county highway and turned onto a rough two-track dirt road into the trees.

"They're my mom's horses."

"Tell me about them. I'm no horseman, but I know they can be as quirky as falcons."

"True. Dad's riding Toby," she said. "Toby's pretty much the boss in the pecking order, even though he's getting older. He's a tobiano paint and he's bombproof in the wilderness."

"I remember Toby," Nate said. "Four white socks with black spots on them?"

"That's him."

"What about the horses we have with us?"

"Rojo in the back is a gelding and he's pretty quick and athletic," she said. "He's also nervous and flighty at times. He worships the ground Toby walks on and he's probably upset and all riled up that Toby's gone. I'll ride him."

"Good."

"Gin's our mare. She's highly trained, but she's lazy. That's why she's the fattest. She can do everything you could want a horse to do, but she doesn't want to. She's not going to be spooked by anything, though."

"I'll take Gin," Nate said. "You know, horses are complicated and unreliable."

"I know that. Would you rather walk?"

Nate didn't reply for a minute. Then he said, "You lead, I'll follow."

"That's kind of what I was thinking," she said.

Nate wore his shoulder holster with his huge .454 Casull revolver in it, and there were three long guns in the cab, all belonging to Nate: his 6.8 SPC Ruger ranch rifle with a fifteen-round magazine, a scoped .270 Winchester bolt-action elk hunting rifle, and an ancient open-sight lever-action Henry saddle carbine chambered in .30-30. The rifles were all placed muzzle-down on the bench seat between them.

"Gee," she said to Nate, "I think we have enough guns along."

"Bite your tongue," Nate said. "One never has enough guns."

Sheridan was filled with relief when they turned from the tight mountain road into an opening and the headlights swept over her dad's green Ford F-150 pickup as well as a new-model Dodge with a long horse trailer hitched to it. They'd found the right trailhead. There was also an empty Suburban.

They parked parallel to the Dodge and climbed out. It was always coldest just before dawn in the mountains and she zipped her coat to her chin and pulled on a pair of gloves. Nate walked straight to her dad's pickup and she followed. Although the truck was locked, Nate quickly located the keys on the top of the driver's-side rear tire, where Joe always hid them. He did it to guard against losing his keys while out on patrol and getting locked out of his own vehicle. Her dad had enough problems with his trucks as it was.

Nate unlocked the driver's-side door and opened it and the

dome light came on inside. She watched through the passenger window as Nate studied the inside of the cab and rooted through the box of hunting regulations and other official Game and Fish Department material. She heard him say, "No more sketches" as he reached over and unlocked the passenger door.

Nate found an old topo map in the door compartment and spread it out across the front bench seat. She opened the passenger door and leaned in.

"It's old, but I doubt the terrain has changed very much," he said.

Inside the cab she could smell a whiff of her dad's Labrador, Daisy. It gave her an eerie feeling to be inside her dad's truck without him in it.

While Nate studied the map, she opened the glove compartment and found a citation book, cigars stored in a ziplock bag to keep them from drying out, a canister of bear spray, and a stubby five-shot hammerless .38 revolver in a black nylon holster. She recalled seeing the weapon before and she knew he used it as a concealed backup gun. Sheridan turned so it wouldn't be pointed at Nate and checked the cylinder to confirm it was loaded, then she slipped it into her coat pocket. The bear spray went into the other.

"It's all about drainages," Nate said inside, following the largest one down the length of the map and pressing the tip of his finger into the bottom of the sheet.

"We are here," he said. "It makes sense that they'd go directly up this big drainage where the trail is. Their camp is probably on it or not far from it."

"Okay," she said.

"So that's where we should go first."

Her fingers were stiff through her gloves as they saddled the horses from the light of her headlamp and a small flashlight Nate clamped between his teeth. She checked Nate's cinch strap to make sure it was tight enough while he lashed two saddle scabbards onto his saddle, one on each side, and one to hers. He slid both the .270 and the ranch rifle into his scabbards and the .30-30 into hers.

"I don't need to have a rifle," she said.

"It's for looks," he replied. "This way you'll look like you mean business and not like some twenty-something girl on a horse."

"That was mean," she said. "Who do you expect we'll run into up there?"

"One never knows," he said. "How many people hate Steve-2 and what he represents? How many people out there just hate billionaires?"

She thought about it. Steve Price was certainly known as arrogant and controversial. "Maybe a bunch of people."

"Well, there you go," Nate said. "Do you have a cell signal?"

She checked her phone. "One bar."

"Text Liv and your mom," he said. "Let them know we're hitting the trail so they can tell the search-and-rescue team when we left."

As she did, Nate said, "My plan is to find your dad and get him back here before noon."

"What about Steve-2?"

Nate shrugged. "What about him? He's nothing to me right now. I've got business to attend to, you know."

"What business?"

Nate climbed into the saddle on Gin's back. "Don't forget we've got a falcon thief on the loose in our own backyard. I let him off the hook yesterday right when I had him in my sights. I'm going to find that guy and shut him down before he ruins everything."

She was encouraged by his optimism and determination to make their mission short and successful. It buoyed her, but she couldn't figure out what he was basing his optimism on. Nate didn't know where her dad was any more than she did, or what had happened to him.

"Okay," she said, sending the text. Then she secured her phone in her jacket, filled a saddlebag with a first-aid kit Marybeth had given her to take along—just in case—and climbed onto Rojo. The slick leather of the saddle was cold, even through her Wranglers and long underwear.

Nate backed Gin up out of her way.

"Ride 'em, cowgirl," he said to her as she passed.

Although it had snowed in the meanwhile, Sheridan noted the churned-up trail leading up and away from the trailhead. She could see deep U-shaped horse tracks beneath the thin blanket of snow in the beam of her headlamp. There had been at least half a dozen horses. Rojo locked in on the purpose of the mission after just a few minutes when he seemed to catch the lingering scent of Toby somewhere along the trail up ahead of him.

Toby's scent gave Rojo motivation to pick up his pace. Nate, on lazy old Gin, had to keep urging the mare to keep up.

While she rode, Sheridan felt a kernel of unease that blossomed the farther she ascended into the dark timber. At first, she couldn't determine exactly what it was. There was plenty foreboding about the immediate situation itself: they were taking horses into unfamiliar mountains in the dark to find her missing father. But there was something else, something Nate had said:

How many people out there hate Steve-2 and what he represents?

She had no idea how many people out there in the world hated Steve-2, or hated technology in general, or hated ConFab in particular. But she recalled there was someone who had railed about him locally.

What was his name? And what had happened to his daughter? The girl was a couple of years behind her at school, Sheridan recalled. She couldn't place her name or face.

Sheridan checked her phone. If she had a signal, she could text her mom to find out more about her suspicions, but there were no bars on the screen.

Still, it ate at her.

TWENTY-FOUR

A short time later, Earl Thomas turned in his saddle and raised his voice and said, "That Joe Pickett is a slippery son of a bitch."

"What was that?" Kirby asked as he rode up next to Earl. His tone was pinched with pain.

"I said, Joe Pickett is a slippery son of a bitch. I wouldn't have thought it, knowing what I know about him, but I haven't seen any sign of him or Price for quite a while now."

Kirby winced as he tried to straighten up in the saddle. "When's the last time you saw a track?"

"Way back there," Earl said, jerking his head back as if punched in the jaw. "I saw water splashed up on a river rock where someone fell in. I haven't seen a damned thing since. I think they slipped us."

"Again?" Kirby asked, incredulous.

Earl didn't reply. Was that a serious question or a snarky

comment? He tried to keep his anger at his younger son in check.

"*Whud's up?*" Brad asked as he neared them with his string of horses.

"We lost them again," Kirby reported.

"*Wha' da fug?*" Brad said.

Kirby translated. "He said—"

"I got it. Shut up, both of you," Earl said through gritted teeth. "They couldn't have gotten far."

He craned around in his saddle and studied the dark slopes on both sides that led down to the creek bed. There was just enough light to see where the eastern ridge was now darker than the predawn sky, but the timber was still impenetrable.

"They either went over the top to the north or the south," Earl speculated. "My guess is they went back over to the south. The north drainage would get them down the mountain too many miles away from the trailhead."

"So they went back to the drainage where we started?" Kirby asked. "That's what you're saying?"

"That's what I'm saying," Earl said softly. One more bit of sarcasm or disapproval from either one of his sons would need to be dealt with fast and hard. Brad was a dolt, but Kirby was a smart-ass. Too bad he needed them both right now, Earl thought.

"*We godda go bag?*" Brad said.

"Your grasp of the obvious is just outstanding," Earl snapped.

Kirby remained quiet. Not accepting, but quiet. In a way, Earl wished his younger son would just put it all out there on the table so he could slap it down and teach him a lesson. His silence was more aggravating than his sarcasm.

"*Where shud we cut to da soud?*" Brad asked, gesturing to the south.

"Right here," Earl said. "My guess is they went over the top but they're still working their way down the mountain like before. They're likely moving parallel to us in the other drainage."

"*Dat sud of a bitch Joe,*" Brad said. "*He'd slippery, all right.*"

Earl rolled his eyes and turned his horse to the left. "Let's pick it up, boys. If we go straight over the top from here, we might head them off right after we clear the ridge up there, so get ready."

It took longer for the party to reach the summit of the ridge than Earl had anticipated. The slope was very steep and the footing for the horses was poor. The animals slipped several times on snow and slick rocks and one of the packhorses decided to sit back on its haunches in protest until Brad whipped it with a coil of rope to make it stand up and proceed.

The trees on the incline were gnarled and tightly packed as well, and Earl had to zigzag through them to avoid pinching himself and his mount between trunks and branches. Earl could hear Kirby cursing behind him and he hoped his son's anger was directed at the predicament they were in and not at the leadership of his father.

With the top in sight and within fifty yards of where they'd cleared the trees, Earl found himself confronted by a vertical rock wall with no obvious opening within it to climb farther. They had to ride east along the base of the wall in a line until, finally, the wall gave way to an ancient rock slide covered in dirt, grass, and exposed scree. They took it and soon found themselves on the flat, windswept top of the ridge itself.

Earl's horse was breathing hard and its gait was ragged and lurchy. Earl bent forward in the saddle and slipped his fingers between the edge of the saddle blanket and horseflesh to gauge its temperature. His mount was hot, tired, and lathered, and his fingers were wet when he pulled them out.

"The horses need a breather," he announced. Earl dismounted and planned to stand there holding the reins until his horse cooled down and stopped huffing. Overheat a horse too much, he knew, and they would be shot for the rest of the day.

"It's getting lighter out," Kirby observed. He stayed in the saddle.

"Do you think I don't know that?" Earl snapped. "Do you think I can't see?"

Kirby shrugged.

"Aren't you going to get off?"

"Don't think I can right now," Kirby said through a grimace.

Earl didn't push it. He'd hate it if Kirby got down and couldn't get back into the saddle because of his injury.

Ten minutes later, Earl pulled himself back onto his horse and nudged it to walk along the length of the ridgetop to the west. Now in the light of the predawn, he could see the tops of other ridges that marked the series of drainages in every direction. Most of them were as treeless as the ridge they were on, and the snow on them glowed.

The morning had all the hallmarks of a nice fall day, he thought.

"What's the plan?" Kirby asked in a whisper from behind Earl. "I thought we were going to go down into the drainage."

"We will," Earl said. "But I want to make sure we get well ahead of them before we climb down. That way, we can intercept them when they come down the creek. We can set up down there and let 'em walk into a crossfire when they come strolling by. I, for one, am tired of chasing them."

"I am, too," Kirby said. "I like that idea."

"I'm glad you like something."

From twenty yards behind, Brad called out, *"Wud are you guys togging about?"*

Earl stopped and turned swiftly in his saddle. His eyes flashed. *"Keep your voice down."*

Brad clamped up and lowered his head, chastised. Kirby hung back to tell his brother what their strategy was in a low tone.

"Jesus," Earl grumbled to himself. "Let's all ride along in profile on the top of this ridge and yell at each other as loud as we can. That'll fucking help."

———

They rode along the length of the ridge for two miles at a good clip, with Earl pushing the pace of his horse and his sons and the pack string keeping up with him. He guessed that they were now well ahead of where Joe and Price should be.

He looked for a trail down to the creek as he moved, and finally found it, the mouth of it located between two truck-sized boulders. Descending on the gentle grade was much easier on the horses than the climb up the ridge had been. Earl leaned back in the saddle and let his horse pick its own way down. Horses were sure-footed that way. They didn't want to slide down the slope, either.

He knew he'd made a mistake to make that climb, but he'd never admit it. Earl didn't acknowledge his errors. He just pressed on.

The party was halfway down the slope and strung out on the trail when Earl looked down the drainage and saw movement in the trees below. Something was passing through a thick grove of aspen downstream of the drainage path. He narrowed his eyes but kept moving.

Had they pushed a small herd of elk out in front of them? he wondered. Had Joe and Price somehow gained superhuman strength and gotten much farther ahead of them than he thought possible?

Then he heard Kirby say, "Riders. Two of them."

And Earl now saw them. Two people on horseback coming up the drainage from below. One large, one small. The small one in front.

Earl turned. Kirby was right behind him and Brad was twenty yards in back, leading the string. The section of the slope they were on was wide open. If the two riders looked up, they'd see them for sure. There was no time to move his party out of the clearing and into the timber out of view.

"Who is that?" Kirby asked. "Looks like a big guy and his daughter."

At that second, the lead rider raised her head and stopped her horse. She'd seen them.

Earl thought for a second. Then he waved at the two riders with as much friendly enthusiasm as he could fake.

"Brad, you stay back with that string of horses. Pull over in that thick timber below and get set up to cover us. Kirby, you come with me.

"Let me do the talking, boys," he said over his shoulder.

TWENTY-FIVE

Joe had been scrambling clumsily down the creek for fifteen minutes, stepping from rock to rock, his lungs aching and his breath ragged, with Price struggling to keep with him ever since he'd heard:

"Wud are you guys togging about?"

"Keep your voice down."

It had been the Thomases, above them. On top of the ridge just ahead of where they were in the drainage. Something was wrong with Brad's voice and Joe guessed it was a result of his injury. But the exchange had been between Earl and Brad, for sure. As he moved, he stole glances up the slope to his right, fearing that he'd see the riders silhouetted against the dawn sky. He never saw them, but he knew they were there.

Either Earl would come down the slope and literally run into them, Joe thought, or the Thomases would arrive downstream

301

and just ahead of them and cut off his and Price's route. Neither scenario was any good.

Joe stopped and leaned forward, his gloved hands on his knees. He was exhausted and he knew he didn't have the physical strength to climb another ridge in order to proceed down the mountain in another drainage.

When he raised his head and studied Price, Joe determined that the man couldn't make another climb, either. Price was hurting. His face was drawn and pale. The wound in his shoulder had helped to take everything out of him.

Joe gestured to the top of the ridge and mouthed, "They're right there."

Price's eyes widened, and he looked for a second like he was about to break down.

"Maybe if we let them get ahead of us," Joe said softly, unsure of himself. "Maybe if we follow them down the mountain instead of being chased by them."

Price shrugged as if he had nothing to add.

Joe said, "I'm running out of ideas."

"At least we can see a little bit now," Price said, indicating the breaking dawn sky.

"Which means they can see *us*."

In the half-light of the morning, Joe studied the hillside to the north. There was a big gap in the trees cleared by a rockslide an indeterminate number of years back. The slide was filled with piles of talus and scree and lengths of trees that had been snapped off in the incident. A pile of huge rock slabs were stacked like a collapsed accordion at the bottom.

There were dark horizontal openings between several of the big slabs. One opening, he saw, looked wide enough that a man could enter it. He couldn't tell from where they were standing how deep it went back and if there was enough space for both of them to fit inside.

Joe nodded toward the slide pile, and Price followed his gaze.

"It's worth a try," Joe said. "We can lay low and let them wonder about us for a while."

Price nodded, and sighed. "So now we're cave dwellers," he whispered. "I started out this trip posting my experiences from my phone to a satellite. We're going backward through human history one hour at a time."

Joe approached the horizontal opening. At its widest, it was about eighteen inches.

"Let me borrow your headlamp," he said to Price.

Joe turned it on and shone it into the mouth of the crevice. He couldn't see how far it stretched back, but it appeared to get narrower the farther it went into the mountain. It *looked* big enough in there for the both of them.

He shone the beam on the crevice floor. There was loose but dry dirt broken up by small white bones and black teardrop-shaped animal scat of some kind. He noted the surface of the dirt was lined like corduroy. Scratch marks.

"We're a little early for bears to hibernate," Joe whispered. "But I can't promise that."

"It looks too small for bears," Price said. Then: "As if I know anything at all about bears."

"I'll go first," Joe said. "If there's enough room I'll curl into a ball so you can come in and get around me. I want to be near the opening with the .22 if anyone gets too close."

Price smiled bitterly. It didn't need to be said that the chances of the cartridge in the rifle firing were fifty-fifty at best. Joe found himself grinning back, filled with a shared dark humor at their situation.

"We're ready for something to go right," Joe said.

"Let me know when that happens," Price said.

Suddenly, out of view but above them on the rockslide, Joe heard Earl say, "*Let me do the talking, boys.*"

Joe slid into the opening on his belly as quickly as he could. It smelled dank and musky inside. He motioned for Price to follow as he jammed himself into the righthand V of where the slabs of rock met. He bent his knees up to make room for Price to scoot by. It was tight quarters, and Price grunted as he clawed his way over Joe's legs and settled in parallel to him behind his back.

At that moment, Joe could feel a slight vibration in the rock ceiling itself. Heavy footfalls right over their heads.

Joe turned to Price and brought his index finger to his mouth. "*Shhhhhhh.*"

Then, through the opening, he could hear the clicks of horseshoes striking rock just a few feet to their left. One by one, the party went by, headed downhill toward the direction of the creek.

TWENTY-SIX

Sheridan tried to keep both warm and alert to her and Nate's surroundings in the early-morning cold as they rode up the drainage. It was difficult to do both because the cold didn't allow her to feel loose and aware. Instead, the chill made her want to fold in her arms and legs and tuck her chin into her coat collar.

Although they'd spooked a few mule deer who had come to water in the creek, they'd seen no sign of her dad or the hunting party. All of the two-day-old horse tracks on the trail were going up the mountain, and none of them were coming down.

She felt movement behind her and Nate clicked his tongue to move Gin along into a faster walk. As he pulled next to her—Nate had learned Gin was a good horse but she needed extra goosing to move along—his head was turned away from her toward the wooded slope to their left. He'd obviously seen something she'd missed.

"What's up?" Sheridan asked.

"Let me get ahead of you. We've got company."

The words sent a secondary chill through her that had nothing to do with the temperature. She sat back in her saddle to signal to Rojo that he should slow down. He obeyed, even though his natural inclination was to keep ahead of other horses who were trying to overtake him.

"What do you see?" she asked Nate. She studied the wooded slope as well. The early-morning sun had not yet penetrated the timber up there.

"Don't stare," Nate said softly as he cut in front of her. "Just ride along as if we don't know they're there."

"As if we don't know *who's* there?"

"At least two riders."

"How far away are they?"

"They're right above us."

Sheridan had learned to trust Nate's uncanny observational skills. He always seemed to see things before anyone else could.

She eyed him as he slipped his right hand up and gently unzipped his jacket. The grip of his .454 Casull was within easy reach under his left arm, but it was concealed from outside view.

I think I see them," Sheridan whispered a few minutes later.

Two horsemen were threading their way through the trees toward the bottom of the drainage. She caught glimpses of them between dark trunks. As they got closer, she could hear the tick of hooves striking loose scree.

"Damn it. I don't think either one is my dad," Sheridan said sourly.

"*Hey there,*" the lead rider called out. "Good morning." He sounded cheery.

"Hello," Nate called back. He pulled Gin to a stop. Sotto voce, he said to Sheridan, "Stay to my side, keeping me in the middle between you and them. If shooting starts, you need to make sure to slide off that horse and find cover. Don't give them a clear shot at you."

"Oh, God," Sheridan whispered.

While she appreciated Nate looking out for her, this was more than she was prepared for. She glanced at the rifle in her saddle scabbard and hoped she wouldn't have to pull it out and try to remember how it worked. She'd fired lever-action weapons at targets before, so she thought she could handle it. But for further assurance, she patted the solid weight of the .38 revolver in her parka pocket.

The two horsemen emerged from the timber in an easy walk. They didn't seem to be trying to be either stealthy or in a rush. The lead horseman was a bulky man in his midfifties with a wide, round face and a growth of silver stubble. He wore a battered short-brimmed cowboy hat, a heavy canvas barn coat, and lace-up outfitter boots. He looked comfortable in the saddle.

Something stirred in her. He looked familiar, she thought. She'd seen him, or a photo of him, before somewhere. She wasn't sure, but she knew he'd been dressed much differently than he was now. Sheridan tried to recall where it had been.

Behind him was a smaller, younger, and darker man. He had a pinched expression, as if he were annoyed or in some kind of pain. The smaller one exuded menace, she thought. He appeared to be dangerous and tightly coiled. The hair on the back of her neck stood up.

Both were heavily armed. Rifle butts jutted up from saddle scabbards and the older man had a holster strapped to his right hip. She couldn't see any handguns on the younger man, but he wore a bulky coat that could hide them. A long leather knife sheath ran the length of his thigh. She caught a glimpse of a bone handle on the knife.

"We didn't expect to run into anyone up here," the older man said to Nate. He displayed a boxlike smile that revealed yellow teeth. His flat, beady eyes were disconnected from the smile on his mouth, though.

He continued in a jaunty tone. "How are you folks doing out here on this cold fall morning? You doin' all right?"

"We're fine," Nate said. "We really didn't expect to run into anyone, either."

She noticed as Nate spoke that he subtly squeezed his legs so Gin would know to take a step ahead. He was keeping himself between the horsemen and her as a barrier.

"I'm Earl Thomas and this is my son Kirby," the older man said. "We're outfitters based between Saddlestring and Shell. We've got clients coming in later this week, so we're up here scouting for elk. What brings you and your daughter up here?"

Nate apparently didn't feel the need to explain too much or

elaborate on Sheridan's relationship to him. She didn't question why not. Instead, she barely heard the exchange over the roar of blood suddenly rushing into her ears.

Earl Thomas.

At the sound of the name, things began to fall into place for her. *Earl Thomas.* He was the man who'd sat three rows ahead of the Pickett family at Lucy's graduation ceremony in the school auditorium. Earl had been dressed differently then, in an ill-fitting gray sports jacket with a black western yoke on the back. He'd been by himself with empty seats on each side, even though the room was packed, as if no one wanted to sit next to him.

What drew her attention to him at the time was his behavior. Although big and rough-hewn, he'd cried openly as his daughter, Sophia, was called to the stage to receive her diploma. His back rocked as he wept, and his head bobbed up and down. People around him acted as if they didn't notice, but they did.

She recalled looking up at Sophia, who was blond, lithe, and tall. Sheridan got a vibe from the girl that although she was attractive, she wasn't very smart. Something about the way Sophia held herself—as if she were unaware of her surroundings and not keyed in to the rest of the ceremony, resulted in the snap judgment.

Sheridan remembered thinking Sophia *had* to know that was her father out there weeping, because he was so loud and demonstrative while he did so. But the girl made a deliberate point *not* to look out at the audience to meet his imploring gaze.

Sophia Thomas, Sheridan thought.

That Sophia Thomas.

We're looking for someone," Nate said to Earl as Sheridan tried to return to the present.

"Really? Who?"

"Wyoming game warden Joe Pickett," Nate said. "He's supposed to be up here guiding a hunting trip."

"I know Joe," Earl said with obvious but treacly surprise, Sheridan thought. It was said like a man who wanted to feign that he was friends with her father, but he really wasn't. "Hell, I've known Joe for years. What's he doin' guiding hunters? Isn't that a job better left to us private-sector types?"

Sheridan squirmed in her saddle. A theory was clicking into place. She tried to remain still when she wanted to shout it out.

Nate shrugged. "I don't know the circumstances, but that's not real important at the moment. Have you seen him?"

Earl turned to his son Kirby and they exchanged a glance. Then Earl said, "I surely haven't seen Joe up here anywhere. But a couple of nights ago, we thought we saw smoke from a camp two drainages over. We couldn't figure out who in the hell that might be."

She thought, *He's lying.*

"Two drainages over?" Nate asked.

Earl indicated the direction behind him and over his shoulder. "Over there," he said.

"Really, that's odd," Nate said. "That seems to be a long way from where he was headed at the start."

Earl shrugged. "Well, I can't explain that other than to say when you're huntin' elk, you go where the elk are. Maybe Joe saw a herd and followed them. But hell, I don't know for sure. We just saw a camp, we thought."

"How many miles?" Nate asked.

"Eight to ten miles away from here, I'd reckon," Earl said. "At least that's where we seen it. They could have packed up and moved by now."

"I see," Nate said.

"Does anyone else know they're missing?" Earl asked. Sheridan thought Earl was trying to pretend he was concerned, but he actually wanted to gather information.

"No," Nate lied.

"When are they supposed to come back?"

"End of the week."

"Ah," Earl said, sitting back and smiling. "You don't need to start worrying for a while yet. They probably got into a bunch of elk and they don't even know what day it is. We've had clients like that who get overexcited, haven't we, Kirby?"

Kirby stirred slightly and winced. "Yeah." But he seemed distracted, she thought. He was too busy trying to get a good look at her on the other side of Nate.

"Are you okay?" Nate asked Kirby, as if on to his game.

Before Kirby could answer, Earl said with a chuckle, "He's fine. He's usually quite the chatterbox, especially when there's a nice-looking female around. But he had a bit too much whiskey last night. He's a hurtin' unit this morning. Aren't you, son?"

"Yeah," Kirby grunted. He looked away. Sheridan was grateful for Nate's intervention.

"I hope you take that as a compliment, miss," Earl said as an aside to Sheridan. She didn't respond.

"What about you two?" Earl asked Nate. "Have you run across anyone else on your way up here? I assumed you must have started at Oh-Dark-Thirty this morning to get up this creek so far."

"We did, and no, we haven't seen anybody but you," Nate said.

"Seen any elk?" Earl asked.

"A couple of cows and calves down low," Nate said.

"If you see some big bulls, please give me a shout," Earl said with a grin. "I'll put my clients on 'em, and I'd be happy to drop off some tenderloin as a finder's fee later on."

Nate didn't respond. She observed him. He looked carefully from Earl to Kirby and back to Earl in silence.

She didn't anticipate an explosion coming, but she couldn't rule it out, either. The entire exchange had felt forced and false to her. She knew Nate could draw his weapon and thumb the hammer back to aim with one swift movement and blow them both out of their saddles. But neither man seemed concerned, which didn't make sense to her, given the circumstances.

Then it hit her. It explained why both men just sat there, seemingly calm. And it was something Nate had obviously already figured out.

It wasn't because Earl and Kirby didn't perceive a threat from Nate, or that they were incapable of drawing first. It was because someone farther up the hill was filling his rifle scope with Nate's head—or Sheridan's. Just waiting for a twitch.

Sophia had been the youngest, but she had two older brothers, Sheridan recalled. Kirby was in front of them. So where was the other one?

"Your daughter doesn't say much," Earl observed while trying to crane his neck to the side so he could see around Nate toward Sheridan.

"Your son doesn't, either."

"Yeah, I guess not."

"Neither Kirby here, nor the one up the slope with the rifle."

Sheridan studied Earl carefully for his reaction to Nate's statement. While Kirby had remained still, Earl's nostrils flared for a millisecond. A tell. Nate was right.

"I don't know why you think that," Earl said.

"Because we're day riders," Nate said. "We don't have pack animals with us. But if you two are up here scouting elk for a few days, you'd have a lot more stock and gear with you. I'm guessing the guy up on the slope is in charge of all of that."

"Maybe we have a camp," Earl said. "Did you think of that?"

Nate hesitated, then shook his head. "No, I didn't," he said, looking abashed. "I didn't think of that at all. Now I'm embarrassed. I'm just being extra-cautious this morning, I guess. My apologies."

Earl seemed confused by Nate's sudden back-down, as was she. Earl narrowed his eyes for a moment, trying to determine if he was being played. Then he said, "You're right. My oldest son, Brad, is up there with the packhorses. We didn't want him bringing them all down here at once. You know how it is when a bunch of unfamiliar horses get together. They've got to establish who's boss of the herd and so on. We didn't want to have a rodeo break out. I don't need to tell you, I'm sure—we see a lot more injuries from horse accidents than anything else up here."

Nate nodded his head as if that made sense, his smile still rueful.

Finally, Earl said, "How about we let you two go on up the creek and we'll stay out of your way?"

"Sounds good," Nate said. "But please keep an eye out for Joe Pickett. If you see him, please tell him we're looking for him."

Earl cocked his head to the side. "I don't believe you told me your names."

Nate said, "We didn't," and clicked his tongue to get Gin moving.

Sheridan fell in behind Nate and they continued up the drainage. Her back felt like it was burning because it was so exposed. The two of them were easy targets.

But Nate rode along calmly, swaying a bit in the saddle. Without turning around, Nate whispered, "Are they still back there?"

Sheridan didn't crane around. Instead, she straightened her

legs in the stirrups and leaned forward as if adjusting Rojo's bridle. While she did it, she shot a glance back under her armpit.

"They're still there," she whispered back. "Standing there by the creek watching us go."

"Good. We're going to ride away, okay?"

"Okay, I guess."

When she presumed they were far enough from the Thomases not to be overheard, Sheridan said, "What are we doing? They were lying to us. I know they were."

"Correct," Nate said.

"So what are we doing?"

Nate blew out a puff of air. "We're up here to find your dad, remember? I could have taken out Earl and Kirby and not found out the answer. Most important, I didn't know where Brad was. I didn't want either of us to take a bullet. If you got shot, I could never look Marybeth in the eye again."

"Never mind that. We're going back, right?"

"Please give me a minute to think. I'm trying to figure out our plan," he said. It was a rare moment of candor from Nate, she thought.

"They don't care about Dad. They're up here to get Steve-2," she said. "I put it together. Earl blames Steve-2 and ConFab for what happened to Sophia."

Nate looked over his shoulder at her, urging her to continue. She spilled out her theory: this was all about Earl Thomas getting revenge on Steve Price. Her dad was just along for the ride.

Afterward, she said, "There were terrible rumors about Earl and Sophia. I never really believed them, because you know how high schoolers are. But he did seem unnaturally close to her, and you should have seen him at her graduation. It was embarrassing. Do you think they know where Dad is?"

"I think they're trying to find him," Nate said. "Just like us."

"Then he's alive," she said with relief.

"My best guess. Your dad can be pretty wily at times. Are they still watching us?"

She did the bridle-adjustment ruse again. "Yes. But they're looking up toward the ridge."

"See that thick timber just ahead?" Nate said.

"Yes."

"As soon as we get into it, I want you to do something."

Five minutes later, with Nate holding Rojo's reins while they hid in the dark copse of trees, Sheridan kept low and scrambled back to the mouth of the trail. She ducked behind a thick spruce trunk and pried the covers from the lenses of the binoculars and focused them on Earl and Kirby below them.

Earl was signaling to someone up on the slope by waving his hand. Kirby sat slumped; his head bent forward with his chin resting on his chest. If it was a hangover, as Earl had said, it was a powerful one.

She rotated around the tree to scan the slope. Within a minute, a younger man even bigger than Earl appeared in a clearing. He was riding a huge horse and he was headed down toward the creek. The man was slowly leading a string of horses behind him. A scoped rifle lay across the cantle of his saddle.

She studied him for just a few seconds before he rode out of view behind more trees. The packhorses, one by one, stepped cautiously down the path.

Sheridan gasped, and leaned into the binoculars so hard they hurt her face as the horses passed through her field of vision.

Then she turned to Nate. "Toby," she hissed. "Toby is with them."

TWENTY-SEVEN

Joe couldn't clearly see or hear what was going on outside through the slit opening of the cave they were in. He knew two riders had gone by earlier because he'd heard them and caught glimpses of horse legs, and he *thought* he'd heard the murmur of voices far below them near the creek. The voices shimmered as if carried away by the breeze.

"Where are they?" Price asked in an urgent whisper.

"Shhhhh." Joe gestured toward the roof of the opening. "Someone is still up there," he mouthed.

Price's eyes enlarged, and he stared up at the slab rock, as if by concentrating he could see through it.

Then Price growled, which startled Joe. The growl was deep and rumbling and guttural. It was a sound that had come from deep within the man's chest. Joe shot him an annoyed look.

"*That wasn't me,*" Price hissed.

There was another growl. It was coming from the dark, beyond where Price lay, from deeper into the cave where it narrowed. Joe felt Price burrow into him and grip his right shoulder so hard he winced.

Slowly, Joe raised the headlamp in the gloom and pointed it toward the back of the cave. Price didn't watch. Instead, he buried his face into Joe's shoulder. Joe could feel the man trembling.

Joe fumbled for the on button and pressed it. The beam of light was startling in the dark and it took a second for his eyes to adjust to what he'd illuminated. He didn't see it in its totality at first. Instead, there was a rapid series of impressions:

Two large round eyes reflecting orange in the beam.

Spike-like teeth glistening wet; black lips curled back.

A low-to-the-ground, heavy body.

Shimmering long hair and folds of skin.

The flash of claws . . .

And the creature was on them, rushing them, grunting, slashing with its claws like single-bladed razors, fighting to get out of the cave.

Price cried out and Joe felt the crush of the animal as it scrambled over the top of him. He guessed it weighed forty or fifty pounds, and its thick coat smelled musky and strong of oil, dried blood, and pine. Like Price, Joe flattened himself onto the cave floor to allow for as much space as possible to allow for the beast to see the opening and rush toward it while slicing away at him the entire time. He could feel rents being ripped through his clothing and piercing cuts in the flesh of his back, legs, and neck.

When it cleared them, Joe opened his eyes to see that the

animal was blocking out most of the light from the opening. For some reason, it had stopped there. Joe hoped it wouldn't wheel around and tear into them again.

But it did.

Before Joe could react and raise the .22, the beast was on him again, trying to roll him over on top of Price, and then he felt an electric jolt in his shoulder as it sunk its teeth into him. Although less than a third of Joe's body weight, the animal had enormous strength and quickness.

Joe grunted and swung at his attacker with his fists. He landed a solid blow on the top of its head with enough force that he heard its jaws snap together.

It was enough. The creature backed away and shot out through the opening.

Huhnnnn.

Huhnnnn.

Huhnnnn.

At first, Joe couldn't account for the repetitious tone in his right ear. Then, as the dozens of cuts and scratches in his back began to scream at him, he realized it was coming from Price. Price was hugging him so tightly that his nose was pressed into Joe's ear. The man's breathing was panicked and ragged.

"It's gone," Joe said.

"Are you sure?"

"I saw it go."

"What in the bloody hell was it? A bear?"

"No," Joe said as he reached down and pried Price's hands from him. "Wolverine. We're in a wolverine den."

"I've heard of them," Price said. "I thought they were extinct."

"They're rare. I've never actually seen one in the wild, but there have been sightings of them here in the Bighorns. Pound for pound, they're considered the most vicious predators in the Rockies."

"I can vouch for that," Price said. "I'm going to have nightmares about that if we . . ."

He didn't finish his thought. No need, Joe thought.

"Will he come back?" Price asked.

"I think it's a she," Joe said. "She's probably going to give birth to kits in the spring. So yes, eventually I'm sure she'll come back."

"Are you hurt?"

"My back is torn to shreds, I think."

"What are we going to do?"

"Right now," Joe said, "I'm going to think about how magnificent it was to see one of the rarest predators in the country up close. I just want to appreciate that for a minute."

"Are you serious?"

"Yup."

"What's *wrong* with you?"

Before Joe could come up with an answer, he felt a vibration in the rock similar to what he'd experienced earlier.

He chinned to the ceiling of the den and mouthed, "Horses. Right on top of us."

Price closed his eyes. His bottom lip trembled. Joe could tell the man was on the precipice of his breaking point and his personal abyss was within sight.

Outside the mouth of the den, Joe watched as horse after horse passed by. He could see only legs because his low angle prevented him from seeing any riders. He knew who was up there, though: Brad. Still leading the string of Thomas packhorses and the stolen mounts they'd gathered along the way. Joe's heart filled when he recognized Toby's unique white socks covered with dark spots.

For a second, Joe considered how tough and resilient Brad Thomas was: still riding and leading horses after being shot in the face. The thought scared him.

Then, from the dark behind Price, came another low growl.

There were two wolverines. This one, Joe guessed, would be the male. Males were known to be bigger, stronger, and more dangerous.

"We've got to get out," Price hissed.

Joe agreed, and the two of them broke and crawled toward the mouth of the den as quickly as they could. The growl behind them settled into an agitated hum, and in Joe's mind's eye he could envision the big male wolverine pacing back and forth while choosing which human victim to target first.

Joe spilled out of the dark into the cold morning high-altitude air with Price right behind him. They emerged on a bed of flattened brown meadow grass studded with protruding

323

rocks. The male charged just as they cleared the mouth, but chose to juke to the side and run back up the mountain instead of tear into them.

Before Joe could breathe a sigh of relief at escaping the close call, he realized that by exiting the den, the two of them had emerged less than thirty feet from the last of the string of horses Brad led slowly down the slope. A line of horse rumps bobbed ahead as the animals worked their way down.

But Joe and Price were completely exposed.

Joe glanced up to see that Brad rode with his broad back to them and apparently hadn't heard them get attacked or clamber out of the den, nor the retreating wolverines. The footfalls of the horses and the breeze in the high branches of the trees must have drowned out the sounds.

He got to his hands and knees and stood up with a wobble. The fresh morning air stung the cuts and scratches on his back. Price remained down in the scree, apparently trying to get his bearings after the trauma they'd just experienced.

Joe attempted to size up their situation on the fly. The caravan of horses moved slowly down the slope, stepping carefully with their heads down, looking for firm footing. Although the rear horse—a gelding Joe recognized as being Boedecker's—had looked back at him, the horse hadn't spooked or whinnied.

Brad could decide to check out his string and therefore look behind him any second, and the two of them would be easy open targets.

Down on the floor of the drainage, Earl and Kirby Thomas

sat mounted next to each other. They were conversing, and neither had yet looked up to monitor Brad's progress. But they could at any moment.

Joe thought: *The Fog of War.* He had no idea whom Earl and Kirby had engaged with earlier or where the visitors had gone— if they were even there at all. Likewise, Earl and Kirby had no idea he and Price were up there. Neither did Brad.

He had three choices, he thought. All of them were bad. He could hunker down with Price and hope against hope that none of the Thomases would see them out there in the open. Or he could try to escape like the wolverines had by running up the steep slope with the hope they could find cover.

Or he could take on Brad while the man's back was turned.

Joe didn't hunker down and he didn't retreat. Instead, he spotted the familiar gait of Toby two horses ahead of Boedecker's gelding. The panniers on Toby's sides bulged with his weapons and gear.

Painfully, Joe jogged ahead. He kept his head low and passed Boedecker's gelding, then a roan packhorse the rancher had brought along, until he got to Toby's painted flank. His horse seemed to recognize him and acknowledge him, but he couldn't and didn't slow down.

While walking alongside, Toby turned his head and tried to nuzzle Joe beneath his chin. Joe turned away.

Instead, he skipped along at the same pace as the horses, trying to unbuckle the straps that held the panniers closed. He hoped to open the stiff container and find his Colt Python, or his bear spray, or at the very least his satellite phone. It was hard to make progress because of the movement of the horses, and he tried to keep his footing as he did so.

Joe loosened the strap and threw the cover back. He reached down into the bag and his fingers felt clothes, extra boots, his sleeping bag, but nothing hard and solid like a weapon. He determined the items he needed must be either in the opposite pannier—or carried by other horses.

Joe glanced up in frustration at the same moment Brad began to turn in his saddle to check the string.

Joe ducked and moved in as close as he could to Toby and tried not to get stepped on. Joe gave Brad a few seconds to look back, then cautiously raised his head as he walked along.

But Brad hadn't resumed his position facing forward. Instead, he glared at Joe in surprise and his eyes got big. Brad's mouth opened to call out, but instead of a cry a thick dollop of blood rushed out and spilled down his chin through his beard.

Before Brad could swing his rifle around, Joe raised the .22 and aimed it at a spot under Brad's right eye and pulled the trigger.

Snap. Another bad round.

Price couldn't pick them, either.

Joe tossed the rifle aside and rushed Brad's horse. As he did, he drew the broken spear out from his belt and gripped it with the point facing up. He ducked again as Brad fired and the concussion itself nearly broke Joe's stride, but he knew intuitively that Brad's awkward position had resulted in a miss right over the top of his head.

Winding up as he ran, Joe thumped headlong into the side of Brad's horse's flank, while at the same time arcing the spear across his body. The tip buried into Brad's upper thigh, but missed bone. Instead, it stopped solidly as the point buried into the skirt of Brad's saddle through the flesh of his leg.

Brad howled while he bolted another round into his rifle, and he spun his horse away. The lead rope he'd been holding for the pack string fell to the ground.

Joe stayed with him out of pure fear, because he didn't know what else to do. When Brad swung the rifle down again, Joe reached up and grasped the warm barrel and pulled, hoping to wrench it away from Brad's grip.

But the man was too strong. Instead of letting go, Brad jerked back and nearly pulled Joe off of his feet. But as he did, he howled again as if the pain from his thigh and his shattered jaw both hit him at once.

Joe placed the sole of his boot on the side of Brad's horse for leverage and leaned back and yanked on the barrel again. This time, it dislodged the big man and he tumbled out of the saddle toward Joe. Brad let go of the rifle as Joe wrenched it free, but the weapon stuck muzzle-first into the ground at Joe's feet.

Brad didn't fall on him with all of his weight because the spear through his leg pinned him to the saddle. Instead, Brad swung down like a pendulum until he was upside down for a second. Then the spear came loose and the big man fell to the ground in a heap.

"*Hey! No! Goddammit!*" Earl shouted from down in the drainage. He spurred his horse and started to charge up the slope with Kirby falling in right behind him. As he rode, Earl pulled his rifle from its scabbard and brandished it.

Joe quickly examined the rifle he'd taken. The muzzle was packed tightly with mud. He had no way to clean it out, and if he pulled the trigger it would likely explode in his face.

The string of packhorses resumed their journey and continued to walk along as if nothing had happened. Horse after horse passed by as Joe stood there with Brad at his feet.

Boedecker's gelding walked past and Joe found himself in the open with Earl and his younger son charging up the slope directly at him. He tossed the useless rifle aside.

As if oblivious to everything that was going on, Price suddenly lurched into Joe's field of vision. He lurched because he was unbalanced from hefting a heavy rock the size of a football above his head with both hands. Which he smashed down on the back of Brad's head with a sickening hollow sound, and the man trembled and went still.

Then Joe caught a glimpse of movement in the drainage, up the creek from where Earl and Kirby had been.

Two figures, one on foot and one on horseback, emerged from a dark tight stand of trees. They charged straight for a place halfway up the slope where they could intercept the Thomases. The rider was Sheridan, her hat flying off her head and her hair streaming behind her as she rode.

To Joe, she looked like a younger, faster, female version of John Wayne as Rooster Cogburn in *True Grit*.

The man on foot with his big revolver out was Nate.

TWENTY-EIGHT

Sheridan swung wide on Rojo just below the tree line when she heard: *"Hey! No! Goddammit!"*

She'd spurred her horse into a full gallop and the gelding had responded as if this was what he'd been waiting for his entire life: to be unleashed. It was hard for her to stay on his back while also seeing what was going on below in the drainage.

Earl and Kirby had also erupted into action. Earl shouted again and barreled up the slope from the creek. She could see he had a rifle in his right hand and the reins in his left. Kirby was behind him and to the side. They were both headed to the same place she was: up the slope, where her dad stood in a clearing with another man near a pile of slab rock.

Was that other man Steve-2?

She leaned forward in the saddle and rode straight toward them. She was moving too fast and the ride was too wild even to consider drawing the rifle out of her saddle scabbard or pulling the pistol. That could come later when she reached her father.

The situation she was in reminded her how unrealistic movies and television shows were when they depicted riders in full gallop drawing their six-shooters and firing away. She was an experienced rider and she could barely hang on.

She noted in her peripheral vision that Earl had pulled to a sliding stop halfway up the slope. At the same time, she realized the reason he'd done it was because he saw her cutting across the incline toward the two men. Earl raised his rifle and he swung it in her direction.

There was a sharp crack as a bullet snapped through the air just ahead of her. Then another behind her that thudded into a tree trunk to her right.

Sheridan leaned forward and hugged Rojo's neck, trying to make herself a harder target to hit.

Nate saw Earl stop and aim his rifle at Sheridan. She was moving fast. Two hurried shots rang out, but she didn't stop. At the same time, Kirby spotted him jogging along the creek and the younger son peeled away from where his father was. He turned his horse toward Nate and spurred it.

As Kirby charged, Nate could see that he'd drawn a rifle out and he held it at his side with a stiff arm. The rifle bobbed up and down as the horse ran toward him.

Nate stopped, steadied himself into a shooter's stance, and leveled his weapon. Kirby was coming hard and fast and he was leaning into it, pressing himself forward along the neck of his horse. Nate thumbed the hammer of his .454, but couldn't get a clear shot. All he could see coming was the horse's head, its nostrils flared.

He hated to shoot a horse, he thought.

But: *BOOM.*

Kirby's mount cartwheeled forward in a violent and complete somersault, throwing Kirby through the air. Kirby was launched and he hit the ground headfirst. Nate clearly heard Kirby's neck snap as he landed. The rifle left his hand and clattered on the rocks of the creek bed.

Kirby lay facedown in the rocks and grass with his limbs thrashing in spasms.

Sheridan, no!" her dad yelled to her when he turned and saw her coming. "Go back!"

She had seen the horse tumble below her and she knew Kirby was down. Nate was now approaching the injured man, following the muzzle of his revolver.

Earl had seen what had happened to Kirby, too, and he'd turned his attention from Sheridan back to her father. He swung his rifle that way, but not before her dad shoved the other man to the ground and dived down himself.

Another shot cracked out. She saw a puff of grit and a shower of sparks on the rocks behind her dad, but she didn't think he got hit.

As she rode within twenty yards of him, she glanced toward

Earl and saw the man drive his horse into a thick stand of tall trees. It walked in with a stiff-legged gait.

Then she lost sight of him.

Kirby was breathing but badly broken. Nate nudged him with the toe of his boot until he could see Kirby's pale, slack face. His nose was broken and bleeding and his head skewed to the side unnaturally.

There was no doubt to Nate that Kirby was motionless because he was paralyzed, his spine snapped at the base of his neck.

Nate looked up briefly in time to see Earl move his horse into the stand of trees. It was a thick group of mature ponderosa pines rimmed by buckbrush in full fall color. The isolated stand stood well above the spruce and lodgepole in the drainage. But the copse was surrounded by clearings on all four sides. There was no way Earl could ride away within the cover of the forest without exposing himself.

"Now that it's all gone to hell, will your dad stand down?" Nate asked Kirby.

A spit bubble formed on Kirby's lips, but his eyes flashed. "No way."

"What does he want?"

"He wants to be with Sophia," Kirby croaked. "That's all he's ever wanted."

A round snapped past Nate's head from the copse and he dropped and flattened himself on the ground next to Kirby. He placed his revolver on Kirby's back and used it as a rest while he moved his front sight through the trees where the shot had come from.

"Get away from me," Kirby hissed. "He can't hit you without hitting me first."

"That's the idea," Nate said.

Sheridan arrived at where her dad was hunkered down and she dismounted on the fly. She hit the ground running, almost stumbled, but ran to where he was and dropped to her hands and knees beside him.

He looked terrible, she thought. There were rips in his clothing, streams of blood coming from fresh cuts on his back and shoulders, and his face and hands were filthy. But he didn't look seriously hurt. And his expression was as warm as ever.

"You're a sight for sore eyes," he said. "Keep down so Earl can't see you."

"Are you okay?"

"Yes. Are you?"

"I've never been shot at before."

He chinned toward the man lying next to him. "Sheridan, this is Steve Price. Steve-2, this is my daughter Sheridan."

"I know who he is," Sheridan said. She realized she was blushing and she couldn't believe it.

Price was distracted and didn't greet her. He had raised his head and was looking down the slope to where Nate was.

"Isn't he your friend?" Price asked.

"Nate?" her dad said. "Yes."

"Then why is he aiming at *us*?"

Sheridan focused on Nate to reveal that, yes, he had shifted his position and was now pointing his pistol in their direction.

BOOM.

Sheridan wheeled in time to see Brad Thomas get hit in the chest and fly backward. Brad had managed to get to his feet and had been approaching them from behind with his shotgun.

"That man is really hard to kill," her dad said.

Back off!" Earl shouted to Nate. "Get away from my son. I've got 'em pinned down up there and if you don't retreat, I'll pick them off one by one."

Nate shifted back to where he'd been before and he concentrated on the stand of ponderosas where Earl lurked within. He couldn't see the man clearly amid the tree trunks, and he guessed Earl was behind them. Nate's fear was that from where Earl was, he could position himself to get a clear shooting angle at Joe, Sheridan, and Price up in the rocks. And shoot them all, as he threatened to do.

Nate squinted, trying to will himself to see better than his vision allowed. And while he couldn't get a good look at Earl himself, still astride his horse, he could make out a contrast of shapes within the vertical trunks.

Specifically, Nate could recognize the rump of a horse on the left side of the thickest tree trunk in the stand, and the head of a horse to the right of it. Which meant Earl was hiding directly behind the tree itself.

Nate steadied his revolver and visualized where Earl's body should be on the other side of the center tree. Then he fired squarely into the trunk six and a half feet from the ground.

A shower of needles fell as the tree rocked with the impact as the bullet passed through it. Earl, practically headless, tumbled to the ground in a heap.

The riderless horse crow-hopped from the surprise, then did a high-stepped canter out of the trees into the clearing with its tail swishing with relief from the sudden absence of two hundred and twenty pounds on its back.

Joe sat back on the rocks with the sun on his face and his oldest daughter next to him and Nate joining them from below. Price paced around them giggling and shaking his head from side to side, saying, "I can't believe we made it."

He was kind of delirious.

Nate scowled at him while he slid his revolver into his shoulder holster.

"I'm sorry," Price said about his laughter, "I've never been through anything like this before. I can't help it."

"You can try," Nate said. Then to Joe: "Are you all right? You look like shit."

"Never felt better," Joe said with a grin. "It's good to see you."

"He saved my life," Price said to Nate about Joe. "So did you and Sally . . ."

"*Sheridan*," she corrected.

"Whatever," Price said, still giddy. "The Thomases tried to kill me, then we nearly froze to death, then we were attacked by wolverines. *Wolverines!*"

Price stopped abruptly. Joe looked up to see Price pointing toward Brad's big body splayed out behind them.

"Shoot him in the head," Price said to Nate. "We need to make sure he doesn't get up again."

"He won't," Nate said. "Neither will Earl. Kirby might survive, but I'm not going to get too worked up about saving his sorry ass."

"He's alive?" Joe asked.

"Barely. Broken neck. Do you want me to finish him off?"

"*No,*" Joe said with vehemence. "Come on, Nate. We can try to get him airlifted out."

Nate shrugged.

Joe noted that Sheridan had watched the exchange with interest, turning from Nate to him as if watching a tennis match.

Then he heard it: the deep bass *thump-thump-thump* of a distant helicopter. He couldn't yet see it in the sky.

"That should be the search-and-rescue team," Sheridan said. "The sheriff finally got things rolling."

"I need to call them in," Joe said. Sheridan helped him to his feet and stayed close to him as he limped down the slope toward the grazing packhorses and his satellite phone. It bothered her that he seemed frail. It was a thought she'd never had before.

"You take first class," Price called to him. "I'll sit in coach this time."

"Is he always like this?" Sheridan asked Joe.

"Off and on," Joe said.

"I can't believe we're here with Steve Price himself," she said with awe. "I mean . . . it's *crazy*."

"It is, I guess," Joe said, putting his arm around her shoulders. "But I'd rather hang out with you."

"Call Mom as soon as you can. She's beside herself."

"Will do."

TWENTY-NINE

Steve Price cradled his phone in both hands with the ConFab app open. He simply stared at it as if it were a Christmas package he was scared to open because he didn't know what was inside. Finally, he looked up to Joe and said, "I don't even know where to start."

They were sitting side by side inside the Bell 206B-3 helicopter as it lifted off from the mountain meadow and made a turn over the timber to fly west toward Saddlestring. Joe was entranced by the forest as they rose above it and the trees and clearings got smaller and smaller in view and became scenery. The contrast was jarring. Just a couple of hours before, he thought, he was down there on his hands and knees in the dirt moving in increments of inches.

Kirby was strapped down on a stretcher and laid across the other two seats of the helicopter. His mouth and nose were obscured by an oxygen mask, but his eyes were open. Because

338

he didn't have a headset on like Joe and Price, he couldn't follow their conversation. But he watched them as if he could.

They'd left the bodies of Earl and Brad Thomas where they'd fallen. They'd be retrieved on the next flight.

Sheridan, Nate, and two deputies had gathered all the horses and were leading them down the mountain to the trailhead. Sheriff Tibbs and the rest of the search-and-rescue team were still on the ground as well, because they were documenting and photographing the scene of the shootout. They'd be up there for a while, Sheriff Tibbs had said sourly, because Kirby had told them there were more bodies to find: Zsolt Rumy, Aidan Jacketta, Brock Boedecker, and Tim Joannides.

Even though Kirby had been helpful to the search-and-rescue team, Joe had told him as they loaded the gurney into the chopper that he still planned to arrest him for his Game and Fish Department violations—if he survived. Kirby had scowled at him before the oxygen mask was attached to his face.

"What did you say?" Joe asked Price.

Price held up his phone. He said, "I don't know where to start. So much has happened. It's like I've been up here a lifetime. I'm nervous about my reentry into my world. How much do I post about what happened?"

"Just tell 'em you're alive," Joe said. "That's what I told my wife."

Price nodded his head, unsure. Then he used his intercom to ask the pilot if his jet would be waiting for him at the airport. The pilot assured him it would be.

"You're leaving right away?" Joe asked.

"Just as fast as I can. I need to get back to work. I need to put all this behind me."

"What about some of those things Brock said about ConFab? Are you going to make any changes?"

Price stared at a spot above Joe's head, then said, "I'll think about it. I'll think about a lot of things."

As Price talked, Joe could see a change in him. The vulnerability and fear Price had revealed in their ordeal was melting away and being replaced by the arrogant and indifferent shell he'd been wearing when he arrived. Even his posture was different.

"I think the sheriff wants you to stick around and give a statement," Joe said.

Price waved it away. "He knows where to find me."

"There's something we never had a chance to talk about," Joe said, hoping his voice didn't sound as uncomfortable as he felt.

"What's that?"

"Governor Allen was hoping you'd be impressed enough with our state that you'd consider locating your big server farms here. He has lots of reasons why it would be a good idea for everybody."

Price looked at Joe without expression. For a good long time.

"I can't," Price said finally.

"Why not?"

Price gestured toward the tops of the mountains out the

window as they streaked along. "This," he said. "All of this. I can never look at this place or think about it again without the image of me smashing that rock into Brad Thomas's head. I was *excited* to do that at the time. I wanted his brains to come out of his ears. In three days, I turned into an *animal*. That's not how I like to think of myself."

Joe sat back. The scratches on his back hurt and his brain was numb and fuzzy. The effects of what they'd gone through were starting to overwhelm him, as they obviously had with Price.

"That's not all," Price said. "Last night in that shack, Boedecker tore me a new asshole. It was just relentless abuse, Joe. That's never happened to me in my entire life—to be treated with such contempt and disdain like that. I've testified before Congress and they were gentle compared to that. It made me realize that Boedecker probably isn't the only person out here who thinks like that.

"These people don't respect what I've done and they don't have a filter. They don't understand that I live in a different world, even though you tried to show me a new one. Joe, I've gone from being scared to death of germs and viruses a few days ago to having my life threatened by violent men and getting ripped up by a fucking wolverine! And trying to brain some mouth-breather with a *rock*. I don't ever want to experience those feelings again."

Price sat back. "No, I need to be with my own kind."

"Maybe I shouldn't have said anything."

"It's okay," Price said. "Your governor thought that maybe

I'd have such a good experience that I'd want to urge my team to build here. That's how things are in my world: everybody wants something from me. It is what it is."

Joe couldn't argue with that.

"This is the last elk hunt I'll ever go on," Price said.

"They aren't all like this," Joe replied.

"I hope not."

"I was really hoping you'd be more open to the governor's request," Joe said. "I'm being purely selfish here. He all but threatened me and my department if it didn't go well for you. And it didn't go well for you at all."

Price placed his phone screen down on his lap. It was an immense concession, Joe thought.

"Tell your governor something for me," Price said, his mouth tightening. "Tell him if he goes after you in any way that I'll sue him. I'll destroy him and his administration. Tell him I think he put me in a position where I lost two of my people and nearly lost my own life because of his negligence. I can throw an army of lawyers at him that will keep him and his administration tied up in court for the rest of his natural life. Tell him *that*."

Joe didn't know how to reply.

"I owe you a well of thanks," Price said. "You're not selfish at all. I know you could have given me up at any time with no cost to you. No one would have even known about it. But you didn't."

"I . . . I just did my job," Joe said, stammering.

"That wasn't your job," Price said. "You went so far beyond your job I'll forever be grateful. I want to reward you if I can."

"You can't," Joe said.

Price made an *I don't take no for an answer* face. He dug in a side pocket of his seat until he found a crumpled blank envelope and a pen. With writing that scrawled with the vibration of the rotors, he scratched out a message and folded it in half and placed it facedown on his lap next to his phone.

"When we land, I'm giving you this. You have to accept it and you can't hand it back," Price said. "I'll tell my people to be ready for your call."

"What is it?"

Price ignored the question. Instead, he tapped out a quick message telling his millions of followers that he was alive and well and that the hunting trip was a "tragic misadventure." Joe could see the screen because they were in such close proximity.

Then Price wrote: *More to come . . .*

As the helicopter descended to the tarmac and Joe could see Price's Gulfstream taxiing over to meet them, Price said, "You're a good man, Joe Pickett. I can't say I've met many like you. It warms my heart to know men like you still exist."

Joe looked away, his face flushing hot.

Before Price unbuckled his seat belt and exited the aircraft, he turned and handed the envelope to Joe.

"Take it," he said.

Joe did, reluctantly. Then Price was gone.

He bounded up the stairs of the jet with more energy than Joe would have imagined the man still had. Before the stairs telescoped up and the door was closed, Price turned and took a last look at the mountains, the sky, and Joe, who was still seated in the helicopter.

Price shouted, "Nature sucks!" Joe couldn't hear the words because of the jet engines wrapping up. But he could read his lips.

Joe unfolded the envelope and read it. Then he read it again. In a childlike wavery script, it said:

I.O.U., Joe Pickett
100,0000 First-Class Shares of Aloft Corp.
Signed,
Steve-2 a.k.a. Steven Price, CEO

He slid the envelope into the back pocket of his Wranglers and stiffly climbed out of the helicopter to solid ground. He was stunned.

Joe thought, *Won't Marybeth be surprised?*

THIRTY

Nate drove home in the borrowed pickup with the now-empty horse trailer clattering along behind him and raising a cloud of dust. As he did, he dug out the cell phone Liv had insisted he take along and powered it up.

The screen showed four missed calls, all from Liv. They'd come within a five-minute stretch two hours before. None came after. She'd not left a message.

Liv *never* did that. Something was wrong. He jammed the accelerator to the floor while calling her back. She didn't pick up and his call went to her voicemail.

Even from a distance, as he topped the hill that led to his compound in the sagebrush prairie, he could tell that things weren't right at home. The symmetrical lines of his falcon mews were crooked and the wire mesh that had been stapled to the frame of it was torn away.

The Yarak, Inc. van Liv usually drove was parked in the open outbuilding next to his home. Meaning she was there but not picking up.

Two of his red-tailed hawks strutted around on the roof of his house. Their hoods had been removed and they'd been set free but had apparently returned.

He blasted by the mews with a sidewise glance as he passed by. There were no live birds inside sitting on their stoops, but there were at least three lifeless falcon carcasses on the ground, their feathers rippling in the wind.

With a flood of adrenaline and outright dread roaring through his body, Nate slammed the pickup to a stop in the front yard and bailed out with his weapon drawn. There was no movement from the closed drapes in the window, because no one was looking out.

He followed his gun through the front door, ready for anything.

Liv was seated in a kitchen chair in the middle of the front room. Her eyes were swelled shut, but he could see her pupils on him through the slits. Her face was bruised and the left side of her hair was flat with matted blood. Her ankles were duct-taped to the legs of the chair and her wrists to the arms of it. Silver duct tape had been wrapped around her head so she couldn't speak.

He was enraged.

"Are they still here?" he whispered.

She emphatically shook her head no. He shoved his revolver

into his shoulder holster and removed the tape from her face. It left a two-inch mark and indentations in her cheeks.

"Kestrel," was the first word she said.

He went cold. "Did they take her?"

"No. I think he would have, but he didn't know about her. I hid her before he came in."

They'd discussed their safe place before, a place Liv was to hide in if danger came to their house. He closed his eyes for a second in relief that both Liv and his baby girl were there.

"I heard him out there in the mews," Liv said as he cut the tape from her wrists and ankles. "When I looked out, I saw him loading the falcons he wanted into his vehicle. He took a bunch of them and he snapped the necks of those he didn't want. That's when I called you the first time. You didn't pick up."

"I'm sorry," Nate said.

"Nate, he scared me. He had a really cold look in his eyes and I think he would have taken Kestrel if he'd known she was here."

"You did the right thing. Are you hurt?"

"I think I'm okay, but he beat the shit out of me," Liv said. "He must have tied me up when I was unconscious."

"Who was it? How many?"

"One man," she said. "But he was strong and he was a demon. When I yelled at him to leave the falcons alone, he came after me and started swinging. I don't think he realized anyone was at home. The SUV had green Colorado plates."

The second she was free, Liv stood up and ran to their bedroom. Nate followed.

Before she could throw the rug back and grasp the steel ring on the floor, he heard Kestrel say, "Da!"

"I'll do it," he said as he opened the panel that led to the crawl space beneath the house. It was dark down there and Kestrel sat on the dirt floor. She clutched her plush dinosaur companion and looked up at him and beamed. When she saw Liv's face, Kestrel was startled and she began to cry.

He snatched her up and his impulse was to hug her so tightly it might crush her. He kissed her chubby cheek and handed her over to Liv. Kestrel clutched handfuls of loose dirt in each hand.

"She's okay," he said.

"She didn't yell out at all," Liv said, nuzzling her baby. "She's such a good girl."

"You both are," Nate said.

On the way to the emergency room with Kestrel strapped into her car seat, Nate said, "After you get looked at, I'm taking you both to Joe and Marybeth's for a few days."

"Joe's okay?"

"Joe's okay."

"Thank God."

"I can't say the same for some other guys."

He briefly told her what had happened in the mountains, and while she took it in, she listened with disbelief. He tried to keep his voice calm as he fought against the cold black rage building up inside of him.

"How long will you be gone?" she asked.

He took a moment to answer. "Just as long as it takes to kill Axel Soledad for what he did to you. And to get my birds back."

ACKNOWLEDGMENTS

The author would like to thank the people who provided help, expertise, and information for this novel.

Sources include "The Egg Thief" by Joshua Hammer, which appeared in *Outside* magazine on January 7, 2019, as well as *Horses, Hitches, and Rocky Trails* by Joe Back, *Packin' in on Mules and Horses* by Smoke Elser and Bill Brown, and *Meat Eater: Adventures from the Life of an American Hunter* by Steven Rinella.

Special kudos to my first readers, Laurie Box, Molly Box, Becky Reif, and Roxanne Woods.

A tip of the hat to Molly Box and Prairie Sage Creative for cjbox.net, merchandise design, and social media assistance.

It's a sincere pleasure to work with professionals at Putnam, including the legendary Neil Nyren, Mark Tavani, Ivan Held, Alexis Welby, Ashley McClay, and Katie Grinch.

And thanks once again to my terrific agent and friend, Ann Rittenberg.

THE MAKING OF *DARK SKY*

For *Dark Sky*, the twenty-first Joe Pickett novel, my goal was to strip everything down. I wanted Joe's world to shrink to its most primitive and basic foundation.

Now in his fifties and in a world teeming with cell phones, GPS devices, the cloud, and social media, our game warden is thrust into a situation where the only thing he has going for him is his wits.

To quote from the novel itself:

Heaving for air and with his hands on his knees, Joe thought:
No horses.
No weapons.
No food.
No way to communicate.
Leaving an easy-to-follow trail in the dirt.
Finally, Price recovered enough to say, "Are we fucked?"
"Yup."

How did he get there? Blame the governor of Wyoming, who has tasked Joe with guiding a billionaire Big Tech CEO and founder of a fictional social media platform called ConFab on an elk hunt in the Bighorn Mountains. What Joe and the CEO don't know when they embark into the wilderness is that a trio of savvy modern mountain men is tracking their every move.

Meanwhile, Nate Romanowski and his new apprentice falconer, Sheridan Pickett, have troubles of their own. Someone has moved into Nate's territory to poach and steal his falcons. The man responsible turns out to be colder, crueler, and more vicious than Nate himself.

Every novelist takes a different approach to a new book. There is no right way and no wrong way.

For me, I start with at least two topics, issues, or controversies and research the hell out of them. Once I feel like I understand the issues as well as I can (whether that means traveling, interviewing experts, or reading), I build an outline for the novel and then start writing it. In my mind, I'm attempting to pull a reader through real-life topics in a page-turning way.

For *Dark Sky,* the two topics are the ethics of Big Tech and social media and the perilous practice of falcon smuggling.

The story's commentary on Big Tech and the power of social media has turned out to be remarkably prescient today.

Here's another quote:

"The novelist Walter Kirn said it best," Price said. "He said, 'Twitter sells conflict. Instagram sells envy. Facebook sells you.' I like to think ConFab doesn't sell anything. We facilitate conversation. We've created a platform where everyone's voices can be heard no matter who they are. Now, I'm sorry if someone posted something that led to this. I truly am. But what can we do? We can't censor people. There's such a thing as a First Amendment in this country. There's free speech. We

have no desire, nor any right, to silence the voices of the people who use our platform."

Hmm.

Many years ago, when I was hanging out with a loose band of outlaw falconers in Wyoming, I was aware that at least two of them were involved in illegally selling falcons to willing buyers in North America, Europe, and the Middle East. It was (and is) a very lucrative trade and it's filled with shady people.

I was reminded of those bad falconers when I recently came across a story in *Outside* magazine written by Joshua Hammer about modern falcon smugglers. It was called "The Egg Thief" and it did a deep dive into the international conspiracy to steal falcon and eagle eggs from their nests and sell them to overseas falconers.

The topic blinked to me in neon: NATE, NATE, NATE.

As you know, on March 12 of 2020 the world changed. I was on the last week of the book tour for *Long Range* when the word came from my New York publisher that the remainder of the tour was cancelled due to the COVID-19 pandemic.

I returned to our small Wyoming ranch to wait it out for what I thought at the time would be a few months. You know the rest of the story. One by one, every event on my calendar, well into the future, got cancelled. Zoom sessions took over from in-person book events, travel, conventions, etc. I could fly-fish nearly every day and I did. And I'd never had more time to write.

I'm not complaining. Although the pandemic has been very tragic for too many, riding it out in Wyoming was not the struggle it was in more populous cities or states. I joked at times to unfortunate city-dweller friends that the hardest part was that it took half the day to find someone to social distance with.

Odd things started happening around us, though. People from around the country fled to our national forests, our campgrounds, our mountains, our riverbanks. Some stayed for months. Some are still there, living in a primitive way that I doubt any of them had envisioned.

I don't think of *Dark Sky* as a pandemic novel. There is a mention or two within the story about the pandemic, but that's not what it's about. I can't imagine anyone really wants to read about the virus and I certainly didn't want to write about it.

There's no doubt, though, that the themes of isolation and loneliness—which were already present in the not-yet-completed book—shouldered their way in even more. Not only is Joe's world suddenly stripped down to the studs, but Nate might be witnessing his newly domesticated life with Liv and his daughter get turned upside down by soulless outsiders.

Dark Sky is a reminder that in our well-connected world, there are still places without connections at all. Huge swaths of our continent are still off the grid.

Joe Pickett has been challenged many times before, but he's never been challenged quite like this.

C. J. Box
Wyoming, 2020